A **COLLAPSE** OF **HORSES**

Also by Brian Evenson
Altmann's Tongue
Contagion
Dark Property
The Din of Celestial Birds
Father of Lies
Fugue State
Immobility
Last Days
The Open Curtain
The Wavering Knife
Windeye

A **COLLAPSE** OF **HORSES**

Stories

Brian Evenson

Coffee House Press
Minneapolis
2016

Coffee House Press books are available to the trade through our primary distributor, Consortium Book Sales & Distribution, cbsd.com or (800) 283-3572. For personal orders, catalogs, or other information, write to info@coffeehousepress.org.

Coffee House Press is a nonprofit literary publishing house. Support from private foundations, corporate giving programs, government programs, and generous individuals helps make the publication of our books possible. We gratefully acknowledge their support in detail in the back of this book.

LIBRARY OF CONGRESS CATALOGING-IN-PUBLICATION DATA

Evenson, Brian, 1966–
[Short stories. Selections]
A collapse of horses : stories / by Brian Evenson.
pages ; cm
ISBN 978-1-56689-413-5
I. Title.
PS3555.V326A6 2015
813'.54—dc23
2015010593

PRINTED IN THE UNITED STATES OF AMERICA

26 25 24 23 22 21 20 19   3 4 5 6 7 8 9 10

for Kristen, with love

CONTENTS

Acknowledgments

The stories in this collection previously appeared in the following magazines and journals:

The American Reader: "A Collapse of Horses"
Black Clock: "The Moans"
Caketrain: "Black Bark"
Conjunctions: "Cult" and "Torpor"
Dark Discoveries: "BearHeart™"
Granta: "The Blood Drip"
Green Mountains Review: "A Report"
McSweeney's: "The Dust"
Monkey / Monkey Business: "The Punish"
Nightmare: "Cult"
Unsaid: "Scour" and "Three Indignities"

And in the following anthologies:

Jesse Bullington, Ed., *Letters to Lovecraft:* "Past Reno"
Ellen Datlow, Ed., *Best Horror of the Year,* Volume 7, "Past Reno"
Ellen Datlow, Ed., *Fearful Symmetries:* "The Window"
Richard Gavin, Patricia Cram, and Daniel A. Schulke, Eds.,
    Penumbrae: "Any Corpse"

Paula Guran, Ed., *The Year's Best Dark Fantasy and Horror, 2014:*
"A Collapse of Horses"
Simon Stranzas, Ed., *Aickman's Heirs:* "Seaside Town"

"Black Bark" would not have been written without Laird Hunt's *Kind One*. "Any Corpse" would not have been possible without William Godwin's *Lives of the Necromancers* (1834). Jesse Ball's "Pieter Emily" is the source for the quoted text in "The Moans." "The Window" came about when Michael Stewart shared the particulars of an attempted break-in with me. I'd also like to extend a heartfelt thanks to a number of magazine and anthology editors who have supported my writing for many years and who seem often to understand my work better than I do myself: many, many thanks, to Bradford Morrow, Steve Erickson, Ben Marcus, David McLendon, Ellen Datlow, Paula Guran, and John Joseph Adams. Thanks are due too to Jeff Vandermeer and Peter Straub, without whom I'd be less of a writer. And to Claro and Motoyuki Shibata, for their fine care with my work in France and Japan, and for catching my typos in English. And finally, my sincere gratitude to Coffee House Press and Chris Fischbach, without whom none of this would be possible.

A **COLLAPSE** OF **HORSES**

—for Laird Hunt

Black Bark

They'd been riding two days straight now, climbing farther and farther up into the mountains in a bitter wind, searching for the cabin Sugg claimed was supposed to be there. Things had not gone smooth. Sugg had taken one in the leg, the thigh, and the blood had dripped down inside his pant leg and into his boot. Now, Rawley saw, the boot was overfull, and Sugg was leaving a drizzle of blood along the trail behind them. The side of Sugg's stolen tovero too was slicked with it, and the slick had taken on a vaguely human shape, as if Sugg's leg jostling back and forth against the horse had been trying to draw someone with his blood.

"We got to stop," said Rawley. "You need to rest."

For a long time Sugg didn't answer. Then he said, in a voice just above a whisper, "It's around here somewhere. Bound to come across it any moment."

"Where?" asked Rawley. There'd been nothing for miles. When Sugg didn't answer, he said, "It's going to be dark soon."

But Sugg just kept on. Or didn't rein his horse in, anyway. Maybe the horse was just following its own path.

They were following a trail that flirted with the fast-moving creek, curving toward it and then away again. At first Sugg hadn't been sure it was the right creek. Now he claimed to be sure, but Rawley guessed he didn't know for certain. He'd been saying for hours the cabin was just around the next curve, around the next bend, but no cabin ever was.

"Going to be dark soon," Rawley repeated. "We should stop, make camp."

Again it took a long time for Sugg to answer, but when he did, his voice sounded a little stronger. "They still following?" he asked.

Rawley shook his head, spat. "Haven't been for hours," he said. "We shook them."

"Maybe they just want us thinking so," said Sugg. "Maybe they're trying to take us off guard."

Rawley shook his head again. "Naw," he said. "It's just us."

Sugg was swaying a little in the saddle. For a moment Rawley eased back on his reins and watched him.

"Sugg," he said. "Sugg, you got to stop."

Sugg didn't say anything, just kept riding.

"Sugg," he called after him. "I'm stopping here. I mean it."

But Sugg didn't look back. He just kept going, still swaying, keeping to his slow, leisurely pace as it took him around a bend in the path and he disappeared from Rawley's view.

Cursing under his breath, Rawley spurred his horse and followed.

He hadn't been far behind, but when Rawley came around the bend, Sugg and the tovero were nowhere. He reined up and took a closer look at the tovero's track, but it just ended, abruptly. He backtracked and looked for a break off the trail they might have taken, but there was nothing he could see. He cursed, louder this time.

"Sugg!" he shouted, and when there was no answer, he took out his pistol and shot it once in the air. He waited the echo out, then listened, but didn't hear any response. He nudged his own stolen horse along with his spurs until it was loping. He followed the trail around the next bend, but Sugg wasn't there either.

He followed the trail up a half mile or so, looking for some sign of Sugg's cabin, but there was still no sign of habitation anywhere. As he climbed, the leaves of the aspens were suddenly already yellowing. The path bucked closer to the creek, and the water's rumble grew louder. He watched the sunlight slide up the side of the slope and disappear, leaving the air suddenly chill, the papery bark of the trees slowly graying in the fading light.

Across the river, he spotted the mouth of a cave, unless maybe it was an old mineshaft. He found a place to ford and splashed his horse across. On the other side he dismounted, tied the reins to a tree, and climbed the bare shale slope, slipping, up to the entrance.

Not a mineshaft. Just an ordinary cave. It was dry inside, with a fairly level floor, and smelled of dust. He couldn't tell how far back it went. Somebody had arranged a circle of worn, ash-smeared stones near one of the walls. A fire pit. Not a cabin, but it was shelter. It'd do.

He started down to gather some wood. There were enough dead and dry branches scattered around that it took just a minute or two to gather a decent stack. Though the sun had slid behind the peak, there was still light left. He tried to gauge how long it would last, but found it impossible to tell without the sun. Could last another five minutes or another twenty. No moon yet, but he didn't know if that meant it was yet to appear or it wasn't coming. He sighed and dropped the branches near his horse, then untied the reins and went back to see if he couldn't find Sugg after all.

He spurred the horse at first and then just settled back to let it take its own way. It galloped for a bit, then loped, then slowed until he spurred it again, rubbing his hand along its neck as he did so, trying to stay friends. Five minutes of decent riding and the light had all but dwindled. A minute later and he could hardly see.

He was readying to rein up and return to the cave when he saw a dim shape athwart the trail. He went close and squinted, finally got down and bent over it. Only by touching it did he become sure it was a man.

"Sugg?" he said. "Where's your horse?"

"Gone," said Sugg. The man was limp, hardly moving, and he smelled of oil and blood.

"You all right?" asked Rawley.

Sugg just gave a low chuckle.

"Come on," said Rawley. "Found a cave."

When Sugg didn't say anything, Rawley hauled him to his feet. Sugg couldn't stand, couldn't keep his feet under him, so in the end Rawley had to drop him. It took a few more tries before he had the man up and across his back and was staggering under his weight. A few good heaves and Sugg was slung over the saddle of the horse, who made it clear it didn't want no part of it. But finally it was done. Taking the horse by the reins, Rawley headed for the cave.

In the dark he missed it at first and had to double back. No moon had come up, none at all. In the end he only found the cave again because he remembered the way the creek had sounded right near it, but it took stopping and setting fire to a dead branch to find where to cross the river, and even then some searching still to make out the cave's mouth.

He put the horse down below to graze, left the torch to burn itself out on the shale, and slung Sugg over his shoulder. Sugg groaned once but otherwise didn't hardly move. Rawley stumbled his way up the shale with him, slipping and falling and once even dropping the man, but finally he pushed the fellow up over the lip and into the cave's mouth. He went back down for the tinder and his bedroll before clambering in for good himself.

"This the cabin?" asked Sugg from the floor, his voice barely above a whisper.

"No," said Rawley. "But it's shelter."

"Not far now," said Sugg absently. "Just around the next bend."

Rawley ignored him.

He seated Sugg against the wall while he arranged the branches, got a fire going. He kept it low, both in case they were still following and because he didn't want to fill the cave with smoke, but there was still some warmth to it if you were close. It wasn't no cabin, but it wasn't open country either. It would do.

In the flickering light, Sugg looked pale, almost dead. Rawley said his name once and then repeated it. Sugg did not seem to hear.

Rawley circled his way around the fire and shook him.

"Here," whispered Sugg. "Still here."

Rawley carefully worked off the other man's boot. He kept expecting him to moan or flinch but he never did, neither spoke nor moved. When the boot finally came loose, it came with a rush of blood, spattering Rawley's hands and his own boots. *How much blood can the man have left in him?* Rawley wondered.

He slit open Sugg's soaked pant leg with his knife, then carefully peeled back the dressing. The skin beneath, once he sopped up the blood, appeared livid, the lips of the wound puckered and swollen. He cleaned it best he could, then bound it up again in the same sodden dressing. Then he circled back to his own side of the fire and sat.

"You're still alive, right?" Rawley asked. When Sugg didn't answer, he came back around the fire pit and prodded Sugg's side with his boot, repeating the question.

"What?" asked Sugg. When he spoke, he didn't move his lips hardly at all, it seemed to Rawley. Or maybe he did. Maybe it was just the flames and shadow that made it seem so.

Rawley leaned over, spat. It didn't hit the fire but sizzled on one of the rocks forming the edge of the fire pit. "You're still alive?" asked Rawley for the third time.

"What kind of question is that?"

"You're going to lose the leg," said Rawley.

There was silence for a long while, then a strange high-pitched wheezing that it took Rawley a moment to realize was Sugg laughing.

Rawley sat still, staring into the fire. He was hungry, but it still felt good to be off a horse.

"Got food in the cabin?" he asked.

"Sure," said Sugg. "Help yourself."

Rawley kept staring. There was something about the way the air drew in the cave that made the fire go from leaping high to nearly guttering, all in the course of a few seconds. He couldn't stop staring.

He breathed in deep. "Tomorrow," he said. "Tomorrow, you stay here. I'll go see if I can find the cabin."

"Tomorrow I'll be just where I am," said Sugg.

"What do you mean?" asked Rawley, confused, but Sugg didn't answer. "That's a strange way to put it," said Rawley. "When are you not just where you are?"

"Exactly," said Sugg.

Rawley stared farther into the fire, deeper this time. When he came to himself, he was not sure how much time had passed. He shook his head back and forth to clear it. "We should get some sleep," he said. He turned and started to stretch out on the cave floor, jostling about to get comfortable. He was almost there when, so softly he wasn't sure at first that he'd heard it, Sugg called his name.

"What is it, Sugg?" he asked.

"Something in my boot I need," said Sugg. "Reach down and pull it out for me?"

"The boot you're wearing or the boot you're not?"

"Not," Sugg said.

"The bloody one," said Rawley, flatly.

"The bloody one," confirmed Sugg.

"Like hell I'm reaching into that blood-soaked thing," Rawley said. He pulled himself up onto his elbows. Across the fire, Sugg still hadn't moved. "It's not sanitary. What you after, anyway?"

When there was no answer, Rawley sighed. He pulled himself over and reached, fumbled the boot up off the stone floor, then rolled until he was sitting up. He upended it, shook it, but nothing came out. He knocked its heel against the floor a few times, then upended it again. Still nothing. He tossed it back. It lay flopped over Sugg's foot.

"What you say it was?" asked Rawley.

"Didn't say," said Sugg. "A good-luck charm."

"No, there's nothing there," said Rawley.

"Figures," said Sugg.

They stayed there watching the fire quiver. It was, Rawley thought, like a living, breathing thing. As soon as he thought that, the fire grew dim, threatened to go out.

"We should stretch out and get some sleep," Rawley said.

"I'm fine," Sugg's voice said over the glow of the coals. "You stretch out. I'm just fine here."

"All right," said Rawley. But for some reason he kept sitting there, staring into the fire and at the dark shape of Sugg across from him.

He didn't know how much time had passed. Maybe a long time, maybe just a little. It was as if the dying fire had hypnotized him, or maybe he'd fallen asleep. But when suddenly he heard Sugg's voice, he wasn't sure if he was dreaming or if Sugg was really talking.

"Know the story of black bark?" Sugg's voice asked. It was completely dark now. Rawley couldn't see even the barest glimpse of the other man. He waved his fingers in front of his face but couldn't see those either.

"Black what?" he asked.

"Bark," said Sugg.

"Like from a tree?"

"Sure," said Sugg. "Why not?"

"What do you mean, why not?" asked Rawley, more awake now, irritated. "Either it is or it isn't."

It was as if Sugg hadn't heard. He was already telling the story. "A man found a piece of black bark in his coat pocket," he said. "He wasn't sure how it had gotten there. It was just there."

He paused for long enough that Rawley asked, "And that's the story?"

"More or less," said Sugg. "The whole of it gathers up in those words, in that beginning. Everything else is just teasing it out."

"What kind of story is that?"

"Shall we tease it out?" asked Sugg.

Rawley shrugged, then realized Sugg wouldn't see it. "Go to sleep," he said.

"You'll sleep soon enough," said Sugg. "For now, listen."

"A man found a piece of black bark in his coat pocket," repeated Sugg. "He wasn't sure how it had gotten there. It was just there.

"He took it out and stared at it. He wasn't sure where it came from, what kind of tree, if it was a tree."

"What else has bark?" asked Rawley, feeling suddenly very strange.

"This man too was the sort of man who only knew about the bark of trees," said Sugg. "Like you. And in his mind, he went through all the trees he knew but couldn't think of any with bark as black as this. Maybe that should have told him something. But he just looked at the piece of black bark for a long while and then tossed it away.

"The next time he put on his coat, there it was again."

"What do you mean, there it was again?" asked Rawley, his voice rising.

"Just what I said. There it was again."

"But he threw it away."

"Yes," said Sugg. "He did."

"Then how did it get back in his pocket?"

"That's not part of the story," said Sugg. "That's the part that gets left out. I'm telling black bark, and I know what's part of it and what isn't. Hush and listen.

"The next time he put on his coat, there it was again. He took that piece of black bark out, threw it down, then reached in his pocket, and it was there again, back in the same pocket. He took it out and threw it into the fire, and a moment later, there it was back in his pocket."

"Why would you tell me this?" asked Rawley.

"No matter where he threw it, it came back to him. He thought he was going mad. Finally he took the black bark out of his pocket, set it on the table, and picked up a hammer. But when he went to hit it with the hammer, it opened its eye and looked at him."

"Its what?" Rawley interrupted.

"Its eye," said Sugg.

"Eye?" said Rawley. "But bark don't—"

"Don't interrupt," said Sugg's voice. "Its eye. Yes, that's what I said. Eye. And don't you try to puzzle it out none and think that it means something other than what I said. Every time you think you have the world figured, trust me, that's just when the world's got you figured and is about to spring and break your back.

"When he went to hit it with the hammer, the black bark opened its eye and looked at him. That was all, just looked. But for a long time, and without blinking. The man looked too, and though he wanted to, found he couldn't look away. Then the black bark closed its eye, and he could look away. So the man lifted it up careful as he could, put it in his pocket, and left it there until he was dead. Once he was dead, it didn't have no use for him."

When he woke up, the morning was well on. His eyelashes had gotten gummed together during the night somehow, and he had to rub them before they'd open enough for him to see clearly. Sugg was gone, though how that could be Rawley had no clue—the man had hardly been able to move, let alone walk. Where he'd been propped up the night before, the cave wall was covered in a swath of blood rendered in a vaguely human shape. Like the shape on Sugg's horse. Hard to believe Sugg still had that much blood in him, considering what he must already have lost. So much blood, and in the shape of a man. *Blood angel*, thought Rawley, then he shook his head, trying to push the words out of his mind.

He stood and rolled up his bedroll, then paused at the mouth of the cave, trying to get as much of a view of the land behind him as possible. No sign of pursuit that he could see. No sign of Sugg either.

He picked his way down to the creek, washed the blood off his face and hands, drank deep. His horse was there, peaceful, the vegetation around it cropped close. He saddled it, rode.

He kept on up the same trail, not knowing what else to do. Maybe the cabin was up ahead somewhere, or some cabin, anyway. He rode through groves of quaking aspen shot through with fingers of juniper pine. The peaks ahead were spattered with snow in places, bare granite where exposed. It was very cold. Why would anybody have a cabin here?

He found a scrubby crab-apple tree and gnawed on a few of the hard fruits just to get something besides water in his stomach. The skin of them made his lips itch. There was still no cabin, nor any sign of one. When a path split off from the trail, he followed it to a boarded-over mine entrance.

By noon, he'd begun to grow dizzy. He found what he thought was some yellow dock, seeds brown and starting to drop. He ate handfuls of them, broke the plant at the stem and stripped back the skin to get at the pith, then sat in the shade until he felt well enough to keep going.

After a while his stomach started to cramp up, his skin grown clammy. He kept riding but slower now, hunched over. A few times he stopped and kneeled at the side of the trail, heaving, but nothing came out.

He drank some water and convinced himself he felt at least a little better, but there were still patches of time when he wasn't sure what or who he was, when he would come to himself on a stretch of trail with no idea how he'd gotten there.

By early afternoon, the trail had begun to peter out, and he had a hard time following it. Soon after, he lost it altogether.

It was near dusk by the time he made it back down to the cave. He was tempted to keep going, down and past it, but he was exhausted, his horse too. No, better to stop a few hours in a place he knew, wait a little, rest a little, continue back down in the morning.

Near the cave, beside the creek, he found Sugg's horse. The blood angel was still swathed on its side, nearly black now in the failing light. "Sugg?" he called in a cracked voice, but nobody answered. Sugg hadn't had the horse yesterday when Rawley found him. It must have just wandered up here on its own, caught the scent of Rawley's own horse, maybe, or of Sugg himself. The horse didn't mean anything.

Still, despite that, when he climbed up the shale slope, he was relieved to find the cave was empty.

He lay on the floor of the cave in the dark, shivering. *Get up,* he kept telling himself, *start a fire.* But he just kept lying there.

Outside he heard the horses neighing. He expected them to settle quickly, but they didn't—something continued to agitate them. He closed his hand over his revolver. If he had to, he told himself, he could go out there and take care of it.

It grew dark, then darker still. It was so dark he wasn't sure where the cave's opening was anymore. Everything seemed the same dark around him. Even if he wanted to gather firewood, he wouldn't know where to go.

After a while, he started feeling warmer, and drowsy. He didn't need a fire, he told himself. All he needed was a little sleep. Tomorrow he'd start out fresh, ride back down the mountain, find food, find shelter, start life over again.

He woke to the warm glow of a fire. He lay there, staring into it, watching the flames weave back and forth. When he looked up, there was Sugg standing over him. He was swaying slightly, one boot missing, his clothing stiff with blood.

"Where the hell you come from?" Rawley asked. Or thought he asked. He wasn't sure if his lips moved. He tried to sit up but found he couldn't move. Sugg stayed looming over him a moment and then shuffled over to the other side of the fire, sitting heavily in the same spot he had been the night before, the spot marked out for him by his blood.

Sugg reached his hand into the fire and stirred it around. Sparks flew up, and the air smelled for an instant of burned hair. The flames didn't seem to bother Sugg, and he pulled his hand only slowly free.

"Comfy?" asked Sugg. "Still alive?"

Inside his head, Rawley asked, *What's happening? What's wrong with me?* Outside, the head didn't move.

"Doesn't matter much one way or the other," said Sugg. Then he opened his mouth wide and smiled. It was a terrible thing to watch. Rawley began to be very afraid.

For a long time Sugg just stayed there smiling. Then, just as suddenly, his face relaxed. "Shall I tell you a story?" he asked.

No, thought Rawley.

"Shall I tell you the story of not black bark?" he asked. "The story of everything black bark left out?"

No, thought Rawley. *Please.*

"A story, then," said Sugg. "A last one for the road. I'll make it a good one." He smiled again, that same terrible smile. Then his lips formed the words "Let's begin."

—*for Jesse Ball*

A Report

A week has passed since I made my report, and since that time, confined as I am, I have turned the words over and about in my mind. Those sentences that initially struck me as fluid and concise now seem poorly assembled and easily picked apart, prone to collapse at a moment's notice. Which, in fact, they must have done—otherwise why else would I be here? What at first I thought to be a model of clarity now seems to turn and spin, refusing to hold in place. Were I asked to deliver the report now, were they to come suddenly and open the door and ask me to recite it yet again by heart, would it be the same report? No. For even though the words would be the same, the report would not be, nor could I deliver it with the conviction I once had. Indeed, I have tried again to recite my report, this time to the walls of my cell. Though I can offer it up, so I believe, verbatim, now the words themselves seem to betray me. Or I to betray them, for my voice cannot give them the resonance they once had.

And yet they have not come for me, nor will they. All I see of them is a flash of the hand that tosses the bowl of food through the slot at the base of the door, but this is quickly gone.

When I was first conveyed here, after delivering my report, I tried to call out. I shouted that a mistake had been made. I begged and pleaded, then cried for help. Very quickly, I heard the other prisoners calling back, telling me to hush, warning me that I was making a mistake. Yet I continued to cry out. I thought, I now believe, that some interaction with the forces that be, even a painful one that might leave me beaten or bleeding, would be preferable to no interaction at all.

And indeed it might well have been. But this was not what I was given.

When there came a noise at the door, I braced myself. Yet instead of the door sliding open, only the slot at the base of it did. A pale hand was quickly thrust in and withdrawn, leaving in its wake only a wadded scrap of paper. I hurriedly took up the scrap and smoothed it and saw written on it these words:

Hush, or we shall burn the soles of his feet.

What? I thought. *This is absurd.* They were not even threatening to hurt me, but threatening me indirectly by threatening someone else. Was I not even worthy of being threatened directly? And who was "he"? What was this he to me? Why did I care if the soles of his feet were burned?

And so I continued shouting, and only stopped when there came a commotion in the cell to the left of my own. There was the sound of the cell door being thrown open, a scuffle of some kind, and a raised and pleading voice, then a sizzling sound and a smell not unlike roasting meat. And then a man screaming, screaming, screaming. The sounds faded, and I heard footsteps walking briskly away and all seemed silent. Indeed, all *was* silent, myself included, with the exception of the groans of the man in the cell next to me, which went on for some hours until, apparently, he passed out.

This was day one.

I rub my feet, the bottoms of them in particular. Ever since I received the crumpled note through my slot I have become hyperconscious of my feet. They are the first portion of my body I am aware of when I awake in the morning and the last of me to go to sleep at night. I rub them and wonder when it will be their turn to be burned.

I cannot help but wonder if I know the man who was tortured. For why would they threaten me with the torture of an unknown man? Still, if I did know him, why would they neglect to inform me of who he is? If it is my father they torture, or my brother, or even a friend, would that not be more effective than simply knowing they are torturing someone anonymous on my behalf?

You would think so, but as it turns out, no. It is worse for me not knowing who the man is—not knowing if I know him, not knowing if the punishment is arbitrary—than being certain he is someone close to me. If he is someone chosen at random, made to suffer for no reason at all, then we are all damned, and this is all the more terrible a place.

Since the first day I have remained silent, or nearly so. I have had moments of briefly calling out or whispering, but have fallen silent long before scribbled notes and threats might begin to arrive through my slot. I have tried to make contact with the man in the cell next to mine, but except for the groans he made on the first and second day, and the curses he gave as he began to walk again on his injured feet on the third, he has not responded to me.

Nevertheless, despite never having seen him, I have a vivid image of him in my head. He may very well be tall and thin, but in my head he is short and nervous. Like me. He wears the round, thick glasses of an accountant, glasses not unlike my own—or he did, anyway, before the glasses were broken, ground to pieces beneath the feet of one of the guards as he burned the bottoms of his feet. Without them the world is a blur, or nearly so.

He is confused as to why he is here. Like me he has never been given an explanation, like me he shouted the first day he arrived, and like me they threatened him by torturing his neighbor until he fell silent. Because of this, I tell myself, he knew what would happen when somebody else started to yell, and perhaps suspected too that eventually it would be he who would fall subject to someone else's punishment.

But when that punishment came, would he accept it and see it as expiation for the punishment he had inflicted on someone else? Or would he resent the person who had refused to fall silent and thus gave it to him? Would he hate those who kept him imprisoned here? Yes, surely, I told myself, some admixture of all of these, though in what quantities and to what degree, who could say? And who could say too if he would go so far as to not only feel these feelings, but to despise as well the words on the scrap of paper he knew must have appeared in the cell next to his—the warning that had been ignored and that had caused his suffering.

And was it always the same warning? Were the feet always what they threatened to burn? Did you always know the punishment that awaited you because of the punishment you had caused to be inflicted upon someone else?

I have to wait until my fourth day to find out. Or not find out exactly, for that is what you can never do, not so long as they keep you confined. You can imagine the man in the cell next to you; you can give him an appearance, borrowed perhaps from your own appearance or an amalgam of your appearance and that of someone close to you—a father, a brother, a friend. But there will always be a gap between name and body. You will never catch a glimpse of him, never know for certain what correlation there is, if any, between your imagination and his reality.

You can imagine too that like you he does not know why he is here. But you are not the only one who can play at this game. Surely he is imagining you as well, and in his mind, you are already other than what you believe yourself to be. Perhaps he is thinking that, like him, you are here for very specific reasons, because of your support of the opposition, say. But you do not support the opposition—you made that very clear in your report, or thought you did—*I* made that very clear in my report, I mean to say, or thought I did; I am getting my pronouns confused—and the idea that he might think this of you, of me, worries me. For if that is the case, who knows what else he has gotten wrong?

And here is the real difficulty with such confinement: it is not that you are kept in, but that the world is kept out. You know the world is out there still—you are given just enough noise (footsteps, muttering, groaning) that you can't help but know this. But you can't construct it fully from the little you have been given. You know there are people around you, just beyond the walls of your cell, but you have no inkling of what they might look like or even why they are here, whether they would embrace you as a friend or destroy you as an enemy. You know there are guards, but you cannot begin to construct them from the brief flash of a hand, sometimes pale, sometimes not, you see twice a day through the slot at the bottom of your door. There must be a guard attached to that hand, or several guards, though even that too begins to feel subject to question: It could be a false hand appended to the end of a stick. Or even a real hand severed from a prisoner, thrust onto a stick, and operated through some morbid sort of puppetry. Not a guard's hand at all.

No, the last thing you were certain of was standing still before them and giving your report, and finding yourself unable to determine their reaction to the report from their faces. Your mouth was uttering the final words of the report, but by this time you were hardly paying attention to what you were saying. Instead, you were wondering if the fact that you were unable to determine their reaction was a good sign or a bad sign. And then you finished your report and stood there, waiting. A moment later, from behind, a sack was thrust over your head, its drawstrings pulled tight enough around your throat to make you choke, then they did make you choke and you passed out, only to awaken here, in this cell. The last thing you remember are expressionless faces listening to your report. The way that even at the very last second, just before the sack engulfed your head, they showed no reaction at all to what was about to happen to you.

I am saying "you" again rather than "I" or "he." And this too is part of the problem.

The fourth day is marked by a commotion. Guards are coming down the hall in what sounds like a large group, dragging something behind them. I lie on my stomach and try to peer through the slot, but no, as always, the slot is kept blocked except when I am fed.

In any case, I hear them pass by. Yes, I am sure they are dragging something. Or someone, I imagine. They open the door to the right of my own, and I hear the sound of someone or something thrown in. Then the door clangs shut again, and the footsteps recede.

For a time after that, nothing happens. A few minutes pass, then perhaps an hour. Then I hear the sound of a groan and I think, *We begin.*

"Hello?" a voice calls after a few moments. "Hello?"

I do not answer. Nobody does.

"Is anybody there?" A little louder this time. Still nobody answers.

"Why am I here?" the voice yells. It is bawling it out this time. "Shhh," I hear someone else say, and the voice grasps eagerly at that. "Hello, hello?" it says. "Can't you help me? I'm not supposed to be here. It's a mistake." And when there is no further response it keeps saying this, louder and louder, yelling now.

I listen to it as long as I can stand, growing more and more anxious until, at last, panicked and frantic, I can't stop from blurting out:

"For God's sake, man, be quiet!"

But, just like my voice did a few days before, this voice keeps yelling. Very quickly it becomes too upset to stop. I can picture the man attached to it—his eyes rolling in his head, the feeling of the sack being thrust over his head and the sensation of being choked still vivid—still amazed that the result of giving his report is this (assuming, like me, he was made to give a report). He is incredulous. No, there must be some mistake. He has always been a supporter of the regime, and he has issued his reports impeccably. No, there must be some mistake!

And in the meantime, here I am, listening to him call out, feeling time running out not just for him, but for myself as well. Yes, I feel all the things I described the man who was beaten on my behalf feeling, and, in addition, a certain resignation. I take off my glasses and lean them carefully in the far corner of the cell, hoping the guards will not seem them, that they will survive intact. And then, not knowing what else to do, I sit down on the ground and wait for what I know to be coming next.

There are the sounds of footsteps in the hallway, slow and measured. The man who is shouting hesitates for a moment, thinking perhaps help has come. There is the sound of his slot being opened and closed, and then the footsteps recede.

For a moment there is only silence. I imagine him uncrumpling the paper and reading it and seeing the message on it. *Hush, or we will burn the soles of his feet.* He does not know that by "he" they mean me, but if he did he would not care.

And so he starts yelling again. It goes on for two minutes, maybe three, before the sounds of the guards' feet are again in the hall, walking past the man's cell and coming toward my own. I clench my teeth and wait.

But they do not stop at my cell. Instead, they continue on, to the cell just past my own, the cell that houses, if I am not mistaken, the man whose feet were burned before, because of me.

The door clangs open. The man is already screaming; his cries are terrifying to hear. There is the smell of his burned flesh and more screaming. Then, mercifully, he passes out. And then, very slowly, the measured sounds of the guards' feet as they leave.

Why not me? I wonder. Did they make a mistake? Did they simply forget it was my turn?

Or, worse, do they always torture the same man? What has he done that they choose to burn the soles of his feet over and over again?

Or, worse still, perhaps there is no system or logic to it at all.

Perhaps it can be anyone at any time, and there is no means of knowing when it will be you, or how often, or if it will ever stop.

Burn me, I am thinking as, lying on the floor, I stare up at the ceiling. Were it not as dark as it is, the ceiling would be a blur for me because my glasses are still in the corner. I know they are there, but I cannot bring myself to get them. What could there be here that I would possibly want to see?

I think about my report. It was simple. I had been asked to observe a man. I was to watch a house, record said man's comings and goings over the course of a single day. This I did, just as they had asked me to do. Then I was to report what I saw.

Coming: The man came to the house, driving a small car. I do not know the make of the car, but I know the car was blue. And small. He got out of the car, made his way to the door, and opened the door with a key.

Going: A moment later, the man was outside again, this time running, a panicked look on his face, his shirt sodden with blood. I could not initially determine if the blood was his own or belonged to someone else. But when, in trying to open the door of his car, he fell first to his knees and then slowly swayed and collapsed completely, I was able to deduce that yes, it was indeed his blood.

This is what I reported. As I had been asked to do, I stayed in position until night fell, then I came and made my report. I thought carefully about how to phrase everything, what to say and what not to say. I gave a description of the car: blue and small. I described the man's shirt, how it looked both before and after the blood. I did not give the man's name because I did not know his name. I had only been shown a photograph of him. I had no idea who he was, nor what importance, if any, he had.

I did not describe the two men who came out of the house perhaps five minutes after the man had collapsed, nor the way one reached the end of the front walk and walked to the left, and the other reached the end of the front walk and walked to the right, each of them seemingly ignoring not only the other, but also the man lying prone in a pool of his own blood. Nor did I discuss how one of the men later doubled back, perhaps two minutes later, and entered the dying or perhaps now dead man's car and either put something into the glove compartment or took something out of it. I had these and other facts ready at my fingertips if they were to ask me about them. But my sense was that unless I was questioned about them, they were outside of the purview of my report. Perhaps, though, I was wrong about this. Perhaps that is why I am here.

I sleep for a while, but it is a fitful sleep. I am awakened for good when the quality of the light in the room begins to change, when the darkness pales a little in the way we know acknowledges the day. By "we," I mean, of course, "I." *I* know. I can only speak for myself—I need to remember that. I am awakened by a reassuring thought: Perhaps they are not burning anyone's feet. Perhaps it is all a trick, a simulation. Perhaps they have a recording of someone being beaten and they simply play that over and over again.

If I can manage to believe that, perhaps it will not bother me nearly as much. Perhaps my feet will stop tingling.

I hear sounds of movement in the cell to the left of me and in the cell to the right of me. If the man in the cell to the right is a recording, he is a very long recording. No, there must be a man there after all.

I would like to say I was shocked by what I saw, by the man dying in front of me. But no, I was not shocked. I have delivered enough of these reports to not be surprised by what happens when I am collecting my data for them. No, I was much more shocked by the sounds I heard as they burned the soles of the man's feet next to me, and by the flesh I smelled burning. Would I have been as shocked if I could see it happening? I don't think so.

After five days, it is too early to wonder if I will ever know why they put a sack over my head and brought me here. And yet, I cannot help but wonder. It is too early to wonder if I will ever be released, and yet I cannot help but wonder this as well.

Sixth day. I think. I awaken to a strange sound, a kind of clicking that at first I think I am imagining, that at first I think resides somewhere within my skull. But then I cover my ears and no longer hear it. I pull myself to my knees and crawl around the cell to try to locate it, but for a time it stops and I cannot. Perhaps, I think, I imagined it after all. But finally it starts up again, and I realize where it is coming from.

Someone is striking the iron door of their cell with something, but doing it cautiously, relatively softly, so as not to attract the attention of the guards. A faint tapping sound. Coming from somewhere to my left, from the cell to my left probably, or perhaps a cell beyond that. Two quick taps, then a slow one, then a more complicated sequence. It is deliberate and oddly syncopated—a pattern, but I can't immediately decipher it. It is not Morse code, nor any other code I know. It is nothing I am familiar with. I try to reproduce the pattern by marking it in the dirt. By doing so I realize that it is a sequence that is repeated—thirty quick and slow taps, then a very long pause, then repeated.

It goes on for a while, then the guards do their rounds, their footsteps echoing through the hall, and the tapping falls silent. When they are gone, it starts again.

How is it being done? I wonder. We have no shoes, or at least I have no shoes. My belt has also been taken from me, and apart from a little scattering of straw, there is nothing in the cell.

And then I remember my glasses.

It takes me a while to figure out how to make a sound, a while after that to make it long enough and at the right moment for the tapper to hear it and to stop to listen to it. But when I play the sequence out, more or less as he has done, he taps four times in rapid succession, which I read as applause. What is it? What am I saying? What message am I repeating? I don't know. But once I have repeated it once, I repeat it again and again and again. I am still wondering about my report, still wondering if I could have or should have done things differently, but the tapping makes me think of it a little less.

I repeat it, and repeat it again, wondering how long I can do it before it destroys the frames of my glasses, which are already bent. I repeat it until, in the silence between repetitions, I hear, tentatively at first, then louder and with more confidence, a repetition of the pattern to my right. I listen, making sure the pattern is correct, is the same as I heard it, and when I decide that yes, it is, or close enough, I give four taps in rapid procession, applauding him and encouraging him. Then the message is receding from me, sent to wend its way somewhere, to someone, down the line of cells. I am part of a chain conveying a message that I cannot understand. But perhaps someone understands it.

For a while I can make out, traveling its way down the hall away from me, the sound of tapping, though quickly it becomes the ghost of itself and I can make little out. And then it fades entirely. I can still imagine that it is traveling on, can still convince myself, rightly or wrongly, that it exists, but I can no longer hear it.

I am waiting for a message to come back. I lie on the ground and think of the report, the words that may or may not have brought me here. It might have been a mistake not to mention in my report having seen the man killed, but then again, perhaps I would have done that and would have been brought here anyway. Who can say? It may be something much simpler than that, and have nothing to do with me. Perhaps every twelfth person who delivers a report is treated as I have been. Or perhaps there is no explaining it.

I consider: If I were asked to deliver a report on this tapping, how would I deliver it?

Perhaps such a report is something that should not properly be delivered at all, at least not until I have figured out what the tapping means to say.

I try to breathe softly. I try not to breathe. I am waiting for the tapping to return.

All night I stay awake, listening for the return of the tapping, the movement of the tapping back the other way. But it never comes.

In the morning, I turn again to the pattern I have scratched in the dirt, the sequence of taps, and stare at it. I try once again to crack the code, looking for frequency of gestures among the sequence that might suggest one letter or another. A vowel, say, or one of our more common consonants. All I come up with is gibberish. I try thinking of the taps coming in pairs, with each pair signifying jointly rather than individually, but get no further with this.

I continue to wait for the tapping to return, either in its original form or in some new sequence, returning from where I sent it back to its source. It still does not return.

Perhaps the tapping hasn't even been started by a prisoner, but by a guard banging on an empty cell from the outside. What, I think for an absurd moment, what if the tapped message I passed along is *Hush, or we will burn the soles of his feet?* No, ridiculous of course, but it reminds me that I am passing along something I know nothing about. It could just as well say *The man in such and such a cell is a traitor and should be killed.* Perhaps the cell mentioned is my own.

And yet, I know if the tapping returns, I will not be able to stop myself from passing it along. There is nothing else for me to do here besides get lost in my thoughts, in my words, in the failed report. It matters less what the message says than the fact that I am among those passing it along, and that there is someone before me to offer it and someone after me to receive it. It is the closest thing I have had to human contact since arriving.

Still no tapping. Should I, I wonder, start it again? I could, but perhaps that would confuse things. If he felt it needed to be tapped again, wouldn't the man in the cell to the left of me do so?

Perhaps there is a man in one of these cells who has no means by which to tap. Perhaps the message has become lodged with him and cannot go forward.

In the end, unbidden, I tap the sequence out again, but it is not picked up by the person in the cell beside me. I tap it again, am still ignored. And so I stop. I sit and wait, and listen. It seems now essential that it come back. And yet it does not come back. I wait until the end of the day, but nothing comes. Finally, I fall asleep.

It is a new day. Eighth day. Or eightieth. Or eight hundredth. Who can say? I listen for the tapping on a door but hear nothing. I listen to the sound of my fellow prisoners but hear them not at all. I might as well be alone here.

And then, suddenly, after seconds, or perhaps minutes, I hear them: the noise of feet in the corridor, the sound of a cell door opening a few cells away, the sound of something, or someone, being thrown inside.

Now I wait. Surely now it shall be my turn. Soon he will regain consciousness, groan, start to cry out. Soon, someone's feet will be burned. Perhaps your own. *Hush,* you tell yourself. *Be quiet, and wait.*

The Punish

I

They called it The Punish, though how they came up with that name Willem later couldn't remember. But it was not The Punishment, it was not The Punisher: it was The Punish. He was sure this was the case, and yes, later still, one of the last things Wilson would do would be to confirm that that was the name, The Punish, that Willem hadn't remembered wrong.

They had been eight years old, both of them. They shared the same birthday, even though in almost every other way they were opposites. He, Willem, was short, sallow skinned, and dark haired, while Wilson was large, ruddy, and blond. They lived on either side of Canyon Road. Willem was in Edgewood, a conglomeration of tract houses, while Wilson was about two hundred yards farther along, on the curve uphill, in a larger house that his father, an architect, had designed. They shared the same religion but did not go to the same church—Canyon Road was the dividing line between one congregation and the other. They did not even go to the same school; once again, the road was the dividing line.

Their parents ran in different circles. And yet, somehow they had become friends of sorts.

How that had happened, Willem wasn't sure. Looking back on it years later, he just couldn't remember. Perhaps they had simply met walking down the street. It was a question he should have thought to pose to Wilson before it was too late.

But they had been friends, there was no denying that, even if the friendship had only lasted a few months, if that. Even if the friendship hadn't outlasted The Punish.

For the first few months after The Punish had ended, Willem thought about it all the time. He not only thought about it, but schemed and planned. He didn't realize at the time that The Punish had ended. He was waiting for his turn. Despite what had been done to him, despite the pain that it had caused him, he still wanted his turn. That was why you submitted to The Punish: once you had submitted to it, it was your turn to run it, to be The Punish itself. He wanted his turn.

And so he had been frustrated when Wilson's mother had kept Wilson away from him after that. Wilson hadn't been the one hurt: Willem had. And his own mother had been too flustered and concerned by what had happened to him to be able to lay the blame clearly on Wilson. She had never gotten the full story out of Willem. She hadn't really tried, and Willem certainly hadn't volunteered. The Punish was personal, private, something between him and Wilson. Or so he had thought. But the fact that Wilson's mother claimed he was never at home whenever Willem came by after that eventually made him realize that Wilson had told his mother about The Punish, that she was deliberately keeping the two of them apart. But even once he realized this, he still kept dropping by, until Wilson's mother finally told him, getting his name wrong as usual, "William, please do not to bother to come again."

After that, he had tried not to go by again. But in the end, after a few months of resisting the urge, he had, only to find that Wilson and his parents were gone, and that there was a For Sale sign in the yard. It surprised him that Wilson's father would leave a house he had designed specifically for himself. But he had, and he had taken Wilson's mother and Wilson himself with him. *Was it because of The Punish?* wondered Willem. And while his head thought *How could that be?* his hand tingled strangely to think that yes, that might be why.

But then, after a few months, he forgot about it. He found friends at his own school who were more like him. He tried with one or two of them to restart The Punish, but nobody understood it like Wilson had. After all, Wilson had helped come up with it. Sure, The Punish was just two kids daring one another, little more than that, each dare a little more serious than the last, but it was more than that too. He couldn't find anybody who understood this like he and Wilson had.

And so he let it go. He forgot about The Punish. He found the slot that people thought best suited him and he crammed himself into it. He grew up. He settled into a life. He went to church and then, slowly, he stopped going, drifted away from it. He got married and had a child, and then the child left for college. His wife, too, left eventually, and he was alone again, working the same job he'd taken out of high school, very skilled with his hands, despite his maimed finger.

II.

His story might have ended there. He might have simply gone on doing what he was doing, living a simple, solitary, and almost monastic life until he died. Instead, one evening after coming home from work, he settled into the Barcalounger, leaned his head back on the grayish doily slung to protect the headrest, and turned on the TV. It was a little after six, in the middle of the local news, and there was someone being interviewed who looked familiar. Even so, he watched most of the segment with only mild curiosity before, near the end of it, they flashed the name again along the bottom, and he realized with a start that it was Wilson. Yes, he could see the eight-year-old boy still in him, incompletely hidden in a body that, like Willem's, was now fifty years old. "Philanthropist" it said next to his name. *What does that even mean?* wondered Willem. Not that he didn't know the word, but what did it mean in Wilson's case?

He went online and found that Wilson and his family hadn't gone far. They'd relocated just a few towns away. Wilson had remained there and, years later, had started some sort of tech business that had gone public and left him inordinately wealthy. With some of this money he had established a foundation, the Wilson Group, focused on education. One of their projects was back here in Wilson's hometown, a new school to replace not the school Wilson had gone to—which had remained well funded and supported—but the school Willem had gone to. There would be a groundbreaking the next day, and Wilson would be there.

That was the first time in years that the words "The Punish" came back to him. At first he couldn't believe they had called it that—it didn't make any sense as a phrase, just sounded wrong: a verb used as a noun, apparently deliberately. But The Punishment and The Punisher didn't sound right either. Sounded even less right, in fact. So maybe they had called it The Punish after all.

He'll be in town, he thought idly. *Why not ask him?*

He thought about it all through dinner, which he made for himself by opening a can and warming up the contents in a saucepan. He had learned to eat directly out of the saucepan, placing a hot pad on the table under it so that it wouldn't melt the vinyl tablecloth. He could save washing a dish that way. *No,* he thought, *The Punish, it must have been that.* But he wasn't sure. Since Wilson was coming into town, why not ask him?

But would Wilson even remember him? It had been so many years ago, and though he remembered Wilson, why would Wilson remember him?

He chewed his food slowly, thoroughly. It was a game he played with himself: try not to look at the labels when opening the cans, then guess what the food is when eating it. Usually he couldn't guess.

But of course Wilson would remember him, he thought. Or at the very least, Wilson would remember taking his finger.

He didn't remember what the early dares had been. He did think—though he wasn't completely certain—that Wilson had been the one to start The Punish, had maybe even been the one to choose the name. Yes, that sounded right: Wilson was from the better part of town, the better house—he would have been running the show. Willem would have let him. He didn't remember the order of the dares or why they had seemed to build so smoothly and easily that both he and Wilson had always been willing to undergo them. He remembered a few of them: Wilson stubbing out a match against the flesh on the back of Willem's knee, Wilson having him hyperventilate and then locking his elbow quickly around his neck to black him out, Wilson putting a thumbtack on a chair and daring him to sit on it. There had been other things he remembered less completely, most of them minor—little, simple transgressions—but a few worse. And there had been things too that Wilson had had to do, certainly. The fact that Willem was having trouble remembering any of them now didn't mean there hadn't been.

The final Punish, they had been at Wilson's house, both of his parents out. They had been idling in the basement, half-watching television, paging through a large atlas spread out flat on the floor, when he noticed Wilson staring at him.

"What?" Willem said.

"Whose turn is it?"

"Whose turn for what?" he asked, although he knew what Wilson meant.

"It's your turn, right?" said Wilson.

He started to nod and then stopped. Was it his turn? No, he would have sworn it was Wilson's. But Wilson, looking at him steadily, seemed so sure. So he nodded.

"Good," said Wilson. "Yes. Let's go upstairs."

They climbed the stairs from the basement. Willem, his mind already moving forward to meet whatever was going to happen, tripped a few times. They came to the top of the stairs and into the hallway leading to the kitchen. Then, instead of staying on that main floor as they'd always done in the past, Wilson led him around the corner to a circular metal stairway leading to the top floor.

Willem followed him up, holding to the center pole and trying not to look over the edge as he climbed. He had never been to the top floor before. The stairs were open on the outside, the treads thin metal rectangles connected to nothing apart from the center pole. He had a hard time understanding what supported them, why they didn't bend under his weight. By the time he got to the top, he was crawling on his hands and knees like a dog, trying to spread his weight over as many treads as possible.

He clambered out onto a carpeted floor, but the carpet was rough and scratchy, almost like rope. Wilson was already there, watching him with a curious expression that Willem didn't quite understand at the time and that he would think about for months afterwards, still without understanding it. Then Wilson moved forward and, with a steady hand, helped him stand.

It had been all of that: Wilson taking charge, and his crawling up the stairs like an animal and then being in a part of the house he hadn't been in before. Alone each thing was very little, but together they added up to something that made him even more receptive to this particular manifestation of The Punish. Perhaps

Wilson had been setting this up the whole way along, through every dare he issued within every manifestation of The Punish. In any case, it was all of that taken together that made him not even hesitate before sticking his little finger to the first knuckle into what Wilson informed him was not his father's cigar cutter, but a finger guillotine.

The rest of it was a blur. That same strange expression on Wilson's face. A surprising lack of pain, but a feeling rather of heat, followed very quickly by an intense, buzzing throb, and then finally pain unlike anything he'd experienced before. Someone was screaming, and only later did he realize it must be him. There was blood everywhere. Then suddenly Wilson's mother was there, her face very white, and she was gathering Willem to her and running out to the car, driving him to the emergency room.

III.

He arrived early at the groundbreaking. Nobody else was there except for a couple of construction workers who were busy cordoning off the area with yellow tape. They kept looking at him strangely. He felt conspicuous. But he just stayed there and waited, trying not to worry about it, and eventually people started showing up and he began to blend in. Then, all at once, a whole crowd of people flooded in and then stood around talking in a tight cluster while the television cameras were set up. Wilson was there among them. *If I just stand here, will he notice me?* wondered Willem. But Wilson didn't seem to.

The ceremony was over almost as quickly as it began, then Wilson and the officials with him were striding back to their cars. Willem had to almost run to catch up with them. When he grabbed hold of Wilson's coat, the man gave a little jerk of surprise, the movement rippling through the people around them.

"Wilson?" Willem said.

"Yes?" said Wilson, his eyes cautious.

"It's Willem," he said, extending his hand to shake. "Don't you remember me?"

Wilson had started to shake his head no, but by then Willem had slipped his hand into Wilson's own, pressing it so that Wilson would feel the missing finger. He watched the puzzlement in Wilson's eyes quickly change to recognition, and watched too the blood drain from his face. Then the same expression came over his face that Willem remembered from the last session of The Punish, the one he still didn't quite know how to read.

"Ah," said Wilson, freeing his hand. "Of course."

"I know you're busy," said Willem. "But perhaps you've got a few minutes later to stop by? To catch up?"

"Ah, well," said Wilson, "I've a limited amount of time . . . I don't think—"

"I had a question for you," said Willem, ignoring whatever Wilson was trying to say. "What was that game we used to play called?"

And though he could see from his face that Wilson knew what he was talking about, Wilson pretended in front of the others that he didn't.

Willem reached into his pocket and took out the scrap of paper on which he had penciled his address. He pressed it into Wilson's hand. "I'm sure you have a punishing schedule." He smiled. "Well, if you do get time, stop by. And if not this trip, maybe the next." And then, feigning nonchalance, he left.

A few minutes later he was back at his house. He bustled around, made sure the porch light was on, the drinks were chilling, a bowl of nuts was set on the coffee table with a stack of paper napkins within easy reach. He did not know if Wilson would come because he wanted to come, because he was intrigued, because he remembered what The Punish had felt like, or if he would come because he was ashamed, or worried that Willem would tell someone that

Wilson had cut off his finger. But either way, he was sure, Wilson would come.

And indeed he did. He came very late and came alone. He stayed standing at the door for some time before finally allowing Willem to coax him in.

At first Willem didn't push him, just made idle small talk, though quickly he discovered that they had very little in common, knew very few of the same people. They had lived two hundred yards away from one another, but they might as well have been in different worlds. So they shared what little gossip they could share, then fell silent.

For a moment, Willem let the silence build, watching Wilson squirm. Wilson, he realized after a time, wasn't exactly sure why he had come. If Willem wasn't careful, he might try to leave.

A little nudge, thought Willem. *Just a little one.*

"Do you remember that game—" he started.

"The Punish," Wilson said. "We called it The Punish. But that was a long time ago," he said. "We were just kids."

"Do you remember some of the things we used to do as part of it?" asked Willem. "Besides my finger, I mean?"

For a moment Wilson did not respond. "I don't know that I want to talk about it," he said slowly, trying not to look at Willem's hand.

"Come on," Willem said. "It's what we have in common. It was so long ago. What possible harm could there be?"

But there *was* harm, a great deal of it, as Willem himself rightly knew. And as Wilson himself would soon find out. For unlike Wilson, Willem wasn't content to stop with a finger. No, with a finger, Willem was just getting started.

Wilson did not undergo The Punish willingly. But in the end, he did undergo it. It was a long time before anybody apart from Willem realized what had become of him.

A Collapse of Horses

I am certain nobody in my family survived. I am certain they burned, that their faces blackened and bubbled, just as did my own. But in their case they did not recover, but perished. You are not one of them, you cannot be, for if you were you would be dead. Why you choose to pretend to be, and what you hope to gain from it: this is what interests me.

Now it is your turn to listen to me, to listen to my proofs, though I know you will not be convinced. Imagine this: Walking through the countryside one day, you come across a paddock. Lying there on their sides, in the dust, unnaturally still, are four horses. All four are prone, with no horses standing. They do not breathe and do not, as far as you can see, move. They are, to all appearances, dead. And yet, on the edge of the paddock, not twenty yards distant, a man fills their trough with water. Are the horses alive and appearances deceptive? Has the man simply not yet turned to see that the horses are dead? Or has he been so shaken by what he has seen that he doesn't know what to do but proceed as if nothing has happened?

If you turn and walk hurriedly on, leaving before anything deci-
sive happens, what do the horses become for you? They remain both
alive and dead, which makes them not quite alive, nor quite dead.

And what, in turn, carrying that paradoxical knowledge in your
head, does that make you?

I do not think of myself as special, as anything but ordinary. I com-
pleted a degree at a third-tier university housed in the town where
I grew up. I graduated safely ensconced in the middle of my class. I
found passable employment in the same town. I met a woman,
married her, had children with her—three or perhaps four, there is
some disagreement on that score—and then the two of us fell gradually and gently out of love.

Then came an incident at work, an accident, a so-called freak
one. It left me with a broken skull and, for a short time, a certain
amount of confusion. I awoke in an unfamiliar place to find myself
strapped down. It seemed to me—I will admit this too—it seemed
for some time, hours at least, perhaps even days, that I was not in a
hospital at all, but in a mental facility.

But my wife, faithful and ever present, slowly soothed me into
a different understanding of my circumstances. My limbs, she
insisted, were restrained simply because I had been delirious. Now
that I no longer was, the straps could be loosened. Not quite yet,
but soon. There was nothing to worry about. I just had to calm
down. Soon, everything would return to normal.

In some ways, I suppose everything did. Or at least tried to. After the
accident, I received some minor compensation from my employer
and was put out to pasture. Such was the situation: myself, my wife,
my children, at the beginning of a hot and sweltering summer,
crammed in the house together with nowhere to go.

I would awaken each day to find the house different from how it
had been the day before. A door was in the wrong place, a window
had stretched a few inches longer than it had been when I had gone

to bed the night before, the light switch, I was certain, had been forced half an inch to the right. Always just a small thing, almost nothing at all, just enough for me to notice.

In the beginning, I tried to point these changes out to my wife. She seemed puzzled at first, then she became somewhat evasive in her responses. For a time, part of me believed her responsible: perhaps she had developed some deft technique for quickly changing and modifying the house. But another part of me felt certain, or nearly so, that this was impossible. And as time went on, my wife's evasiveness took on a certain wariness, even fear. This convinced me that not only was she not changing the house, but that daily her mind simply adjusted to the changed world and dubbed it the same. She literally could not see the differences I saw.

Just as she could not see that sometimes we had three children and sometimes four. No, she could only ever see three. Or perhaps four. To be honest, I don't remember how many she saw. But the point was, as long as we were in the house, there were sometimes three children and sometimes four. But that was due to the idiosyncrasies of the house as well. I would not know how many children there would be until I went from room to room. Sometimes the room at the end of the hall was narrow and had one bed in it, other times it had grown large in the night and had two. I would count the number of beds each morning when I woke up, and sometimes there would be three, sometimes four. From there, I could extrapolate how many children I had, and I found this a more reliable method than trying to count the children themselves. I would never know how much of a father I was until I counted beds.

I could not discuss this with my wife. When I tried to display my proofs for her, she thought I was joking. Quickly, however, she decided it was an indication of a troubled mental state and insisted I seek treatment—which, under duress, I did. To little avail. The only thing the treatment convinced me of was that there were certain things one shouldn't say even to one's spouse, things they are just not ready—and may never be ready—to hear.

My children were not ready for it either. The few times I tried to fulfill my duties as a father and sit them down to tell them the sobering truth, that sometimes one of them didn't exist, unless it was that sometimes one of them existed twice, I got nowhere. Or less than nowhere: confusion, tears, panic. And, after they reported back to my wife, more threats of treatment.

What, then, was the truth of the situation? Why was I the only one who could see the house changing? What were my obligations to my family in terms of helping them see and understand? How was I to help them if they did not desire to be helped?

Since I am a sensible man, a part of me couldn't help but wonder if what I was experiencing had any relation to reality at all. Perhaps there was something wrong with me. Perhaps, I tried to believe, the accident had changed me. I did try my level best, or nearly so, to see things their way. I tried to ignore the lurch reality took each morning, the way the house was not exactly the house it had been the night before, as if someone had moved us to a similar but not quite identical house as we slept. Perhaps they had. I tried to believe I had three, not four, children. And when that did not work, that I had four, not three, children. And when that didn't work, that there was no correlation between children and beds, to turn a blind eye to that room at the end of the hall and the way it kept expanding out or collapsing in like a lung. But nothing seemed to work. I could not believe.

Perhaps if we moved, things would be different. Perhaps the house was, in some manner or other, alive. Or haunted maybe. Or just wrong. But when I raised the idea of moving with my wife, she coughed out a strange barking laugh before enumerating all the reasons this was a bad idea. There was no money and little prospect of any coming in now that I'd had my accident and lost my job. We'd bought the house recently enough that we would take a substantial loss if we sold it. We simply could not afford to move.

And besides, what was wrong with the house? It was a perfectly good house.

How could I argue with this? From her perspective, of course, she was right, there was no reason to leave. For her there was nothing wrong with the house—how could there be? Houses don't change on their own, she told me indignantly; this was not something that reason could allow.

But for me, that was exactly the problem. The house, for reasons I didn't understand, wasn't acting like a house.

I spent days thinking, mulling over what to do. To get away from the house, I wandered alone in the countryside. If I walked long enough, I could return home sufficiently exhausted to sleep rather than spending much of the night on watch, trying to capture the moment when parts of the house changed. For a long time I thought that might be enough. That if I spent as little time in the house as possible and returned only when exhausted, I could bring myself not to think about how unsound it was. That I would wake up sufficiently hazy to no longer care what was where and how the house differed from before.

That might have gone on for a long time—even forever, or the equivalent. But then in my walks I stumbled upon, or perhaps was led to, something. It was a paddock. I saw horses lying in the dirt, seemingly dead. They couldn't be dead, could they? I looked to see if I could tell if they were breathing and found I could not. I could not say honestly if they were dead or alive, and I still cannot say. I noticed a man on the far side of the paddock filling their trough with water, facing away from them, and wondered if he had seen the horses behind him, and if not, when he turned, whether he would be as unsettled as I. Would he approach them and determine they were dead, or would his approach startle them to life? Or had he seen them dead already and had his mind been unable to take it in?

For a moment I waited. But at the time, in the moment, there seemed something more terrible to me about the idea of knowing for certain that the horses were dead than there was about *not* knowing whether they were dead or alive. And so I hastily left, not realizing that to escape a moment of potential discomfort, I was leaving them forever in my head as not quite dead but, in another sense, nearly alive. That to leave as I had was to assume the place of the man beside the trough without ever being able to turn and learn the truth.

In the days that followed, that image haunted me. I turned it over, scrutinized it, peered at every facet of it, trying to see if there was something I had missed, if there was a clue that would sway me toward believing the horses were alive or believing they were dead. If there was a clue to reveal to me that the man beside the trough knew more than I had believed. To no avail. The problem remained insolubly balanced. *If I go back,* I couldn't help asking myself, *will anything have changed?* Would the horses still, even now, be lying there? If they were, would they have begun to decay in a way that would prove them dead? Or would they be exactly as I had last seen them, including the man still filling the trough? What a terrifying thought.

Since I'd stumbled upon the paddock, I didn't know exactly where it was. Every walk I went on, even every step I took away from the house, I risked stumbling onto it again. I began walking slower, stopping frequently, scrutinizing my surroundings and shying away from any area that might remotely harbor a paddock. But after a while, I deemed even that insufficiently safe, and I found myself hardly able to leave the house.

And yet with the house always changing, I couldn't remain there either. There was, I gradually realized, a simple choice: either I would have to steel myself and return and confront the horses, or I would have to confront the house.

Either horse or house, either house or horse—but what sort of choice was that really? The words were hardly different, pronounced more or less the same, with only one letter having accidentally been dialed up too high or too low in the alphabet. No, I came to feel, by going out to avoid the house and finding the horses I had, in a matter of speaking, simply found the house again. It was, it must be, that the prone horses were there for me, to teach a lesson to me, that they were meant to tell me something about their near namesake, the house.

The devastation of that scene, the collapse of the horses, gnawed on me. It was telling me something. Something I wasn't sure I wanted to hear.

At first, part of me resisted the idea. No, I told myself, it was too extreme a step. Lives were at stake. The lives of my wife and at least three children. The risks were too great.

But what was I to do? In my mind I kept seeing the collapsed horses, and I felt my thoughts again churn over their state. Were they alive or were they dead? I kept imagining myself there at the trough, paralyzed, unable to turn and look, and it came to seem to me my perpetual condition. In my worst moments, it seemed the state not only of me, but of the whole world, with all of us on the verge of turning around and finding the dead behind us. And from there, I slipped back to the house—which, like the horses, seemed in a sort of suspended state. I knew it was changing, that something strange was happening. I was sure of that at least, but I didn't know how or what the changes meant, and I couldn't make anyone else see them. When it came to the house, I tried to convince myself, I could see what others could not, but the rest of the world was like the man filling the horse trough, unable to see the fallen horses.

Thinking this naturally led me away from the idea of the house and back instead to the horses. What I should have done, I told myself, was to have thrown a rock. I should have stooped and scraped the dirt until my fingers closed around a stone, then shied it at one of the horses, waiting either for the meaty thud of dead flesh or the shudder and annoyed whicker of a struck living horse. Not knowing is something you can only suspend yourself in for the briefest moment. No, even if what you have to face is horrible, is an inexplicably dead herd of horses, even an explicably dead family, it must be faced.

And so I turned away from the house and went back to look for the paddock, steeling myself for whatever I would find. I was ready, rock in hand. I would find out the truth about the horses, and I would accept it, no matter what it was.

Or at least I would have. But no matter how hard I looked, no matter how long I walked, I could not find the paddock. I walked for miles, days even. I took every road, known and unknown, but it simply wasn't there.

Was something wrong with me? I wondered. Had the paddock existed at all? Was it simply something my mind had invented to cope with the problem of the house?

House, horse—horse, house: almost the same word. For all intents and purposes, in this case, it was the same word. I would still throw a rock, so to speak, I told myself, but I would throw that so-called rock not at a horse, but at a house.

But still I hesitated, thinking, planning. Night after night I sat imagining coils of smoke writhing around me followed by rising flames. In my head, I watched myself waiting patiently, calmly, until the flames had reached just the right height, then I began to call out to my family, awakening them, urging them to leave the house. In my head we unfurled sheets through windows and shimmied nimbly to safety. We reached safety every time. I saw our escape so many times in my head, rendered in just the same way, that I realized it would take the smallest effort on my part to jostle it out of the realm of imagination and into the real world. Then the house would be gone and could do me no more damage, and my family and I would be safe.

I had had enough unpleasant interactions with those who desired to give me treatment since my accident, however, that I knew to take steps to protect myself. I would have to make the fire look like an accident. For this purpose, I took up smoking.

I planned carefully. I smoked for a few weeks, just long enough to accustom my wife and children to the idea. They didn't care for it, but they did not try to stop me. Since my accident, they had been shy of me and rarely tried to stop me from doing anything.

Seemingly as a concession to my wife, I agreed not to smoke in the bedroom. I promised to smoke only outside the house. With the proviso that, if it was too cold to smoke outside, I might do so downstairs, near an open window.

During the third or perhaps fourth week after I took up smoking, with my wife and children asleep, it was indeed too cold—or at least I judged that I could argue it to have been such if confronted after the fact. So I cracked open the window near the couch and prepared the images in my mind. I would, I told myself, allow my arm to droop, the tip of my cigarette to nudge against the fabric of the couch. And then I would allow first the couch and then the drapes to begin to smoke and catch fire. I would wait until the moment when, in my fantasies, I had envisioned myself standing and calling for my wife and children, then I would do just that and all would be as I had envisioned. Soon my family and I would be safe, and the house would be destroyed.

Once that was done, I thought, perhaps I would find the paddock again as well, with the horses standing this time and clearly alive.

And yet, the fabric of the couch did not catch fire, instead only smoldering and stinking, and soon I pressed the cigarette in too deeply and it died. I found and lit another; when the result was the same, I gave up on both the couch and the cigarette.

I turned instead to matches and used them to ignite the drapes. As it turned out, these burned much better, going up all at once and lighting my hair and clothing along with them.

By the time I'd flailed about enough to extinguish my body, the whole room was aflame. Still, I continued with my plan. I tried to call to my wife and children, but when I took a breath to do so, my lungs filled with smoke and, choking, I collapsed.

I do not know how I lived through the fire. Perhaps my wife dragged me out and then went back for the children and perished only then. When I awoke, I was here, unsure of how I had arrived. My face and body were badly burned, and the pain was excruciating. I asked about my family, but the nurse dodged the question, shushed me, and only told me I should sleep. This was how I knew my family was dead, that they had been lost in the fire and the nurse didn't know how to tell me. My only consolation was that the house, the source of all our problems, had burned to the ground.

For a time I was kept alone, drugged. How long, I cannot say. Perhaps days, perhaps weeks. Long enough in any case for my burns to slough and heal, for the skin grafts that I must surely have needed to take effect, for my hair to grow fully back. The doctors must have worked very hard on me, for I must admit that except to the most meticulous eye, I look exactly as I did before the fire.

So, you see, I have the truth straight in my mind, and it will not be easy to change. There is little point in you coming to me with these stories, little point in pretending once again that my house remains standing and was never touched by flame. Little point coming here pretending to be my wife, claiming there was no fire, that you found me lying on the floor in the middle of our living room with my eyes staring fixedly into the air, seemingly unharmed.

No, I have accepted that I am the victim of a tragedy, one of my own design. I know my family is gone, and though I do not yet understand why you would want to convince me that you are my wife, what you hope to gain, eventually I will. You will let something slip, and the game will be over. At worst, you are deliberately trying to deceive me so as to gain something from me. But what? At best, someone has decided this might lessen the blow, that if I can be made to believe my family is not dead, or even just mostly dead and not quite alive, I might be convinced not to surrender to despair.

Trust me: whether you wish me good or ill, I do hope you succeed. I would like to be convinced, I truly would. I would love to open my eyes and suddenly see my family surrounding me, safe and sound. I would even tolerate the fact that the house is still standing, that unfinished business remains between it and me, that somewhere horses still lie collapsed and waiting to be either alive or dead, that we all in some sense remain like the man at the trough with our backs turned. I understand what I might have to gain from it, but you, I still do not understand.

But do your worst: disrupt my certainty, try to fool me, make me believe. Get me to believe there is nothing dead behind me. If you can make that happen, I think we both agree, then anything is possible.

Three Indignities

1.

During the surgery they peeled the ear off his head, severing the nerves so they could get at the tumor that had spread its fingers across his jaw and up one side of his neck. Then the ear was forced back down, sewn into place. *The nerve had to be sacrificed*, the doctor told him when, disoriented and nauseous, he awoke. What was there, if anything, to do about it now?

"Sacrificing the nerve" apparently meant that the link between ear and body was mostly gone. There was still *something* there—he could tell by the way the dead ear pressed against his skull when he tried to sleep on his side—but whatever was there no longer made sense. He could feel around it, piece it together with his fingers, but in a very real way the ear was no longer a part of him.

The severed nerve throbbed, pulsed. At times, inside his skull, he almost could feel the ear there again, but it was no longer an ear. He could feel it trying to tap in to the nerve. And then it did momentarily tap in, and he felt it unfurl like a fan and then, suddenly, clench like a fist. It was no longer his ear, no longer an ear, but its own creature, a separate animal—sewn firmly to one side of his head but not part of him, no, not at all.

2.

There had been premonitions. Back before he had had the surgery, they had herded him into a room that contained a large medical hoop, plastic and metal, and had inserted him into it—not all of him, just his head and neck. A male nurse, a Croat or a Serb—unless he was an Albanian—had bluntly informed him they would have to inject him with *contrast,* and there was a chance, albeit minuscule, that this would kill him. *Please sign here.*

He signed. He waited patiently while the nurse attempted to insert an intravenous needle into one arm, failed, tried again, failed, then called another nurse in to inflict the needle painfully but successfully into the other arm. He lay there as the bench he was on slid jerkily into the hoop, an apparatus within the ring spinning around, whirring. Then the whirring stopped. *That's all?* he thought, relieved.

But that was not all. As it turned out, that was only the test run. When he was slid again deep into the hoop, and the so-called contrast was injected, he felt a surge of intense, unbearable panic. It didn't last long, only a few seconds, but by the time it was done, he was, he felt, no longer the same person. Or, for that matter, even a person at all.

3.

Months later, just as he was beginning to get over it, just as he had reached the point where the panic was all but forgotten and his ear, though still numb, had begun again to feel as though it belonged to him, something else went wrong.

It took him some time to notice it, but after that things moved very rapidly. In a matter of minutes he found himself lying on a table. He was wearing a paper gown with a hole cut to allow the extrusion of his penis, a mercilessly attractive nurse having pushed a hypodermic's worth of Novocain through his urethral opening, after which she clamped his penis off midhead.

And then, with a polite smile, she left him alone.

For five minutes, maybe ten, it was just him alone in the room, trying not to look down at his clamped-off and bloodless penis, which was numb in some parts and stinging in others. Five or ten minutes, or maybe twenty. But however long it was, it felt longer.

It went on so long that he was relieved when the doctor finally arrived. But only briefly. When he saw the telescoping apparatus the doctor was armed with and learned that he intended to force this up his urethra and squirrel his way around until he had forced it into his bladder, he was filled with something akin to panic.

"This is going to hurt a little," the doctor said. The attractive nurse was somehow beside him again. She smiled and took hold of his wrist. It was only once she also took hold of the other wrist that he realized she was not trying to comfort him, but was holding him down.

"Maybe even a lot," the doctor admitted, unclamping his penis and grasping it firmly.

The doctor was not, as it turned out, lying. A lot was exactly how much it hurt, or maybe more than a lot. When it was done, the question he had to ask himself as he lay there shivering was what, if anything, was there left of him worth saving?

As far as that question goes, he, or whatever now stands in for him, still doesn't know the answer.

Cult

It had been terrible from the start. He knew it was a disaster, knew
from the very beginning, maybe even from the very first instant,
that they were not, no matter what she claimed, *meant for each other,*
that he should get away from her as fast as he could, if not faster.
And yet, somehow, he couldn't. He'd always experienced a certain amount of inertia, but it was something other than that. What
exactly it was, though, he wasn't sure.

After a few weeks, he knew not only that they weren't meant
to be together, but that he didn't even *like* her, but by then she had
already moved in. The months that followed—the whole relationship, if he was being honest with himself—had been like being
brainwashed, if you could be brainwashed while still knowing with
a painful clarity what was happening to you. It was as if he was
watching someone else move from humiliation to humiliation but
was powerless to do anything to stop it. But the problem was that
this someone else was not someone else: it was him.

No, they never should have been together in the first place. He
knew that even then, but he couldn't do anything to stop it. If she

hadn't stabbed him, they'd probably be together still. Even the stabbing had been just barely enough to propel him out of the relationship. Even lying there on the floor, clutching his side, waiting for her to call the ambulance, he had already begun to forgive her, to consider how her stabbing him had been, in a way, if you really thought about it, his fault. And she hadn't been trying to really hurt him—if she'd been trying to really hurt him, she would have used the butcher knife. No, she had just used a little knife, not even as long as a steak knife, a knife he didn't even know the name of. How was she to blame if the knife had been sharper than she expected?

Of course, she had said none of this to him—he had thought it all out for himself, had even said some of it to her before he passed out the first time. No, it took his friends days, if not weeks, to begin to convince him that even if she hadn't said it, she'd made him the kind of person who would say it for her. She had gotten into his head and rewired it, changed it. So much so that when he became conscious again and found she wasn't there, he hadn't told himself *She's deserted me* or *She's fled because she's afraid she'll be arrested for stabbing me*. No, instead he'd thought, *She must have gone for help.* It took passing out twice more before he could bring himself to crawl across the floor, pull the phone off the coffee table, and dial 911. Not because, he told himself even as he dialed it, he thought that she hadn't done it, but only because if both she and he called, an ambulance would be more likely to come.

It took weeks, but in the end they convinced him. She had never called 911. She had stabbed him and fled, perhaps thinking she'd killed him. Even then, he might not have been convinced if he hadn't realized that she'd had the presence of mind to pack up her few possessions and take them with her when she left. Simply fleeing he might have been able to forgive, but fleeing with all her clothes and worldly goods was another story.

Even then, he might have forgiven her had she called, had her voice again activated what he'd come to think of as the control mechanism she had rigged in his mind that kept him in exile from himself. But his friends, his true friends, the ones who nursed him back to health, the ones who stayed in the hospital beside him day after day after the stomach wound turned septic and he nearly died, hid his cell phone. If she called, they deleted her calls, and when he asked about her, they told him to fuck off. They had given him tough love, but that was what he'd needed to climb out of the trough that had been their relationship. And once they had given him back his phone, the few times she had called they had been there and had taken the phone bodily from him, had told her he didn't want to talk, that she should not call again, that she should never call again, that if she called even once more he would press charges. And soon, even if they weren't there, he could simply not answer the call of his own accord, could simply delete the message.

After a while she stopped calling. He felt great relief. From time to time, at greater and greater intervals, he wondered what had happened to her. But soon—even though a few months before he wouldn't have thought it possible—he stopped thinking about her altogether.

II.

He was driving and his phone was ringing, but no name was coming up above the number. *Unlisted.* It was not his local area code but maybe was somewhere close, Pennsylvania maybe, unless he was confused and it was Ohio. Probably a telemarketer. So he didn't answer. It rang until voicemail picked up, but nobody left a message. So, a telemarketer. Or an election pollster. Or maybe some sort of robot call. He let the phone fall onto the passenger seat and kept driving.

A few minutes later the phone started up again, buzzing against the fabric of the seat. He just kept driving, glancing over at its screen until the buzzing stopped. Again, no message left.

When the same number came up a third time, he considered powering the phone down, but his hand was already reaching for it, raising it to his ear.

"Hello?" he said. "I think you must have the wrong number."

But no, she did not have the wrong number: she knew exactly who she was calling. The last thing he had considered was that it could be her. But *her* was exactly who it was.

She was calling from a convenience store, she explained. God, she said, how she missed him. She couldn't believe she'd finally got through, how great it was to hear his voice! Had they been keeping her from him? She really needed him.

Blood was beating in his ears. He hadn't managed to utter a word.

"I joined a cult," she told him. "I just up and joined it."

"Excuse me?" he said. His mouth was dry, and the words came out sounding strange.

"Of course, at the time I didn't think it was a cult, but now I see it was. They kicked me out." She laughed. "Who gets fucking exiled from a cult?" she said. "Me, I guess. I was always—"

"You must have the wrong number," he tried again.

"Wrong number?" she said, and her voice took on a hard edge. "I recognize your voice. It's me, Star."

"Star?" he said, genuinely confused.

"Oh, sorry," she said. "That's the name I took. You'll have to get used to it. I'm not going back to Tammy. I always hated that name. And Tamara's even worse. They can exile me from their fucking cult, but they can't take away my new name."

She stopped speaking. He didn't say anything, just swallowed. He kept the phone pressed tight to his ear.

"Hello?" she said. "Hello? You didn't hang up, did you?"

He hung up.

Later, after the worst had happened, he told himself that if only he hadn't been alone and driving, he would have been okay. Or even if he'd been driving, if only he hadn't been on the turnpike and had had an exit or a place he could have pulled off, he would have been okay. If he was honest with himself, he didn't know if this was true, but it made him feel better to think it.

She called back less than thirty seconds later. He didn't answer. Then she called again, and again, and again. *I should roll down the window and throw the phone out,* he thought. But it was a new phone, still under contract; he couldn't bring himself to do it. In the course of eight minutes she called fifteen times, and each time the phone rang, he felt a little piece of himself weaken.

After four or five minutes he knew he'd pick up, but still he tried to resist, hoping she'd give up and stop calling. If she gave up, he could still be saved.

But no, she was persistent. He tried, as the phone kept ringing, to plan out what he was going to tell her. He would tell her he wasn't her friend anymore, that he didn't want to talk to her. He would ask her to have the simple human decency to never call him again. He would remind her how she had stabbed him—not only stabbed him, but stabbed him and fled and left him for dead. How could she expect him to ever talk to her ever again? What was wrong with her?

And yet, when he finally did answer, he could not bring himself to say any of this. Indeed, at first he said nothing at all.

What *she* said was, "What happened, did your phone go dead? Cell phones just aren't reliable. Which carrier do you have? Do you still have the same one as when we were together? I tried to get you to change it then, do you remember? I bet you never did."

"Tammy . . . ," he started.

"Star," she said. "Who's this Tammy? There's no Tammy here. It's Star. The name is Star."

"The thing is—"

"Did I tell you I was in a cult?" she said, a sharp edge to her voice. "The Children of Light, they're called. How do you think I ended up there? Whose fault was that?"

It's your fault, a small voice in his head was already saying, a voice he thought had long ago been throttled out of existence. *You drove her to it.* At least the voice was still saying "you," he told himself. When it started saying "I," then he would be in real trouble.

She waited for him to answer and, when he didn't, said in a softer voice, "I need someone to come get me."

"Come get you," he repeated flatly.

"I need you to come," she said. "I need *you.*"

"No," he said, ignoring the dissenting voice growing inside his head. "Absolutely not."

"I don't have anybody else," she said. "I only have you."

"You don't have me," he said.

"Look," she said, "I don't like this any better than you do, but I don't know where else to turn. If you just do this for me, I'll never ask anything else of you again."

"Never?" he asked, but he knew from how quickly she answered yes that she was lying.

"No," he said. "I'm sorry. I can't do this."

"Thank you," she said, ignoring him. Very quickly she spat out an address, a little convenience store near the Pennsylvania border. "I'm counting on you," she said. Then, before he could say anything else, she hung up the phone.

III.

He tried to call the pay phone back, but nobody answered. *Typical,* he thought, *just like her.* He tried not to go, really he did, but it was too late, the damage was done. A part of him, an admittedly infinitesimal part, thought that it was just possible there had been a reception problem, that she did, honestly, think he was coming. It was ridiculous, the rest of him knew, but that doubt, no matter how small it was, was not something he could navigate smoothly past.

He kept thinking of her, alone, waiting at the convenience store, night coming, nowhere for her to go. She was a terrible person, he knew that—she had stabbed him and left him—but if he didn't go, wouldn't that make him a horrible person too?

He wasn't a horrible person, he knew it. And he could prove it. He could just go and get her, just drive her somewhere, then his obligation would be done. Then, he told himself, he'd never have to see her again.

At the next exit he got off the turnpike and went back the other way.

It took four hours, each one harder on him than the one before. The farther he went, the more he felt as if his mind was no longer his own, as if he was once again a man driven out of his own body, as if once again she, Tammy, or rather now she, Star, was in charge.

The whole drive he turned over in his head what he might say to her and what she was likely to say back, how the conversation might turn and twist and where in the end it might possibly end up. But no matter how he turned and twisted it, no matter how generously he slathered it with luck, no matter how willfully he tried to squint away what she really was and the control she had over him, he could not see any way in which things would turn out well for him. At best, at absolute best, he would see her and it would devastate him. Even if it did turn out that she really was asking just one more thing, that after this she would be willing to walk away and let him go, it would still take him weeks, if not months, to recover.

And that was only the best possibility. Chances were he'd be back in a relationship with her, suffering for months, if not years, until the time she once again stabbed him and, probably, this time killed him.

For a while he tried not to think about it, but how could he help it? He turned on the radio as loud as it could go, tried even for a few miles to sing along to drown out his thoughts, but all the songs were about mending shattered relationships. They were giving ammunition to the wrong part of his subconscious.

When he stopped for gas at the service area just shy of Buffalo, he got out and stretched his legs. He used the bathroom and then sat in the food court for a while. On a whim, he looked up "Children of Light" on his phone. Nothing listed as a cult, but there was a collective on the edge of Pennsylvania. Nonreligious hippies, it seemed, running a farm and a craft store. Hardly a cult. Idealistic anarchists at best. Not the kind of people to kick anybody out unless they absolutely had to. But knowing Tammy, knowing Star, they'd probably had to.

He tried the phone number she had called from again, but he still got nobody. He climbed back into the car, kept driving.

It was dark by the time he reached the convenience store. It was at the corner of a two-lane state highway and one of the long roads dividing one set of farms from another that came in these parts only every mile or so. There wasn't much else to be seen beyond farmland. The lot of the convenience store was lit by a single sickly floodlight rigged on a corner of the roof.

She was sitting there on the edge of the curb just below the pay phone, her arms wrapped around her knees, her back against the building wall, staring straight ahead. Next to her was a well-worn paper bag, clothes spilling from the top of it. When he pulled in, she put a hand up to her face to block the light. She looked, he thought, harmless. Deceptively so.

Watching her, he suddenly remembered the strange way she had drawn her hands over and around his body when they first kissed, her fingers whispering just over his clothes, touching but not touching, as if she was making a cage around him that was only just barely larger than his body.

He put the car in park and turned off the lights. He waited, but she didn't move. *Maybe she's dead,* he thought hopefully.

But she was not dead. From time to time she moved a little. Maybe she was asleep? But no, he could see the gleam of her eyes; they were open.

She wants me to get out and come to her, he thought. A dull anger began to grow within him. He would just wait her out, he told himself; he was not her slave.

But a moment later, he could not stop his hand from opening the door. He watched his body climb out and move toward her.

She did not respond when he spoke her name. She waited until she felt his hand on her shoulder and then immediately she was up and holding on to his arm.

"I knew you would come," she said in a voice he wanted to describe as breathy. He couldn't tell if she was genuinely out of breath or if it was simulated. "I was waiting for you and you came. You still love me after all."

I will take her where she wants to go, he told himself. *I will drop her off. I will never see her again.* But there was more to it. They weren't on the road, not yet. No, she had to go back to the cult and get the rest of her things.

"They're not a cult," he said. "I looked them up."

"Who would know better, me or you?" she asked. They would go back to the *cult,* and they would get her things. It wasn't far, she claimed, probably not more than a few minutes by car.

But it was more than a few minutes. It was maybe twenty, and it felt much longer. She talked nonstop, about him, about them, their relationship, which she didn't seem to realize was over and done. She was there beside him, leaning over the center console, stroking his arm. He kept flinching away, but she either didn't notice or didn't care. Now that she was in the car with him, she would have her way.

He felt worse than he had felt in years, worse, in fact, than when she had stabbed him. She was talking, talking. He just tried to ignore her. They would get a little house together, she was saying, unless, of course, he already had a little house, did he? Somewhere where they could be together, separate from the world and safe, living in exile from everybody else, just the two of them together, nobody but the two of them.

Oh, God, no, he thought, though somewhere within him, his heart leapt like a stag.

They would have a baby, she went on, they owed it to the world to have a baby, but please, God, make it look like her rather than him. Sure, he had his good qualities, but after all, they could both agree that she was the one with the looks. She would stay at home with the baby and with the baby's nanny, and he would support them and watch the baby at night.

Yes, that small and more insistent part of him was beginning to assert. *She has a good point.* He shook his head, tried to stay himself.

Look at him now, she said. Who had chosen that shirt? Had he stolen it from a homeless man? Didn't he know he needed someone to take care of him, to keep him from humiliating himself?

And then, mercifully, they were there. He was out of the car and heading toward what he guessed to be the main building of the so-called cult, waving her back, no, he would get her things, no, they had kicked her out, she couldn't come in, he would do it, it wasn't any bother.

She was still calling something after him through the open driver's side door of the car when he started knocking on the door. He tried not to hear what she was saying. The door opened and a thin woman with a windburned face revealed herself.

"Yes?" the woman said.

He introduced himself, awkwardly shook the woman's hand. "I'm here to gather Star's things," he told her.

"Star?" said the woman. "You mean Tammy, right?"

"Didn't you rename her Star?"

"Us? She started calling herself Star, all right," said the woman. "We went along with it for a while. I mean, why not?" The woman craned her neck. "Is that her in the car?"

"That's her," he said.

The woman nodded. "She should stay right there. Come on in," she said. "I'll lock the door behind you."

He was led down a central hall and through some sort of dining area containing five big tables and eight stacks of chairs. Past that, the hallway began again, doors punctuating it. The woman led him down near the back of the building and opened a door on the left.

"There you go," the woman said. There were two black garbage bags balanced on a narrow cot. Each looked half full, the tops knotted closed.

"What's in them?" he asked.

The woman shrugged. "Nothing much," she said. "Worldly goods. So-called chattel. The millstone round the neck. Nothing anybody needs, least of all her."

Puzzled, he just nodded, then moved forward to gather the sacks.

"She's bad news. Still, we would have sent them to her," the woman said from behind him. "We would have paid her bus fare too. You didn't have to come fetch her."

"I didn't want to," he said.

She gave him a sharp look. "Then why did you?"

Why had he? It seemed so far away now, days in the past. But no, it had only been a few hours. Already he was back at the bottom of the trough, and there was no getting out.

He sat heavily on the bed. He didn't realize that he had sat down until the woman was beside him, asking if he was okay.

"I just," he said, "maybe just, a moment to catch my breath."

The woman nodded. She watched him incuriously for a little bit and then left.

IV.

How long can I stay here? he wondered, a garbage bag to either side of him. How much time had actually gone by? Ten minutes? Fifteen? When would she have had enough and come after him?

Wouldn't they stop her from coming after him at all? She was, after all, exiled, was not allowed to come back. The front door was closed and locked. Even if she wanted to, she wouldn't be able to get in.

Maybe he could claim sanctuary with the Children of Light. He could fall on his knees and beg them to save him from himself. As long as he was here, he would be safe.

He took a deep breath. Yes, he would stay here. He wouldn't move from this spot. Here he was safe. There was no reason for him to ever leave, no reason to ever see her again. Losing the car was a small price to pay. Losing his connection with the outside world a small price to pay, as long as he could stay himself, as long as he never had to see her again.

Yes, he would stay, he told himself again.

He took another deep breath and then, gathering the two bags, went outside to his own destruction.

Seaside Town

1.

In past years, Hovell had simply not bothered to vacation away, but the arrival of Miss Pickaver had changed that. Her arrival had, in fact, changed a lot of things. In the past, Hovell's idea of vacationing had been sitting around in his ratty sweater and khakis in his bedroom, reading the newspaper very slowly, savoring it even, letting his cigarette ash fall where it would, each day like the next until he had to return to work. But then Miss Pickaver had swept into his life and into his bed, taken him to hand and slowly taken him to task, and now, yes, he'd been made to understand that, as a vacation, this simply wouldn't do.

"But where would I go?" he pleaded.

"*We*, you mean," said Miss Pickaver, "where would *we* go? Because it isn't just you anymore."

But Hovell didn't care to go anywhere. A man of regular habits, he was an incurious person. He did not care to learn about new things. Even the old things he already knew about he often thought it was better to forget. He still lived in the house he'd been born in, the house he'd inherited when his mother died. He had some difficulty understanding how it was that Miss Pickaver had suddenly jimmied her way into his life, coming in a matter of weeks to have so much of a say in everything.

"To Europe," Miss Pickaver said decisively.

"Europe?" he repeated, as if confused.

"You have the money. You've never been to Europe. It has to be Europe, James."

It made Hovell wince when she called him by his first name—nobody called him by his first name, and even to himself he was simply Hovell, but he had given up correcting her. Miss Pickaver had a first name she used, but he suspected he would always think of her as Miss Pickaver.

And so, Europe. He did not, he was surprised to find, immediately give in. He had the presence of mind to at least let her know that if he had to go to Europe, he wanted to stay put, to stay in one place. And once he told her that if she wanted, she was welcome to do one of those tours—six countries in four days or some such—as long as he could go somewhere and stay put, she agreed. She'd stay with him for a few days on either end of the trip, she told him, get him established at the beginning and help him pack at the end, but in the middle he'd be on his own. She couldn't help it if he didn't want to make the most of the trip. But no worries, she said: she would be sure to tell him all about everything he missed.

The flight alone all but killed him. Though Miss Pickaver had managed to sleep for most of it, Hovell had hardly even blinked. When they landed in Paris, Miss Pickaver had delicately stretched and given a little yawn, exposing what had always looked to Hovell like too many teeth, as if she had an extra row, then proceeded to lead Hovell implacably through the nightmare that was French customs. Did monsieur have anything to declare? No, monsieur did not. Was monsieur sure? Would monsieur please open his bags? The sight of the officers fingering their way through his carefully folded underthings while Miss Pickaver tittered was too much for him, and when he lost his temper it was only Miss Pickaver's quick action and heartfelt apologies on his behalf that kept him from ending up detained in a back room for hours. When he tried to sleep later, on the train to the seaside town whose name even the French themselves were apparently unsure how to pronounce, she told him no, considering what time it was, he would be better off staying awake until night came. Thus, every time he began to nod off, she would nudge him awake.

He arrived at the seaside town disoriented and half blind with fatigue. There were no taxis waiting at the train station, and Miss Pickaver wasn't willing to wait while they figured out how to call one, so they walked along the road and into town, him pulling both bags while she turned the map over and about, trying to figure out where they were heading.

"But I thought you'd been here before," complained Hovell.

"I have been," said Miss Pickaver. "With that German gentleman I used to know. But he was the one who knew the place. I just followed along in his tracks."

"German gentleman?" he asked. "I'm staying in a house you stayed at with some previous lover?"

"Surely I told you about him," she said. "It was years before you and I met. Well, months anyway." She frowned, smoothed the map over her belly. "And I can't imagine what objection you could possibly have to me taking you to a place I've been to before and can vouch for," she added, as if the whole reason for her taking a German lover had been entirely for his benefit here, now.

Sighing, he trudged on.

The place was part of a gated community, a little triangle of buildings full of apartments, some of which had motorized metal shutters that could be brought down at night, sealing you in like a tin of preserved meat. The courtyard between buildings seemed deserted—no sign of habitation visible through the windows and no people out walking on the compound grounds.

Miss Pickaver found the right building, managed to extract a key from the concierge despite Miss Pickaver having no French and the concierge having no English. They were on the third floor, room 306. The tiny elevator was too small for him to ride in with the suitcases, and so she went up first, and he sent the bags up one at a time to her. When, finally, he climbed in, he found it to be even smaller on the inside than it looked from the outside, a kind of lacquered wooden box with a sliding grate for a door. He felt as if he were riding in a coffin.

As the elevator slowly trundled up, creaking, he felt panic beginning to rise. By the time he reached the third floor, he was a nervous wreck.

"Don't be so dramatic," she said. "It's just an elevator."

And true, yes, it was just an elevator, but he had lived fifty years of his life to this point never having to ride in such an elevator as this. Why should he have to ride in one now?

She had already turned away, was looking for their apartment. There was one long, dingy hallway stretching away, apartment doors dotted to either side of it, odd on one side, even on the other. They ran out at 305. There was no 306.

"Are you sure the concierge said 306?" he asked.

But the look she threw him made him wish he hadn't asked. Yes, of course she was sure—she was always sure. Even though there was no number on the key fob, she still claimed to be sure.

"It's simply not here," he said.

Stubbornly she went down the hall again, scrutinizing each door in turn with such intensity that Hovell wouldn't have been surprised if 306 did suddenly appear. But, of course, it didn't.

"There must be another third floor," she said.

"Another third floor," he repeated dully.

"Sure," she said. "That you can't get to from this elevator. That you have to get to from another elevator."

He was dispatched to question the concierge, but he refused to take the elevator this time, trudging instead down the tight winding stairs that circled the elevator shaft. The light in the stairwell was dim, and he had to grope, but it was better, even if just a little, than the elevator.

He reached the bottom to find the concierge's lodge locked, and nobody answered when he rang the buzzer. He waited as long as he dared, then trudged back up to deliver the bad news to Miss Pickaver. Miss Pickaver, he knew from experience, did not take bad news well. But when he arrived on the third floor, he found only the pile of their bags; Miss Pickaver was nowhere to be seen.

He trudged nervously up the hall and back. He opened the elevator and looked in. And then, quietly, and somewhat hesitantly, he called her name. There was no answer. Maybe she had gotten tired of waiting and taken the elevator down to find him. But surely, if that had been the case, he would have heard the elevator, would likely have even seen her in it when he crossed the first- and second-floor landings on his way back up. Or at least seen the cable moving.

He knocked again on the concierge's door for good measure. Still no answer. He poked his head out of the building, but it was still just as deserted outside the building as it had been before.

When he finally headed back upstairs, she was there, arms crossed, waiting.

"Where have you been?" she said. "I've been calling for you."

"I was just . . ." he started, then took off his glasses and rubbed his eyes. He didn't want to fight. But he wasn't sure he could help himself. "Where were you?" he asked, trying not to sound accusatory.

"I," she said, drawing herself up, "was busy finding our place." And then she led him up the dim stairs, up halfway between the third floor and the fourth, where, in the round wall of the stairwell, off one tread, was a small door.

He leaned in close, peered at it in the dim light. He had to squint to read the numbers.

"It says 309," Hovell said.

"That's a mistake," Miss Pickaver said. "It has to be. You saw the hall only went to 305, and there are no other halls."

"I thought you said there had to be another elevator," he said. "Another third floor."

"Don't be difficult, James," said Miss Pickaver. "This is the right room."

But there had been no rooms in the stairwell between the first and second floors, or in the stairwell between the second and third floors. Why would there be a room here? Maybe it was just that he was tired, but it didn't seem right to him.

"It says 309," he insisted.

"Someone must have taken the 6 out and put it in upside down, as a joke."

"What kind of joke is that?" he asked.

She ignored this. Instead she pushed past him, jostling so that he almost slipped and tumbled down the stairs. A moment later the door swung open.

"The key works," she said. "It has to be the right place."

But even after that, as he hauled the suitcases one by one up the stairs and inside, as he ducked down and shouldered his own way in, as he watched Miss Pickaver opening the windows and airing out the apartment, he still wondered if they were in the right place.

2.

From the window, the courtyard looked not busy exactly, but at least not deserted like it had when they had come in. At a distance, he could hear the sound of the waves. He watched people come and go.

He had slept for hours, had awoken disoriented with no clear idea of what time it was. Miss Pickaver looked refreshed and relaxed, the exact opposite, he supposed, of how he looked. She had been out to purchase some groceries: olives in a reddish goo, strange tubs of pureed meat, cheese pastes, drinkable yogurts, boxed milk, tins depicting sauerkraut and tiny sausages, dried packets that apparently could be reconstituted into soup or, at least, broth. He stared at it all as if stunned.

"Feeling better?" she asked brightly.

He nodded weakly. She had done her hair, he noticed now, and had applied a thick, unnaturally dark shade of lipstick. "Are we going out?" he asked.

She gave a peal of laughter. "I've been out, darling. There's no point in your going out, especially not now. It's nearly night again. You slept the sleep of the dead."

The sleep of the dead, he thought now, nursing a bowl of tepid tea as he sat at the window, staring out. The other apartments, the ones on the real third floor, all had balconies, but all theirs had was the window. He watched, on one of the balconies below, the backs of a man and a woman, the man holding the woman around the waist as they stared out across the courtyard and through the gap in the buildings to the sea beyond.

He followed their gaze. The light, he had to admit, was beautiful, just as Miss Pickaver had suggested it would be, and if he sat at just the right angle, he had a glimpse of the beach. It was littered with bodies. Mostly Eastern Europeans or Germans, he guessed, based on the gold chains they wore and the fact that the women were blonde and seemingly topless. The men, he noticed now, mostly wore nothing at all, lying baking nude in the sun, their flesh leathery, as if being cured.

"Is it a nude beach?" he asked.

But Miss Pickaver, in front of the bathroom mirror plucking her eyebrows, humming softly to herself, didn't seem to hear. He couldn't bring himself to repeat the question. He did not want to be accused by Miss Pickaver of staring at the nudes on the beach. That seemed a humiliation.

When he looked back down at the balcony, the couple was no longer there. He shifted his chair. In the courtyard below, a couple crossed back and forth, their heads bent toward one another. Was it the same couple? He didn't know. The man was about his age, the woman, roughly the age of Miss Pickaver. There was, now that he thought about it, a physical resemblance as well, both to him and to Miss Pickaver, but they were in the long shadow cast by the building, and their faces were turned away, so perhaps that was partly imagined. But when he realized from the cloying smell of her perfume that Miss Pickaver had left the mirror and was standing behind him, he pointed them out to her.

"Like us, no?" he said, smiling.

She leaned forward and squinted, then drew slowly back. "I don't see the resemblance," she said. Then she kissed him on the top of his head. He imagined the dark stain the lipstick must have left there. "Will you help me carry down my bag?" she asked.

"Your bag?"

"I catch the train in an hour," she said. "For my little tour."

"You're leaving already?" he said, beginning to panic a little.

She crossed her arms, stared at him. "This is what you wanted," she said in a clipped voice. "You wanted to stay put. This is what we agreed on."

But had it been? They'd barely arrived and already she was going. He didn't know the place, he hardly knew how to get to town, but when he voiced these complaints, she opened the fridge and gestured at its contents.

"You needn't go to town," she said. "You have everything you need right here." She patiently batted away his objections until, fifteen minutes later, a plain white car pulled into the courtyard below and honked.

"There's my ride," she said.

"But it's not a taxi," he said. "It's just someone's car."

"That's how taxis are here," she claimed.

"But—"

"Who's been here before?" she asked. "You or I?"

Confused, he hauled her bag down the stairs and to the elevator and sent it down. "No point in you coming down. I'll have the driver come in and get it," she said. "You don't need to bother."

He lingered at the window until darkness and then lingered a little longer. Long after dark, there was the noise of the couple walking around below, the gentle murmur of their voices. Though, over time, that murmur became less and less gentle, finally concluding in a shriek from one or the other of them. He kept listening, wondering if he should go down and check on them, but there was only silence. After a while, he closed the window and went to bed.

But he couldn't sleep. His body had no idea what time it was, and he had slept too long during the day, and so he lay in the dark staring up at the ceiling. Perhaps he should have gone with Miss Pickaver. Perhaps he should have done twelve countries in ten days or whatever it was, expanded his horizons a little—no, this was only nervousness about being left alone. He did not want to see twelve countries. He did not want to see even one country, but now that he was here in this one, there was little he could do.

He lay in bed obsessing, tossing and turning until quite late, one or two in the morning, before he got up and found a book. He tried to read, but the words weren't sticking with him, and after a few pages he had no idea what he'd read. So he turned off the light and went back to the window, resting his elbows on the sill.

There was a moon out now, pale and nearly bitten through but still casting a fair amount of grayish light. If he leaned far enough out, he could see, below and to the left, the pale, white glow of the balcony for the room closest to him on the real third floor. There was a dark shape on it, large, though difficult to say whether it was the man or the woman. From time to time it moved a little or settled in a different way.

Down below, on the paving of the courtyard, a dark blotch of some sort, largish, much bigger than a man. Hard to say exactly what it was, however, and it was in any case motionless. Maybe it wasn't anything at all, a trick of the light. But if it wasn't a trick of the light, what could it be?

He stayed there staring down, eyes flicking from the shape in the courtyard to the shape on the balcony, until, after a while, close to morning, he began to feel sleepy and went to bed.

3.

When he stumbled awake it was well past noon. He poured out something pink from a jug in the fridge, found it to be slightly sour, but whether it was supposed to be like that or not he was at a loss to determine. He put it away, poured himself a glass of rusty water from the tap.

Before he knew it, he was back at the window, looking down. Whatever had been in the courtyard the night before had left no sign of its presence. When he leaned out he could see the balcony below, but it was bare, no drink glasses or shoes or bits of clothing to indicate who had been there.

What would he do today? He could find the town, wander through it, just to expend a few hours. Or he could stay here, up in the apartment, read a little, relax, stare out the window.

There was a buzzing sound, unfamiliar but insistent. At first he thought it must be the door, but then it continued and he realized it wasn't coming from the door, but from the kitchen, from the telephone on the wall there. *Why bother to answer it?* he wondered. It wouldn't be for him—nobody knew he was here, at least nobody who mattered. He would just ignore it.

But it was hard to ignore. It just kept ringing and ringing. After a while, he got up and went into the kitchen and stayed there, staring at it. Each time it rang, it shook slightly in its cradle. No, he wouldn't answer it. But it was all he could do not to answer it.

It rang perhaps thirty more times and then stopped. He took a deep breath and slowly let it out, then headed back to the window. By the time he arrived there, the phone had started ringing again.

It might be Miss Pickaver, he told himself this time, less because he believed it and more because the idea of hearing the phone ring over and over again seemed impossible. *Maybe it* is *for me after all.*

But when he picked the phone up, the connection was odd, thick with static. "Hello?" he said. When he had no response, he added, "Miss Pickaver?"

A voice that sounded very distant said something in another language, maybe French, maybe not. Or maybe it was just the distorted echo of what Hovell had said. He waited a long moment for the voice to say something else. When nothing was forthcoming, he hung up the telephone.

Late in the afternoon, he managed to make it downstairs. The concierge was there now, sitting in the lodge just beside the door. It wasn't the same man as yesterday, or at least he didn't look the same. Maybe it was a job shared by two different people, or maybe it was just one person who, depending on what he wore and his mood, could look very different.

Hovell tried to make the man understand what he wanted. *Town* he repeated, again and again, then the actual name of the town, with both pronunciations he had heard, but the concierge just looked blank. The concierge said something back in French, a question judging by the intonation, but Hovell couldn't understand a word of it.

After a while he gave up and went toward the front door. But quickly the concierge was in front of him, between him and the door, gesticulating, pushing him back.

"What's wrong?" asked Hovell. "I just want to go outside."

But when he reached for the door again, the concierge knocked his hand away.

Under normal circumstances this would have been enough to turn Hovell around, send him back up the stairs, but with everything else that had gone on, he was not himself. He reached out and grasped the concierge by both shoulders and moved him out of the way, then went out the door. This time, the man did not try to stop him.

He crossed the courtyard to find the gate he had originally come through locked, so he circled around the edges of the compound until he found a place where the fence met a wall and he was able to climb up and over. Nothing on the other side looked familiar. Immediately he was lost, and when he started out in what he thought might be the direction of the town center, he found himself squirreling around small little streets that gradually became larger and emptier, the houses sparser and sparser. He'd been too tired to pay any attention when Miss Pickaver had led them from the train station. He should have paid attention. He tried to work his way back to the complex, but the streets seemed different going the other way on them, and quickly he was off course. There were streets and houses, but no town center. And then, suddenly, he was at the beach.

He felt immediately conspicuous, dressed as he was in the same khaki trousers, ratty sweater, and worn, gum-bottomed shoes he wore to putter around the garden at home. He was overdressed. The most anyone on the beach was wearing was a thin strip of fabric over their fork, if fork was the right word, and the majority were not wearing even that. Most were nude, scattered in clusters here and there on the beach, and in the few moments he looked out over them none of them moved, as if the sun had reduced them to a sort of paralysis.

"Please?" said a voice behind him in a thick, guttural accent. Russian, maybe.

He turned to see a tall, bronzed man who was completely bald and completely nude, greased from head to toe with some sort of oil. A gold watch glinted on his wrist. His eyes were hidden behind a pair of goggles with dark protective lenses.

"I seem to have gotten lost," said Hovell. It was disconcerting, he realized, to talk to a man naked except for a watch and goggles.

He felt as if some sort of rule of etiquette was being violated but wasn't sure whether he or the bronzed man was the one violating it.

"This you can say," said the bronzed man, crossing his arms. "This they all say."

"But it's true," protested Hovell.

"If you care to have your look, we shall have our look too," the man said, and he reached out to take hold of Hovell's sweater.

Hovell recoiled, stepping rapidly backwards. For a moment the man held on tight and then he suddenly let go. Hovell stumbled and almost went down in the sand. He rushed quickly away, the giddy laughter of the bronzed man ringing loudly behind him.

It was nearly dark by the time he found the complex again, which revealed itself to him just at the moment when he'd finally given up looking for it. The gate was still locked, and though he rang the buzzer, the concierge never came to open it. He circled the complex until he found the place he had climbed over and climbed back in that way. It was more difficult coming back in than going out, and he tore open the knee of his trousers.

In the twilight he crossed the courtyard. The same couple, or a couple very much like them, were there once again tonight, walking arm in arm, heads inclined toward one another, and he thought again of the resemblance of the middle-aged man to himself and of the younger woman to Miss Pickaver. He was tempted to approach them, and indeed had started toward them. But as he came closer, he realized that something was happening between them, that what he had taken to be a genial arm-in-arm was the man holding the woman's arm so tightly she couldn't release it. He was pulling her forward, and the reason her head was so inclined was because it was hard for her to do otherwise. And yet, the woman did not cry out. Surely if she was in trouble, if she needed him, she would cry out.

Unsure, he drifted toward them anyway until, with a sudden burst of speed, they darted away. He stayed there for a moment confused, looking after them, before he went inside. The concierge was there, waiting, and immediately began to wag his finger at him, but whether for climbing the fence or for some other reason, Hovell was at a loss to say. Hovell pushed past him and climbed the stairs.

By the time he reached his own window and was looking out of it, the couple had gone. There were however two men wearing what looked, in the growing darkness, like uniforms. Police perhaps, or people dressed to look like police. What did the police over here dress like anyway? He watched them walk in a unified step across the courtyard and enter his building.

The next hour he spent waiting for them to knock at his door. They did not knock, but knowing they could at any moment was enough to keep him agitated and upset. In his head he imagined what he would tell them about climbing the fence, about accidentally wandering onto the beach. He found his hands moving, gesticulating his innocence to the empty air. He tried for the first time to close the metal shutters over the window, to keep them from seeing him through the window, but though the mechanism made a humming sound, the shutters did not come down. Eventually, he took a blanket and a pillow and locked himself in the bathroom to wait for morning. There had been no need to leave the apartment— why had he done it? He would not, he promised himself, leave the apartment again until Miss Pickaver returned.

4.

He was awoken by a narrow strip of light coming under the bathroom door and shining into his eye. He was sore all over from the hardness of the bathroom floor, from having to prop his feet on the bidet as he slept. No, in the light of day, it seemed foolish to have panicked. He hadn't done anything wrong. There was no reason the police would have come for him. He had let his imagination run away from him.

But still, he did not leave the apartment. He moved from room to room, reading, looking idly out the window. He sampled more of the unfamiliar tins Miss Pickaver had bought, and though he wasn't fully taken with any of it, some of it was at least slightly better than edible. It was good to relax, he told himself. Before long, he would feel like himself again.

Twilight found him at the window watching for the couple, but tonight they were nowhere to be seen. Or, rather, now there was only the man, walking and pacing the courtyard all on his own, in a seemingly agitated state. Perhaps Hovell had started watching for them too late, after the woman had already gone in. Or perhaps the woman was elsewhere tonight. Or perhaps—but no, what other reasonable possibilities were there? No point letting his imagination run away with him.

He would read and then fall asleep, Hovell told himself. No late night for him. Not tonight. But instead he found himself still at the window, the lights of the apartment extinguished behind him to allow him to see better. How much time went by, he wasn't sure. An hour maybe, or maybe more. And then, suddenly, he noticed again the shape on the balcony, the man there—he was almost sure now it was the man—visible in the moonlight and in contrast to the pale metal of the balcony. Another watcher, much like himself, unable to sleep. But what was there to see at night?

And then the clouds shifted, and he realized it was there again, on the paving stones of the courtyard: the large black shape, the heap or mound of something. One moment it hadn't been and then now, suddenly, it was. What was it? He felt the hair rising on the back of his neck as his mind darted from terror to terror, offering each as a way to fill the mystery.

But no, it was ridiculous to think this way. He was letting his imagination escape him again. There must be an explanation. If he went down, he'd find what it was.

He did not move from the window.

The figure on the balcony, he noticed, didn't move either. It must be staring down at the same black heap, just like me. *Unless,* he suddenly realized with a start, *it's staring up at me.*

It was as if the figure had taken this thought of his as its cue. He watched as it clambered onto the rail of the balcony, and then, before Hovell could do anything or even cry out, it jumped.

He clattered his way down the stairs, heart pounding, and rushed past the closed concierge's box and out into the courtyard. The body was nowhere to be seen, no human figure was sprawled on the pavement below the balcony. But wasn't the fall enough to kill it? Or him, rather? Maybe he had crawled away.

He moved farther out into the courtyard and thought for a moment he'd glimpsed it, but no, what he saw was too big to be a human figure—it was instead a large, dark heap.

He almost turned and went back but he just couldn't. Now, so close to it, he wanted to know.

He moved forward, wishing he had a tiny flashlight. When he came quite close, he could feel the warmth rising off it, and he thought for a moment it was a compost heap or some other form of refuse. But then he came closer still and touched it and felt fur and realized it was a horse.

It was dead, or seemed to be. The body was still warm, but cooling rapidly. It must have been black, or a very dark brown, or he would have been able to see it better from above. But even close to it, even touching it, he had a hard time making it out clearly.

It wasn't possible. It was immense in the darkness, the biggest horse he had ever seen. Where had it come from? And what had the heap been on the earlier night? Surely it couldn't have been the same dead horse on both nights.

But what about the man who had leapt from the window?

He pulled back his hand as if stung and stood up. There, near the door now, between him and the door, stood a figure, apparently a man. At first he thought it was the concierge, but when it

began to move toward him with a stuttered, broken stride, he was
no longer so sure.

For a moment he hesitated, wanting to understand what was
happening, to give it a logical explanation. This turned out to be
his undoing.

5.

When Miss Pickaver returned, she had seen four countries in four
days, but since they were not new countries to her, not countries
she had not seen before, they hardly counted. What did count was
that she had seen them in the company of the German gentleman she used to know, who had footed the bill. She would not
tell Hovell about that—he wouldn't be likely to understand, not
in the way he should. But she would tell him about the four countries and what she had seen over the course of those four days.
Or, to be honest—which she would not be—*two* days, since she
and the German had not left his room in town for the first two days.
After all, she had told herself at the time, she was a Miss, not a
Mrs. What she did with her leisure time was nobody's business
but her own.

The concierge greeted her with a torrent of French and gestures
she could not understand. She just shrugged and nodded until he
either thought he'd gotten his point across or decided to give up—
with the French, how could you know what they were thinking?

Upstairs, she found a man in grubby overalls, a maintenance man
of some sort, at the door of their apartment, nailing the 6 in 306
back in place, the right way up, so it no longer could be read as a 9.
Inside, Hovell was at the same window he'd been at when she'd left,
still staring out into that deserted little courtyard.

"Hello, darling," she said. "Have a nice time?"

He grunted in reply, turned just long enough to give her a wan
smile and pat her arm. *Same old James,* she thought. And then, suddenly, he did something that surprised her.

He turned fully toward her. "Shall we take a walk?" he asked, in a voice so confident it seemed hardly his own. "A turn arm in arm in the twilight?" And then he smiled in a way that seemed to her not like him at all. "Come on," he said. "It'll be fun. Nothing to be afraid of."

He stood and put his arm around her and began tugging her toward the door.

The Dust

I

A few days after they arrived, the baffles started to clog. They had expected the baffles to clog—that wasn't a surprise. Grimur had been trained to unclog them, and now he trained one of the men. Trained Orvar, in fact. They were a skeleton crew, just enough of them to prepare for the arrival of the full contingent three months later if the site proved productive, so there was little for Orvar to do at the moment.

At first Orvar protested. As head of security, cleaning baffles was not part of his job description. Grimur just stared patiently, with his pale, steady eyes, and waited, impassive, for Orvar's protestations to run down. When they did, Grimur simply opened the contracts file, called Orvar's up, and appended a clause assigning him the cleaning of the baffles. Then he turned the screen toward Orvar for his thumbprint.

"Supposing I refuse?" asked Orvar.

"You won't," said Grimur.

Orvar looked uncomfortable. "You could clean them," he said. "You know how to do it already."

Grimur shook his head. "I have other things to do," he said. "You don't. Not yet."

That wasn't entirely true, Orvar thought. Though there were only seven men, not counting himself and Grimur, there had already been a fight, a drunken one. It had nearly cost a man an eye. Orvar had broken it up, separated the men, but there was no brig yet—that would come later, after the arrival of the next vessel. For now, all they had was the space that would become a brig: three doorless, unreinforced walls, exposed ductwork. There was no way to hold someone in.

So he had had to improvise. He had chained the uninjured man, Jansen, to the rock drill halfway down the shaft and left him bellowing there to grow sober. The other man, Wilkinson, he'd restrained with nylon cord before closing the cut above his eye with suture tape. When he was done, he propped Wilkinson up against the wall in what would one day be the brig.

"What gives you the right?" the man complained in an uneven slur.

"What gives me the right?" repeated Orvar, surprised. "This is my job."

But Wilkinson wasn't listening. He had already passed out.

Orvar stared at the screen for another moment and then pressed his thumb against the scanner, just as he and Grimur had always known he would. Grimur nodded once, curtly, then stood.

"Come on, then," he said.

They clambered through the partially built complex, past the workers' bunkroom, around the piles of boxes, and through the stacks of paneling to arrive at the system that brought in the unbreathable air from outside and scrubbed it. There was, Orvar felt, always a bad taste to the air afterwards, a taint to it. He had been feeling light-headed. If he ran or otherwise exerted himself, as he had when breaking up the fight, his head throbbed.

Some of the particulate matter was so fine that it passed through the filters and baffles, Grimur was telling him. That was the problem with the filters, he said: they had not been designed for this environment.

He showed Orvar how to close the baffles and shut the filtration down, then how to remove the filters and clear them. When he took one out, Orvar could see the sides of the channel were coated in a thin layer of dust. Grimur banged the filter softly against the metal wall, and a haze of dust arose and floated in the air. The cloud stayed there, motionless. Orvar could see it, but when he passed his hand through it, he felt nothing. When he drew his hand back, though, it had taken on a faint sheen.

"Ideally," Grimur said, "we'd do this in a contained space. But we haven't built one yet."

Orvar nodded. "Only the necessities," he said.

Grimur pointed at the remaining filters. "I'll leave you to do the others. Clean them and slide them back in, then turn the system on. Put your hand up here," he said, pointing to the first vent in the ductwork above. "If you feel air pushing out, then all is as it should be."

"And if I don't?"

"Then take the filters out and clean them again."

It was not a hard job. There was, to be truthful, nothing to it, and it gave Orvar something to do. He'd been languishing, he realized. Cleaning the filters helped him pass the time.

There had been no more fights. When he'd unchained Jansen, the man had been sheepish and embarrassed. He'd asked immediately how Wilkinson was.

"He lost an eye," said Orvar initially, but when he saw Wilkinson's pained expression, he decided to drop it. "Or could have, anyway," he said. "No more fighting."

As for Wilkinson, when Orvar had asked what he'd said to set Jansen off, he'd just shrugged. The man had been so drunk he didn't even remember the fight. He had been surprised to awaken chained up. Why, Wilkinson wanted to know, had Jansen attacked him?

"I always liked him," Wilkinson said. "I thought he liked me too."

"He does like you," said Orvar. "And how do you know that you weren't the one attacking him?"

"Was I?" asked Wilkinson.

Orvar didn't know. "You didn't lose an eye," Orvar told him. "You probably won't even have a scar." And then he made him promise to be careful next time he drank.

So, no more fights, but more and more dust in the filters. He banged them out twice daily; sometimes, especially first thing in the morning, he would have to knock them against the wall repeatedly before he'd feel a healthy current of air flowing from the vent. After a week or so, even the airflow from the just-cleaned vents seemed to be growing weaker. Or was he just imagining it?

Working hours were lonely, with half the crew drilling in the shaft and the other half analyzing and sorting samples in the makeshift space that might one day be a lab. For now they made do with a series of plastic sheets tacked to the ductwork above to form a rough square enclosure, sheets that did little to keep out the dust that now seemed to be everywhere. It was on them all, a kind of pollen-like layer that made their skin gray. Every night Orvar would use enough of his water ration to dampen a cloth in order to wipe his body down, but the dust seemed to be on him again immediately. It wasn't gritty or grimy; he could hardly feel it. But there was still the nagging awareness of it being there, on him, on everything.

Find anything? he'd ask each man at some point in the day, sometimes more than once. They always shook their heads. The site was not, or at least not yet, productive. They had another month, perhaps, to make it so before the company would have to decide whether to dispatch their reinforcements or simply send a vessel to retrieve them.

Sometimes Orvar would go to watch the progress being made in the shaft, the men shouting at one another over the noise of the rock drill. He would stand at the entrance, feeling the rumble in his legs, then he would turn and go back.

At other times he would go to the office, the only room in the complex that qualified as finished. It was sparsely furnished—computer system, communications console, and a series of control panels regulating the temperature of the complex, monitoring the environment, or in some cases just in stasis awaiting the arrival of the machinery that they would monitor. There was the single metal desk, foldable but nonetheless solid, and a set of metal folding chairs, all stacked against the wall except for the one Orvar habitually used. Grimur's chair was different, an upholstered and wheeled thing that, despite the vessel's space restrictions, he had managed to fit in. Behind it, near the wall, was a bedroll. Grimur slept alone in here rather than in the bunkroom.

Grimur always seemed to be busy, though what he was doing was hard for Orvar to say. He suspected Grimur had even less to do than he did, yet the man was always at his computer, always typing. He often kept his hands poised over the keys while they spoke.

He would ask Orvar how he was, then nod in acknowledgment no matter what Orvar answered. He would ask about the men and nod there as well.

"No more fighting?" he might say, one eyebrow raised. And Orvar would explain that no, everything seemed to be going well.

"Ah," Grimur would respond, half distracted. "And the drilling?"

"They haven't come across anything yet," said Orvar.

Only then might a shadow flicker across Grimur's face. Orvar did not know what sort of involvement his superior had had in choosing the site, what he was likely to lose if the site proved nonproductive. But he could tell Grimur would lose something.

At least the rock they were boring into was igneous and solid—they had gotten that right, even if the site wasn't proving productive. No dust coming out of the shaft. The dust had instead seeped in, drifting into the shaft through the filtration system. The men had noticed this. It seemed to be everywhere now, a little thicker every second. It hung in the air, a delicate haze that gave a blur to the lights.

Moving about the complex, dragging a finger against the wall, Orvar began to think of himself as being underwater. It was as if he were walking along the ocean floor and had come upon the remnants of a city, flooded somehow and forgotten, never meant to be found again.

And yet, he thought, *this is where I live.*

The men were huddled together talking, but fell silent as he came farther down the shaft. All of the men were present, not just the extractors—the testers were there as well.

"Everything all right?" he asked.

"Just taking a break," one of them said. Lewis.

"Find anything yet?" Orvar asked. Another of the men, Yaeger, he thought, kept brushing off his arms, over and over again. A sort of nervous tic.

"What do you mean?" asked Gordon.

Orvar stared. "What do I mean? The same thing I meant yesterday."

"The site's not going to be productive," said Gordon. "If it was, it would have happened already."

"Shut up, Gordon," said Durham. "Don't harass Orvar."

Orvar shrugged. He was trying not to pay attention to Yaeger, to the restless, endless movement of his hands, brushing, brushing.

"Maybe they made a mistake," he said. "We knew that was a possibility. That's why they send a skeleton crew first. We could still find something."

Gordon shook his head. "I've been on a project that folded," he said. "By now, we should be packing up."

"Maybe Grimur thinks there's still a chance," said Orvar.

But Gordon, an experienced extractor, did not want to be appeased. "No," he said. "Something's going on."

"Don't be paranoid," said Lee.

"I don't know what it is," said Gordon, "but it's something."

"Gordon," said Orvar, looking him steadily in the face. "There's no hidden project. I promise."

"You trust Orvar, don't you?" Durham said to Gordon. "You can see he's telling the truth."

Gordon reluctantly nodded. "Maybe Grimur just hasn't told him."

"No," said Orvar. "I know Grimur. He'd tell me. Do you want me to ask him?"

"He'll probably lie," mumbled Gordon.

"I'll ask him," said Orvar. "I'll know if he's lying."

"And you'll tell us," prompted Jansen.

Orvar reached out and touched Gordon on the shoulder. The man flinched.

"I'll tell you," said Orvar. "I promise."

The shaft seemed longer on the way back. He was out of breath by the time he'd gotten within the complex walls again. He was having trouble gathering his thoughts. *What's wrong with me?* he wondered, but he shook it off. No sense letting Gordon's paranoia infect him. Still, what if Gordon was right? What if there was a hidden project? But Grimur would have told him. As security officer, it made sense that he would be told. Didn't it?

Even if he hadn't been told, Grimur wouldn't be able to hide it from him. Orvar was sure, or almost sure, that that was true.

He started toward the office but then, reconsidering, doubled back to check the filters.

When he held his hand up to the vent opening, there was a slight trickle of air, but only very slight. He turned off the system, opened the baffles, removed the filters. Before he could start cleaning, Wilkinson was there, next to him.

"What's wrong?" asked Wilkinson. "Broken?"

"Routine cleaning," said Orvar. "I do this every day."

Wilkinson narrowed his eyes. "But you already did it once today," he said.

Orvar hesitated. Then, slowly, he explained that yes, he had already done it once today, but most days he did it several times, just to be safe. All the while he was thinking, *Wilkinson has been watching me. Why?* Wilkinson was doing the same thing with his arms that Yaeger had been doing earlier, brushing at them again and again, though not quite as frequently. *What's wrong with Wilkinson?*

He watched the man's eyes flit hurriedly about their sockets. *Maybe it's nothing,* he thought. *We'll all be a little nervous until the site proves productive.* He tried to remember what it was that Wilkinson actually did.

"Which team are you on?" Orvar asked.

"Team?" said Wilkinson, surprised. His hands stopped in mid-brush. He squinted. "Are there teams? I thought we were all in this together."

"No," said Orvar. "Where do you work, I mean. The drill or testing the samples?"

Relief washed over the man's face, but it was quickly lacquered over by a gnarled layer of suspicion. "Why do you want to know?"

Orvar spread his hands in front of him. "It's just a question, Wilkinson," he said. "Nothing to worry about."

Wilkinson thought about this for a moment, then finally said, "The drill?"

"And you're on break now?" asked Orvar. "Is this how you usually spend your break?"

"I should be getting back," Wilkinson said. A moment later he was retreating, casting nervous glances over his shoulder.

Grimur was hunched over his computer. He barely glanced up as Orvar entered and took a seat.

Orvar waited, his gaze wandering around the room. Nothing to look at, really: Grimur's crumpled bedclothes just visible around the desk's corner, the monitoring panel lit up with green and amber lights, the computer's lid, past which he could see Grimur's haggard face. He hadn't shaved. His eyes were bloodshot.

Finally Grimur closed the computer, leaned back. Over tented fingers he stared at Orvar.

"Well?" he said.

"They still haven't found anything."

"Then they should keep digging," Grimur said. "They haven't stopped, have they?"

Orvar shook his head. "They're still digging," he said. He hesitated. He was turning the question over in his head, trying to decide how best to phrase it. Whether to phrase it at all. Now that he was here, sitting across from Grimur, it seemed ludicrous. There was no conspiracy, he told himself, only Grimur still doggedly hoping to find something. The simplest explanations were usually correct.

Grimur gestured to the monitoring panel. "You see the amber lights?" he asked.

"Yes," said Orvar. "What about them?"

"Air quality," he said. "You need to clean the filters."

"I just cleaned them," Orvar said.

Grimur shook his head. "As time goes on and the dust builds up, you'll have to clean them more often."

"I've been cleaning them at least twice a day."

"Ah," said Grimur. "I see."

"Shall I clean them again?"

"No, no," said Grimur, absently. "Maybe the monitoring system hasn't caught up." But then he said, "You know, on second thought, it can't hurt. Clean them again."

He stood, then moved around to sit on the front edge of his desk. He was brushing his arms, Orvar noticed. Not exactly like how either Wilkinson or Yaeger had done it, but still. *Am I doing it too?* wondered Orvar. He glanced down at his hands. For a moment they seemed like someone else's.

"What do you think it's doing to us?" asked Orvar.

"What?"

"This dust," he said. "If it's building up like this in the ventilator, what's it doing inside our bodies?"

Grimur was staring at him, frowning. "What makes you think it's doing anything?"

"Maybe it's not," said Orvar, suddenly cautious.

"The body metabolizes it," said Grimur. "It isn't hurting us. The company wouldn't send us out here if it was."

"You know that for a fact?" asked Orvar.

Grimur didn't answer. Instead he stopped brushing his arms and sat back down. "Clean the filters," he said. "Make sure there's air coming out of the vents afterwards."

But Orvar didn't stand. "Some of the men are worried," he said.

Grimur shrugged. "There's always a chance a site won't be productive," he said. "They know that. They get paid either way."

Orvar shook his head. "No," he said. "It's more than that. They think that we're here for some other reason."

"Like what?"

"They don't know," Orvar admitted. "A hidden project."

Grimur guffawed, spread his hands. "Out here? What could it possibly be? Don't be ridiculous."

Orvar watched the man's face as he said this. It was calm, relaxed, giving nothing away. There was no reason not to believe him, but no reason to believe him either.

"They think there's a conspiracy," Orvar said. "They think you're part of it."

Grimur gestured to the computer, to the control panel. "I have enough to worry about without their paranoia," he said. He leaned forward, the corners of his mouth turning down. "Who's the security officer here?"

"Me," said Orvar.

"Then it's your worry."

There was no reason to distrust Grimur. No, the men were simply restless, dissatisfied that the site wasn't productive. They couldn't understand why Grimur kept them working. But Orvar understood. At the very least it kept them busy, stopped them from having more fights. And yet he understood something else: there would come a time when everything tilted the other way, and the paranoia caused by fruitlessly continuing to dig would do greater damage than shuttering the site.

All this dust, he thought, knocking the filters clean again. Or not clean, exactly—they weren't coming close to clean now. *Maybe the dust's the problem.* He'd felt dizzy ever since they'd landed. The air tasted strange, and he could feel the particles on his skin, clogging his pores, in his throat, thickening. Wasn't it possible the dust was clogging not only the vents but him? Wouldn't it be in their lungs? Their blood?

And what if the dust wasn't just dust, but something else entirely? *Like what?*

He didn't know. Something organic, something alive.

He shook his head and forced a laugh. *Now who's paranoid?* He was the security officer. He was supposed to be keeping things stable. How could he do that if he started to think such things?

He raised his hand and held it just below the vent. No air coming out, none at all.

For a moment his heart caught in his throat: sheer blind panic. Then he realized he'd simply forgotten to turn the system back on.

When he checked again, there was a little current of air. Nothing substantial, but it was there, a little air, definitely flowing. He wondered if the lights in Grimur's office would be green now.

He wondered too how worried he should be.

Halfway to the shaft, he realized someone was following him. At first he thought he was imagining it, the dust-ridden air echoing his own footfalls back at him, but then he tripped, and for a moment he heard the sounds behind him separate from his own.

He turned quickly and looked behind him. He would have thought less of it if he'd been anywhere else, but there were no surprises here. Nothing alive for tens of thousands of miles except for himself and the others. There was only the corridor, ill lit, littered with boxes and stacked paneling and various supplies. Plenty of places for someone to hide.

He considered retracing his steps, going after them, but instead he kept going. He undid the fastener of his holster, holding his hand loose and ready just above the pistol's butt. *Probably nothing*, he told himself. But he still had to force himself not to hurry.

He turned into the bunkroom and flattened himself against the wall, gun drawn now. He held his breath and waited.

For a long moment nothing happened, and then he heard the quiet scraping of shoes in the hall. Once they'd gone past the door, he risked a look out. Gordon, at a little distance, just turning down the mouth of the shaft.

Probably nothing, he told himself. *Probably Gordon wasn't following me. Or if he was, it was just to prove to himself that I am on his side.*
Am I? he wondered.

The men were disturbed, upset. And as Grimur had reminded him, it was his responsibility to handle them.

At the mouth of the shaft, he met Yaeger. The man jumped, startled. *Startled because I surprised him or for some other reason?* wondered Orvar.

"All well?" asked Orvar, trying to render his voice hearty, reassuring.

"Yeah, sure," said Yaeger, not quite willing to meet his eye. But he lingered. He was rubbing his arms again, a little more quickly now.

"I spoke to Grimur," said Orvar.

"Yeah?" said Yaeger. "So what is it?"

"What's what?"

"Why are we really here?"

Orvar shook his head. "No," he said. "I was right. It's business as usual."

"You heard Gordon," said Yaeger. "If the site was productive, it already would have happened. How's that business as usual?"

"No," said Orvar. "Gordon was on a very different site on a very different planet. He doesn't know."

"If you say so," Yaeger said.

"I do say so," Orvar said. "I'm not lying, Yaeger."

"I'm not Yaeger," said Yaeger. "I'm Lee."

This threw him. "You're Lee?" Orvar said. "I could have sworn you were Yaeger."

"Yeah, well," said the man Orvar couldn't help but think of as Yaeger. "I'm Lee."

"Okay," he said, and the ersatz Yaeger twitched and brushed his arms again.

Was he really called Lee? It was impossible for Orvar to believe he'd been wrong all this time. But why would the man lie?

"What's wrong with you?" Orvar asked before starting down the shaft. "Can you stop doing that?"

"Doing what?" asked Yaeger or Lee. When Orvar mimicked him, the other man folded his arms.

"It's this dust," he said. "It's everywhere."

II.

A few days later, the ventilation machinery began to rattle. At first it was hardly noticeable. Had Orvar not been standing there silently, holding his hand to the vent to feel if the air was flowing, he might not have noticed. But it was a little louder every time he went back after that. He was cleaning the filters four times a day now. Soon he would have no time to do anything but clean filters.

By the time he informed Grimur, the rattle had become a grinding. They both stood beside the ventilator, staring.

"How long has it been doing this?" asked Grimur.

"Not long," said Orvar, evasively. Yes, in hindsight, he should have told Grimur earlier. "How are the readings?"

"Always amber now," Grimur said. "You're cleaning the filters diligently?"

Orvar nodded.

"Then we have a problem," said Grimur.

They stopped the machine and opened the access panel. On their knees, they stared through the narrow opening and up at the engine, Grimur shining his penlight at it. The whole thing was coated with dust, thick with it. Dust stuck to the engine like mold.

"Wipe it off as best you can," said Grimur. "They'll be here in less than a month."

"It's not going to do much good," said Orvar. He gently appropriated the penlight and shined it through the holes in the housing. Inside, the armature was thick with dust.

"You can vacuum it," said Grimur.

"With what?"

"They'll have something with the drilling equipment," the man said. "I think something was on the manifest. If not a vacuum then some kind of a blower."

And indeed, they did have a vacuum, Lee admitted a few minutes later. A small handheld thing they kept on the sample table.

"Only there's a problem," Lee added.

"Problem?"

"It stopped working,"

Together they unscrewed it, only to find the whole casing packed with the powdery, polleny dust. The motor was burned out, the circuitry shot.

"How did it get so bad?" Orvar asked.

Lee shrugged. "There's a lot of dust," he said. "It destroys everything."

When Orvar returned to close the panel, Gordon was on his back staring up into the machine.

"What are you doing?" Orvar asked.

"What's wrong with it?" asked Gordon.

"Nothing's wrong," claimed Orvar. "I'm just cleaning it. Move over." He fell to his knees and wiped at the machinery as well as he could with a rag.

"That's not going to help any," said Gordon.

Orvar ignored him.

"What's wrong with it?" asked Gordon again, but Orvar chose not to answer.

He closed the cover and stood, brushing the dust off his pant legs, his arms. He opened the baffles, shook the filters out, slid them back in place. Gordon just watched.

"Nothing to worry about," Orvar claimed again.

But when he started the machine up, it made a grinding noise.

Orvar, not knowing what else to do, shrugged and left. Gordon stayed near the machine, listening.

Later, when it began to smoke, Gordon was still there. By the time Orvar had been called and managed to open the access panel, the motor was dead.

Grimur, when Orvar finally went to him, looked even more haggard than usual. He already knew something was wrong: behind him, the entire control panel was winking red.

"Any chance of fixing it?" Grimur asked.

"I don't know," said Orvar. "Jansen and Lewis both have mechanical experience, but neither seems to be getting anywhere."

Grimur sighed. "I've sent a message. Or tried to. Communications have been intermittent at best."

"What do we do?" asked Orvar.

"We wait until the full crew arrives. They either repair the ventilation system or carry us out of here."

"We can't wait that long," Orvar said. "There's not enough air. We'll suffocate."

"No," said Grimur. He brandished a crumpled stack of paper and handed it to Orvar. Orvar took it, looked through it. Measurements, computations of volume, followed by pages of equations. At the end, on the final page, was a single circled number, *24*, drawn awkwardly—the *2* a quick single stroke, the *4* traced over several times.

"That's the number of days," said Grimur. "That's how long we'll last without ventilation, assuming I've properly calculated the cubic footage of the structure and figured the current oxygen mixture correctly, and assuming the oxygen spreads evenly and that everybody's oxygen consumption is a quarter liter per minute. No exercise, no strenuous activity, and we should be fine."

"When are they coming for us?"

"Twenty-one days, nine hours, fifty-two minutes," Grimur said. "We should be fine," he repeated. "We'll have air to spare."

"All right," said Orvar.

"Still, we should fix the ventilator if we can," said Grimur. "Just in case."

"We'll keep trying," said Orvar. He handed the bundle back. "Why paper?" he asked.

"Excuse me?"

"Why do the calculations on paper? Why not the computer?"

"I started them on the computer," Grimur said. "But then the computer started to act strangely. Eventually it died. Too much dust," he said.

"All right," said Orvar. "Let's stay positive. We have enough air. That's a good thing. What are you going to tell the others?"

"Nothing," said Grimur.

"Nothing?"

"No point in upsetting them."

"You have to tell them something," said Orvar.

"Why?"

"Even if there's enough oxygen, they'll feel worse as it diminishes. They'll experience hypoxia. So will we. Headaches, fatigue, shortness of breath, nausea. We'll stop thinking clearly. If it gets bad enough, we'll hallucinate—we'll fade in and out of consciousness. If they don't understand what's happening, it'll be all the worse."

"How do you know so much about it?" asked Grimur.

"I've been through it before," said Orvar. He didn't volunteer more. "You need to tell them, Grimur," he said again.

Grimur just shook his head. "No," he said.

"If you won't tell them," said Orvar, "I will. They have to know."

"All right," said Grimur. "Tell them. But I won't be responsible for what happens."

He entered the shaft, told the men to turn off the rock drill.

"Orders from on high?" asked Gordon eagerly. "We're giving up?"

"Not exactly on high," he said. "But the drill is off for good."

Together they all went to the testing area. He stopped the tests there too. Leaning against the table, he told them what was happening.

"I knew it," said Yaeger, or perhaps Lee, brushing his arms more frantically now. "I knew the dust would be the death of us."

"Ashes to ashes, dust to dust," said Wilkinson, smiling wryly.

"Shut up," said Lewis. He turned to Orvar. "What are we supposed to do?"

"We'll keep trying to fix the ventilation system," he said. "Maybe we'll get somewhere. We'll take apart the drill and scavenge it."

Lewis shook his head. "Nothing doing," he said. "The company makes them vandalproof. We'd need some serious equipment to open it up."

"Well, do what you can," said Orvar.

"When do we run out of air?"

"We don't," said Orvar. "They're scheduled to arrive long before that. We won't have much oxygen, but we'll have enough to survive."

"You've been told to say that," said Gordon. "Grimur doesn't want us to know we're all going to die."

"No," said Orvar. "I've seen the equations. We're going to be okay."

"Then why bother trying to restart the ventilation system?" asked Jansen. "There's something you're not telling us."

"I'm telling you everything I know," said Orvar.

"Then why bother with the ventilation system?"

"Just in case," said Lee, or perhaps Yaeger. They did, in fact, Orvar noticed, look somewhat alike. "Just in case the pickup is late. Just in case we end up using more air than they've calculated we should. There's no conspiracy, Gordon," he said. "Orvar's our friend."

III.

He left the others to talk among themselves, giving them time to get their heads around it. It was only then, once he had fulfilled what he saw as his responsibility, that he had a moment to reflect on what was happening.

He lay there on his bunk, staring up at the unfinished ceiling, the flimsy metal panels, the sealant binding their edges, the snarl of electrical wire and exposed ductwork. Had Grimur taken into account that the ceiling was exposed, that that might give them just slightly more oxygen? If so, had he taken into account that a good part of that space was occupied with wires and other infrastructure? For that matter, how had Grimur accounted for the boxes and other items scattered down the hall, each of them a place where oxygen could not be? What about the men's bodies, the space they occupied?

It made him nervous. So many variables. Despite the pages and pages of equations, what if Grimur had gotten something wrong? Even a small error at the wrong place in the equation could mean they wouldn't have enough oxygen.

And what about the shaft? That was space Grimur probably hadn't considered. It was fairly long now, probably several thousand cubic feet of air. If Grimur hadn't taken that into account, then they had a great deal more oxygen than he believed. Perhaps even enough that they would be saved well before the hallucinations started.

No, on second thought, he shouldn't ask if Grimur had considered the shaft. It would only make things worse if it turned out he had. Better not to know. Better to hope.

The last time this had happened to him he had, by the end of it, been mad enough that he thought he might never come back from it. Just three of them, alone on a free-floating craft, waiting for help to come—it had been all he could do to stop himself from opening the hatch and letting the little air that remained rush out. Not because he had wanted to kill himself or the other two, but because with the way his mind had begun to work, the way it had gnarled itself, the void beyond the hatch had seemed like salvation. How would his mind respond this time? Would he survive it?

Neither of the other two men had survived. He couldn't remember their names—or rather he could, but wished he couldn't. One had gotten his throat cut, though Orvar was never quite sure whether the man had done it to himself or if their other shipmate had done it. Orvar was certain, or fairly certain, that he hadn't slit the man's throat himself. But after they'd rescued Orvar, they'd refused to answer any of his questions about what had happened. Probably understandable, considering the state he was in. But surely they could have answered them later, once he was himself again.

The other man had gotten it into his head that he'd have a better chance of surviving if he was the only one breathing a particular stretch of air. He'd forced his way into the hold and then disabled the lock. But the hold was quite a bit smaller than the rest of the ship, which meant the majority of the oxygen was out with Orvar rather than in with the other man. This was probably the only thing that had saved Orvar. Again, he was sure, or almost sure, that he hadn't forced the other man into the hold and disabled the lock. Though he had to admit it was difficult to remember.

The thing he remembered best was this: the man's hand pressed against the reinforced glass of the door panel once he stopped trying to get out. The hand just resting there, seemingly ordinary, and then shriveling, just a little. First the tips of the fingers, then, gradually, the rest of the hand, turning blue, until Orvar himself was raving and couldn't pay attention to anything, let alone that.

He was talking to Grimur, trying to be helpful. *Properly administered synthetic morphine,* he was suggesting. Grimur shook his head.

"No, just listen," said Orvar. "We sedate them, make them breathe shallowly. They'd use less oxygen. We're all sedated except for one of us, who keeps the others under."

Grimur shook his head. "We have enough oxygen to survive," he insisted.

"But what if your calculations are wrong?"

"They're not wrong," said Grimur.

"But what if—"

"It's all useless speculation anyway," he said. "We don't have any morphine, synthetic or otherwise."

He insisted on examining the medical kit himself—he was the security officer, after all, that gave him the right—but yes, Grimur was right, there was nothing there. Had there never been any morphine in the kit, or had someone filched it, either on this project or on some project before? Didn't matter really. Not now, anyway.

There were still other things, other ways to ensure their survival. There must be. All he had to do was think of what they were.

Jansen and Lewis by turns worked on the generator motor, cleaning it as they went. Yaeger and Gordon and Durham spent most of their time at the rock drill, trying to break apart the housing in a way that would leave the motor useful and intact. Nobody was getting anywhere.

What am I doing? wondered Orvar. *Wandering a little, stumbling a little.*

Where are Wilkinson and Lee? he wondered, and a moment later came across them around the turn of a hallway, sitting cross-legged. They were whispering back and forth, taking turns brushing one another's arms, faces, hands.

"Orvar, Orvar!" hissed Lee. "Come here," he said.

"What is it?" said Orvar. He approached them cautiously, hands loose and ready, just in case.

"Can we trust you?" asked Wilkinson.

"Sure," said Orvar.

"No, I mean really," said Lee. "Can we really trust you?"

Orvar shrugged. "I don't know," he said. "Can you?"

The pair locked gazes until, finally, Wilkinson nodded slightly. "Yeah, we can," Lee said. "It's just this," he said, irritated, and then gestured again. "Come closer," he whispered, "closer."

Orvar stooped, brought his ear close to their bearded faces, their cracked and quivering lips. "What is it?" he asked again.

"Just this," said Lee. "You know the air?"

"The air?"

"Air's not the problem," said Lee.

"What's the problem then?"

"Dust," said Wilkinson.

Lee patted Orvar on the shoulder. "Yes," he said, "dust."

"It's everywhere," said Orvar. "Yes, you already told me."

"But that's only part of the problem," said Lee.

"Only the start of the problem," said Wilkinson.

"And what's the rest of it, you ask?" said Lee.

"I don't—" said Orvar.

"The rest," said Lee, his fingernails digging into Orvar's shoulders, "is that the dust is one."

"One," said Orvar, keeping his voice level.

Wilkinson nodded. "You know how we keep all our cells inside our bodies, carrying ourselves around like a sack? The dust is what happens if you don't have a sack. It's still all one thing, but spread everywhere."

The conversation left him strangely unsettled. They were paranoid, nervous, maybe delusional. *But what*, a very small part of him asked, *if they were right?* What if there was something about the dust? What if it wasn't just bad luck that the generator had failed? That Grimur's computer had failed? That the communications system, as Grimur now admitted, had failed? A slow, invisible, systematic destruction of all their equipment. By what? By dust. If humans had managed to incorporate colonies of bacteria into every part of their organism, into their very cells, who was to say the reverse might not also be true—that a certain sort of consciousness did not necessarily need a body to contain it? Hadn't he believed during his last oxygen shortage that consciousness was not something that resided deep within the body but rather something that hovered on his skin's surface, like sweat? What happened if something flicked the sweat off? Where did it go?

He shook his head. No, he didn't believe it. He was just looking for something to distract himself.

IV.

Three days after the ventilation failed, Orvar had a dream. He was trapped in a pressurized metal sphere, surrounded by water. He was alone, having trouble breathing. He knew there was a rebreather system, with a soda-lime scrubber, but when he turned it on, water began to seep in—he felt the pressure building within his ears. Hurriedly he turned it off. He checked the circuit, checked the tubing, but could find nothing wrong. But when he turned it back on, out came water, not air.

He turned it off, but it was too late. The metal of the sphere ' groaned around him. One side of the sphere dimpled, and a drop of water formed at the top of the porthole, slowly rolling down. There was a sharp pain in his head and a wetness in his ears and down his neck. When he touched the wetness with his hand, he found that it was blood. Another thump, another dent, then another, until the crumpled sphere was hardly bigger than his body, the pressure still building in his head.

He awoke to find Yaeger kneeling beside him in the darkness, shaking him. He pushed the man back, heart thudding.

"Jesus, Yaeger," he whispered, "you scared the shit out of me."

Yaeger lifted his finger to his lips. "They're dead," he said. "You have to come."

"Who's dead?" he asked.

"Come on," Yaeger whispered. And then he wandered out.

Hurriedly Orvar pulled his clothing on. Someone was sitting up in one of the other bunks, watching him, but the light coming through the entranceway was not strong enough for Orvar to tell who it was.

He reached for his holster but found it empty, his gun missing. He cursed. A voice asked him something, but he didn't quite hear what it was. He looked under the pillow, then fell to his knees, looked under the bed. The gun was definitely gone. Nothing to be done now. He made his way quickly through the doorway and out.

Yaeger was halfway down the hall, abeyant. Catching sight of Orvar, he continued forward, picking his way through the boxes.

What the hell? wondered Orvar.

He watched Yaeger turn a corner and followed in his wake. About halfway to the corner, he began to wake up, to think more clearly.

Yaeger's hardly the most stable of us, he was thinking. What was Orvar doing following him down a corridor while everybody else slept? Where was the man taking him? What had Yaeger done? Who was dead? Why?

Am I in danger? he wondered.

Hypoxia, he thought. And then repeated, like a mantra: *headache, fatigue, shortness of breath, nausea, elation.* Hallucinations? What about paranoia? They were part of it too.

He shook his head, laughed it off, continued on. Still, he was careful going around the corner, just in case. Yaeger was already at the next turn, waiting. He waved frantically at Orvar and then disappeared around it.

Right, then right again. He's taking me in a circle, thought Orvar.

He began to look around for a weapon. Scooped a length of pipe off the floor, hefted it in his hand. It would do.

He turned right, expecting to see Yaeger at the next corner. Instead the man stood hesitating at the mouth of the shaft. When he saw Orvar, he just nodded, stared pointedly at the opening.

When Orvar approached, Yaeger pushed a flashlight at him. "Down there," he said.

"Who is it?" he asked.

But Yaeger just shook his head.

Orvar hesitated a moment, then took the flashlight. He started down. When he turned and looked back, he could see Yaeger standing there, leaning against the wall of the entrance, waiting, motionless for once.

He moved forward, throwing the flashbeam just a little way in front of him. There was only rock, slightly discolored from the dust, shiny in some places from some vagaries in the stone or due to the way a drill bit had slipped. As his eyes adjusted, he could see a gleam that solidified to become the curve of the drill. Besides that, it was just the shaft, nothing else, nothing out of the ordinary.

At least not at first. As he went farther, he began to see a discoloration streaked along the tunnel floor. It was hard to make sense of, initially. But then suddenly he knew it was blood.

He reached down and ran his fingers through it where it was shiniest. Wet still, but tacky. It had begun to dry. Moving farther into the tunnel, he could see the swath of it curving around the front of the rock drill. There was more and more blood, enough that he was certain that whomever it came from was dead.

He moved forward on the balls of his feet, pipe raised.

Halfway around the drill he saw the man's feet. One foot was still shod, the other bare. They rested at very different angles, as if not belonging to the same body. He went farther and saw the legs, then the man's gashed chest. He crouched beside the corpse, steadying himself against the drill with one hand. He could smell blood and the rubber of the rock drill's tire and the dust. All three together were somehow much worse than the smell of blood alone. The man's throat had been slit ear to ear, the cut very deep and vicious, almost severing the head. The head, too, had been bashed in on one side, beaten until it was pulpy, bits and pieces of bone mingling with the dust. It was hard for Orvar to think of the body as human, though he knew it must be. It took him some time to recognize who it was. Wilkinson.

He felt himself growing dizzy. He stood and took a few steps back. He closed his eyes. He only opened them upon hearing the soft footsteps behind him. He turned and saw Yaeger there, a dim ghost.

"Did you kill him?" Orvar asked.

Yaeger shook his head. His eyes in the darkness looked glassy, vacant. *If he did kill him,* thought Orvar, *why would he have guided me to the body?* He would have only done so if he were very clever, or quite mad.

He cleared his throat. "There's only one body here," he said. "But you said 'they.'"

Yaeger nodded. He turned and started back up the shaft.

This time Orvar kept pace. Yaeger did not have to turn and wait and coax him forward. He led him to the end of the shaft and then down the hall, back to the ventilation system. There, he stopped.

For a moment Orvar didn't see him. Or, rather, it. Yaeger was not in the right position, had stopped too soon. He stood there, waiting for Yaeger to continue forward, and when he didn't, he came a little farther forward himself and saw the open access panel, the interior wet with blood.

He crouched and looked in. The body had been forced clumsily up past the motor housing in such a way that it was clear its back had been broken. The throat was cut again, more jaggedly this time and not as deep. The legs seemed intact, unbroken, and the head had not been beaten. Both the eyes had been cut out. It was, he was pretty sure, Lee, the man's gaunt face even more gaunt now that the blood had started to pool lower in the body.

Orvar reached out and touched the body's cheek. It felt waxy. He wasn't sure what that told him. He reached through the access panel and took hold of the arm, bent it at the elbow. It resisted a little, and once bent stayed in the new position. That, he knew, should tell him something about how long the body had been dead.

"Aren't you contaminating the evidence?" asked Yaeger from behind him. It was hard not to flinch.

"I'm trying to figure out how long he's been dead," he said.

"Ah," said Yaeger. And then, as Orvar continued to manipulate Lee's arm, "How long *has* he been dead?"

"I don't know," Orvar admitted reluctantly. He let go of the arm and worked his head inside the housing. With his face so close to the body, the smell was intense. He shined the flashbeam around, trying to decide if he should drag the body out and get a closer look at it.

"Is it the same killer?" asked Yaeger.

"Why wouldn't it be?" asked Orvar. And then added, "How do you expect me to know?"

"You're in charge of security," said Yaeger simply. "You're the one who should know."

I'm the one who should know, Orvar thought. *If that's the case, then we're in trouble, because I don't know anything.*

"Wait here," he told Yaeger. "I'll be right back."

It took a while for Grimur to open the door. When he did he was wrapped in a blanket, his hair mussed.

"Do you know what time it is?" asked Grimur, irritated.

"No," said Orvar. "Do you?"

"Not exactly," Grimur admitted, "but I'm certain that we both should be asleep."

"We have a problem," said Orvar.

"Besides the ventilator?"

Orvar nodded. "Two men are dead," he said.

"Of what? Suicide?"

"Someone killed them."

For a moment Grimur just stared at him. And then he slowly began to close the door.

"Wait," said Orvar, blocking the door with his foot. "Didn't you hear what I said?"

"I told you not to tell the men," said Grimur. "But did you listen? No, you didn't."

"This isn't my fault," said Orvar.

"You're security," Grimur said. "It's your fault."

"What should I do?"

Grimur sighed. "Make sure nobody else gets killed."

"But how does that fix anything?" asked Orvar, confused.

"What's wrong with you?" asked Grimur. "We're still days away from running out of oxygen. You should be thinking more clearly."

But maybe Grimur was the one not thinking clearly, thought Orvar. "We need to solve the murders," he said. "They were both obsessed with the dust."

"The dust?" said Grimur. "What does that have to do with anything?"

"They thought the dust could think."

Grimur shook his head. "That's ridiculous. How can dust think?"

"I'm not saying it can," said Orvar. "I'm just saying what they thought."

Grimur sighed, rubbed his face. "Don't try to solve anything. You'll just make it worse. You're not a policeman. You're just a glorified security guard."

Orvar sighed and took his foot out of the door.

"On the plus side," said Grimur, "whether my calculations were right or not, now we have plenty of air." He shut the door.

...

Yes, thought Orvar on his way back, *there was that.* Two people dead meant enough air. They had nothing to worry about now. They would reach the stage where they had headaches perhaps, but surely they would be rescued before they started hallucinating. Or before the worst hallucinations, anyway.

Sometimes it felt as if he was living through something he had lived through before. What kind of luck did you have to have to twice end up in a situation where there wasn't enough oxygen to go around? What was wrong with him?

He was still puzzling out that question when he reached the entrance to the sleeping quarters. Yaeger was waiting there for him.

"Do you know who did it?" he asked.

Orvar shook his head. "I thought I told you to wait with Lee."

"You need help to sort it all out," said Yaeger.

"I'm not supposed to sort it out."

Yaeger's arms suddenly stopped moving. "Why not?"

"They'll be here soon," he said. "When they arrive they'll have someone trained to do that sort of thing. A proper investigator."

"Will they?" asked Yaeger. "In my experience they don't."

Orvar shrugged. "That's what Grimur claims."

Yaeger nodded. "Won't the evidence be lost by then?"

"I don't know," said Orvar. "Maybe."

"There's a killer here. Right now. What about that?"

"I'll keep there from being more killings," said Orvar. "That's something I'm supposed to do."

Yaeger opened his mouth and then closed it. Finally he opened it again. "Don't you think," he said, "that the only way to stop the killings is to catch the killer?"

The remaining men were huddled inside, talking. When he came in they stopped and then, tentatively, began asking the same questions as Yaeger. Who had done it? Why? How did he plan to catch them? Orvar answered evasively. There was, he realized now, no advantage to suggesting that he would not even try to solve the murders.

"Shouldn't we move the bodies?" asked Jansen.

Orvar shook his head. "Not until they've been thoroughly investigated."

"When will that be?" asked Jansen.

Orvar shrugged. "When the ship gets here."

"And how do you advise us to avoid being killed?" asked Gordon.

"Stick together," Orvar said. "Always be in a group. That's the only way to be sure to stay alive."

V.

And yet Orvar was one of the first to break with that advice, choosing to patrol the halls alone before returning to bed. What did he hope to find? There was only Grimur plus the five men plus himself—he wasn't going to suddenly discover a new person he could blame the killings on. No, it had to be one of them. Everyone was a suspect. The only thing he knew was that it wasn't him.

Even Yaeger, despite the fact that he'd drawn Orvar's attention to the murders, could have done it. Showing Orvar the bodies could have been a ploy.

So, paranoia after all, whether the oxygen was depleting or no. And, of course, to the others *he* was a suspect. Perhaps they would believe that was why he wasn't investigating the murders: because he had committed them.

It would make for a difficult few weeks. But there was nothing to be done. They just had to hold on until they were rescued.

He reached the shaft, paused, then followed it down, despite knowing what he would see. It was strange to move down past the drill with the body already looming up in his mind before it began to actually appear. He saw at first the spattering of blood, dry now, duller than before. The body was just a little farther in than he remembered.

He shone the light on it, regarded it. It looked just like it had before. *Why am I here?* he wondered. *What am I hoping to accomplish?*

He didn't know. He stared at the body for some time, trying to fix it in his mind. Did that qualify as evidence? Did it preserve anything? Would it be useful to whoever actually did try to solve the crime?

He didn't know.

He examined the other body again too, the way it was crammed up along the housing of the ventilator motor. It must have been hard to get it up there, he thought, must have required a certain amount of strength. Who was strong enough? Again, he didn't know. Maybe any of them. But maybe not. Likely the crew working in the shaft—they were used to physical labor. Those testing the samples: maybe, maybe not.

He had to aim the flashlight at just the right angle to get a clear view. Again, he tried to fix the body in his mind. He wasn't sure what he was accomplishing, but it felt better to be doing something.

He expected to see Yaeger in the halls but didn't. He wasn't in the bunkroom either. Orvar went around a second time but still didn't find him. Perhaps they just kept on missing one another. Or maybe he was talking to Grimur, or deliberately hiding. Orvar didn't know what, if anything, he should do to find Yaeger, and so he ended up doing nothing.

Back in the bunkroom, the remaining men had left their huddle and moved back to their own beds. They were either asleep or pretending to be. He made sure they were all there: Jansen, Lewis, Durham, Gordon. Still no Yaeger.

Jansen's eyes were slightly open; Orvar could see them shining in the darkness.

"Seen Yaeger?" whispered Orvar.

Jansen propped himself up in his bed, shook his head. "He wasn't with you?" he whispered.

Orvar shook his head, drifted back to his own bunk. He stood there for a moment, hesitating, then sat down. He considered his mental pictures of the bodies. Something was troubling him about one of them, but before he could determine what, Jansen was there beside him.

"Shouldn't you be out looking for him?" he asked.

"I've already looked," Orvar said.

"Did Yaeger do it?"

"Do what?"

"Kill them," said Jansen. "Lee and Wilkinson."

"Yaeger?" said Orvar, surprised. "No, I don't think so."

"He has an alibi?"

"An alibi? No, not exactly."

"Then you can't rule him out?"

"No," said Orvar, slowly. "I can't rule him out. To be honest, I can't rule anybody out."

"Not even me?"

"Not even you."

"I didn't do it," said Jansen.

"Go to sleep, Jansen," said Orvar.

"If I do," asked Jansen, "how do I know I'm going to wake up alive?"

The air felt close, too tight in Orvar's throat. In the dark he listened to the sound of his own breathing, imagining his lungs filling with dust. Perhaps Yaeger *was* the killer. Or perhaps it was one of the others. Or perhaps, somehow, the dust itself. He had a vague sense of being on the verge of choking. Falling asleep felt a little like drowning.

VI.

He awoke feeling he had heard something but was not quite sure what. His head ached, flaring a bright line of pain. Some of the others were stirring as well. Gordon's bed was empty.

He sat up and pulled his boots on.

"What is it?" asked one of the dark shapes around him. Jansen, probably.

"I don't know," said Orvar. "I thought I heard something."

"Wait," said Lewis, a little panicked. "We'll come with you."

But he was already in the hall. A noise, a loud one: that was what had woken him up. Unless he'd dreamed it.

Out in the hall, he began to faintly smell cordite. So, not a dream. He made his way down the hall in one direction until he realized the smell seemed to be growing fainter, then he backtracked. The others were now clustered in the doorway.

"What is it?" Jansen asked again.

"Gunshot," he said simply, then kept going.

Gordon or Yaeger, he thought. Those were the only options. All the others had been in the bunkroom. Either Yaeger shooting Gordon or Gordon killing Yaeger. Or one or the other of them killing Grimur.

He took a turn and threaded his way through a stack of boxes. Had they been arranged like that before? He was already past when he realized what he'd glimpsed and went back. There, stuffed upright in the middle, was a body. Its face was pushed against the wall; he couldn't see clearly who it was.

"Hello?" he heard a voice call from down the hall. "Who's there?"

He pulled himself back behind a box, heart pounding. "Gordon?" he called out. "Is that you?"

"Orvar?" said the voice. "Is that you?"

He heard the sound of approaching footsteps. He tensed, waiting.

"I thought I heard a shot," said the voice, closer now. "Where are you? It's me. Grimur."

And yes, he realized, it was Grimur—he should have recognized the voice right away. He stepped out to meet him.

"Did you fire a shot?" asked Grimur.

"Somebody did," said Orvar.

"It wasn't you? You're the only one with a gun."

Orvar shook his head. "My gun's gone missing," he said.

Grimur frowned. "Some security officer you are," he said. "Who has it?"

"I don't know," Orvar admitted. "Yaeger, probably. Unless that's Yaeger there." He gestured between the boxes where the body was. "If so, then it'd be Gordon."

Grimur came closer, squinted. "Shit," he said. "Is that a corpse?"

Instead of answering, Orvar started moving boxes. For a moment the corpse balanced there, leaning against the wall, then it slowly spun and toppled, fell to the floor. There was no gun in the gap, despite the blood spatter against the wall. Definitely not a suicide.

"That's Gordon," said Grimur.

"Then Yaeger has my gun," said Orvar.

"How the hell did you let Yaeger get hold of your gun?"

"He took it, somehow. Without me realizing," said Orvar.

"Why are you brushing your arms like that?" asked Grimur.

"What?" said Orvar. Surprised, he looked down at his moving hands. "It's this goddamn dust. It sticks to everything," he said. "It's like it's alive."

Grimur shook his head. "It's just dust," he said.

"How do you know?" asked Orvar. His voice was getting louder. He was helpless to stop it. "How can you be sure it's not doing something to us?"

"Because it's just dust," said Grimur simply. "I'm going to go back to my room. Try not to let anybody else die."

Back with the others, he explained that Gordon was dead and Yaeger nowhere to be found. There was every indication that Yaeger had killed Gordon and the other two as well.

"So you solved it," said Jansen. "That was quick. Yaeger's our killer."

"Yaeger wouldn't do that," said Lewis.

"It's Yaeger," Orvar said.

"Then where is he?" said Lewis.

Orvar shrugged. "Hiding," he said.

"Hiding where?" asked Lewis.

"Why are you brushing your arms?" asked Jansen. "Are you cold?"

Only with enormous effort was Orvar able to stop. "I don't know where," he said. "I'm searching for him."

"How do we know that you didn't kill them?" asked Durham.

"Why would I do that?" asked Orvar.

"Why would Yaeger?" asked Lewis.

"No," said Jansen slowly. "You heard the shot, Durham. Orvar was here when Gordon was killed."

"He could have set something up," said Durham. "Some sort of trap to make the gun go off automatically. And then as long as he's the first one to the body, he could hide the trap."

"Don't be paranoid," said Jansen.

"There are three dead bodies," said Durham. "We'd be fools not to be paranoid."

"Be careful," said Orvar. "Stick together. That's the best thing you can do. That's what will keep you alive." He moved toward the doorway.

"Where are you going?" asked Jansen.

"To find Yaeger."

He looked through the halls and down the shaft and then started poking through boxes, but there was no sign of the missing man. He couldn't find Yaeger anywhere. How was this possible? He had to be somewhere. Eventually Orvar went back to the bunkroom. Everybody was pretending to be sleeping.

"Has Yaeger come back?" he asked.

Nobody responded. Taking that as a no, he went back out again.

He leaned against the samples table in the research area, thinking. Where could Yaeger be? There was a chance he was hiding undetected in one of the boxes, that Orvar hadn't checked thoroughly enough. Or that Yaeger had simply been circling through the halls in a way that deliberately avoided Orvar. It would have been difficult, but it was possible.

Or he could be in Grimur's room.

Yaeger could have snuck in when Grimur came out after hearing the gunshot. Perhaps he was still there, hidden.

But no, thought Orvar, picturing the room in his head, there was nowhere to hide. If he was there, either he was holding Grimur hostage at gunpoint, or Grimur was dead.

What was the best way to go about it? He stood outside Grimur's door, hesitating, and then finally knocked lightly. There was no answer. He pressed his ear to the door. No indication of movement inside. Perhaps Yaeger was lying low. Or perhaps he'd left. Orvar knocked again, louder this time. When there was still no answer, he slowly pushed down the door's handle, opened the door, and slipped inside.

The room was dark. He let the flashlight play slowly along the walls. Nobody there, nobody standing anyway. He moved a few steps in and pointed the light down and saw, behind the desk, Grimur's makeshift bed. In it was a human shape, mostly covered in blankets, facing the wall.

Very slowly he approached, the light mostly covered, just enough to make out vague outlines. He moved closer and finally fell to his knees, crawling the rest of the way until he was very close, close enough to be fairly certain that it wasn't Yaeger. It must be Grimur.

Yaeger had already killed him, Orvar thought. He couldn't tell if the sounds he was hearing were the body's breathing or his own. He held his breath, but it didn't help.

He reached out and softly touched the neck. Warm. Still alive. He pulled his hand back but already the body was moving, a blur in the half dark. Something struck him hard in the face and he fell to one side, the flashlight clattering away. Two heavy blows to his ribs and suddenly he couldn't breathe and then the body had clambered on top of him and had its hands wrapped around his throat.

Everything went darker still, then the world seemed to stutter and stop entirely.

A light. Slowly, his eyes began to focus. Grimur was crouching over him, watching him closely, a disgusted expression on his face.

"Coming around?" he asked.

Orvar just groaned.

"I could have killed you," Grimur said. "What were you thinking?" He reached out and helped Orvar sit. Orvar groaned again, his head throbbing. "You can't do that," Grimur explained. "I thought you were trying to kill me."

"I thought you might be dead."

"And that's how you figure out if I am?" he said. "What were you thinking? Do you know how much oxygen we must have wasted struggling like that?"

"I was looking for Yaeger," said Orvar.

"Yaeger? Why would he be here?"

"We can't find him."

"You must not be looking in the right places," said Grimur.

"We've looked everywhere."

"Obviously not," said Grimur. He helped Orvar to his feet. "Go look somewhere where he might actually be," he said. "Do your fucking job."

Do my job, thought Orvar, a little dizzy, confused. *Do my job.* He made his way back to the bunkroom and lay down. The others were in the beds, dark, motionless shapes. They were probably alive. There was no reason to assume they were not. As long as he didn't know they were dead, he could think of them as alive.

He stared into the semidarkness, thinking. *Do you know how much oxygen we must have wasted struggling like that?* he heard Grimur say again in his head, saw again his look of mingled concern and disgust. He thought of the diminishing oxygen, the air thick with dust, and through those little twisty mental passages scrabbled his way back to the other time he had been trapped without air. What had gone on exactly? How culpable was he? He hadn't killed the others; he was sure, or almost sure, he hadn't slit the first man's throat. And the man who died in the hold, that had been his own fault. But Orvar hadn't tried to get him out.

He took a deep breath and let it out. A little more oxygen gone.

He shook his head. No, he couldn't think like that. They were still days away from running out of air. It wasn't going to be like last time: they had enough oxygen to last until the company came to get him.

But then he found Grimur's words rising again in his mind. Why had he said that? Now that three people were dead, there was no danger: they had extra air.

So why would Grimur be worried?

He kept thinking too of the ventilator, and of the body stuffed in it. Or not thinking of it, exactly. Just *seeing* it over and over again in his mind. Each time it felt just a little off, as if his mind was revising it.

What did it all mean, all these various things cycling through his mind? How did it all come together? He didn't know. He stared into the dark, willing himself to see a pattern. But he didn't see anything.

Until, suddenly, he did.

VII.

He got up and pulled his boots on. He made no effort to hide what he was doing, but he wasn't noisy either. He grabbed the flashlight. If the others were going to say something, then let them say it. If they were not, if they were just going to pretend to be asleep, then so be it.

He went down the hall to the ventilator. Once there, he fell to his knees and stared up into the housing. There was the body, just

as it had been before—or almost. Yes, that's what he'd been trying to understand: it was a body, but it wasn't the body he'd first
seen there. The head was twisted away from him, but it wasn't
hard to stick his hand up into the housing, wrap it in the hair, and
tug hard. With a crinkling sound, the head came around to reveal
Yaeger's face.

He worried the body back and forth until it came loose and
spilled out onto the floor. His gun clattered out with it. Back in
the housing, pushed farther up, was the other body, the one missing its eyes. The killer had been smart: he'd hidden Yaeger's body
somewhere that nobody would think to look: disguised as another
body. But he'd been careless too. If he'd taken out Lee's body and
put Yaeger's above it, Orvar would never have realized it. He would
have gone for days thinking Yaeger was on the loose, when in fact
the killer was someone else.

He examined Yaeger's corpse. It hadn't been shot. One side of
Yaeger's head was soft. There were marks, too, around the neck,
the bruises of fingers. He'd been strangled, probably shoved up into
the housing long before Gordon was killed. Someone had killed
Yaeger, forced Lee's body up higher, pushed Yaeger in, then gone
after Gordon.

Orvar checked the gun's chamber. Five shots left. He holstered
it. *And now,* he thought, *my turn to go after the killer.*

A few moments later he was knocking on Grimur's door. What
time was it? Early? Late? He didn't know anymore.

He heard a voice rumbling inside but not what it said. He tried
the door's handle, but it was locked. He knocked again.

He heard slow, patient movement within. He tried to imagine
Grimur rubbing his eyes, getting up, getting dressed, approaching the door.

"Who is it?" Grimur's voice asked from just inside.

"Orvar," said Orvar.

"What do you want?"

"To come in."

For a moment there was only silence. "What is it this time?" Grimur finally asked.

"Somebody else is dead," Orvar said.

At first nothing happened. Then the lock clicked and the door slid open.

"Who?" asked Grimur. His eyes, Orvar saw, were curious, but when Orvar said "Yaeger," something changed.

"Ah," Grimur said. "I see." He waved Orvar into the room. "You haven't done your job very well, have you?" he said.

"On the contrary," said Orvar. "I figured out who killed them."

Grimur stopped. He turned around. His surprise, when he saw that Orvar was pointing the gun at him, seemed genuine.

"You're the killer?" said Grimur.

"Me?" said Orvar. "No, of course not. It's you."

Grimur slowly shook his head. "You're mad," he said. "You're getting confused."

"Don't try to confuse me," said Orvar. "It has to be you."

"Does it?" said Grimur. "Why?"

"No," said Orvar, waving the gun. "Let me explain it to you. We were all in the bunkroom when Gordon was killed. Except for you."

"What about Yaeger? Was Yaeger in the bunkroom?"

"No," Orvar admitted. "He wasn't. But he was already dead."

Grimur swallowed. "Are you sure he was dead by the time Gordon was killed?"

"What?"

"How do you know there aren't two killers? Maybe Yaeger killed Gordon and then someone else killed Yaeger."

"Who would the other killer be?"

Grimur shrugged. "Who knows? It could be anybody. Did you watch everybody? Did you have your eyes on them all the time?"

"You're trying to confuse me," said Orvar. He licked his lips. His mouth felt too dry.

"No," claimed Grimur. "I'm trying to make you think straight."

"Why would any of them want to kill Yaeger?"

"Why would I want to?"

"No," said Orvar. "You said it. I heard you."

"What did I say?"

"Do you know how much oxygen we must have wasted?"

"So?" said Grimur.

"Why would you care?"

"Why would I care?"

"With the others dead, we have more than enough oxygen to survive. It doesn't matter how much oxygen we wasted."

Grimur once again looked genuinely shocked. "That's your evidence?"

"You lied," Orvar insisted. "You told us there was more oxygen than there was, but you knew some of us would have to die if the rest were to survive. You knew you could kill them and that I, because of what had happened at my last posting, would be blamed."

"What happened at your last posting?"

"You know," said Orvar. "Oxygen shortage. Everybody died but me."

Grimur shook his head. "This is all news to me."

Orvar tried to think back. How much had he told Grimur? He couldn't remember exactly.

"How long has it been since you slept?" asked Grimur.

"That doesn't matter," said Orvar.

"It does matter," said Grimur firmly. "You're panicked. You've become paranoid. There's something wrong with the air. The dust in it. You're letting it get to you."

Was he? He shook his head. It ached.

"Orvar," said Grimur gently. "Don't you see? I've spent days figuring out how much oxygen we have and how long it will last us. Doesn't it make sense—even if I know we have enough to survive—that the first thing I would think of is oxygen?"

Orvar looked at him. The gun shook in his hand. He had been so sure when he had found Yaeger. Wasn't he sure now?

"This has all been a misunderstanding," said Grimur. "I understand why you thought it was me, but surely you see now that you were wrong?"

Orvar didn't answer. *Yes, what if you're wrong?* a part of him was thinking. Alone, in his head, it had all made sense, but now, with Grimur calmly talking, he wasn't sure anymore.

But if it wasn't Grimur, who was it?

No, it had to be Grimur. It had to be.

"Orvar," Grimur said, his voice serene. "Put down the gun."

"No," said Orvar.

Grimur spread his arms slowly. "You're going to kill me over a slip of the tongue?"

"It wasn't a slip."

"Are you crazy? Is that proof? Is it really enough?"

"It's all I have," said Orvar desperately. And when he saw that Grimur, confident now, was going to continue talking, was going to talk Orvar out of killing him, he pulled the trigger.

VIII.

He holstered the gun. The shot was still ringing in his ears, and the room reeked of cordite. *Maybe I should have waited,* thought Orvar. *Maybe I should have just immobilized him somehow, tied him up.* But if he'd done that, Grimur would have convinced the others that Orvar was mad, and before he knew it, Grimur would be free and Orvar himself tied up.

There was blood all over his shoes, glistening and then slowly growing dull as the dust began to adhere to it. Blood had spattered onto the wall, and there was a swath of it across the floor. There was no point trying to clean up. It was too much to hide.

And it doesn't matter, he told himself. *I didn't do anything wrong. I just killed a killer.*

There was blood on his sleeve. He would have to change his shirt before the others saw. If he didn't, they would think *he* was the killer. *But I'm not the killer,* he told himself. *Grimur was.* He was almost certain that was the case. All but certain. Less so, admittedly, than before Grimur had started talking, but still. He looked once around the room and then went out, closing the door behind him. *At least now,* he told himself, *it's over.*

But is it really over? his mind was already asking only halfway down the hall. What if he'd gotten it wrong, taking what was plausible for what was actual? What if he'd killed an innocent man? Was there any way to be sure the killer wasn't still on the loose?

No, he told himself just outside the bunkroom, *there's no way to be sure.* What, really, did he know? One, the ventilators were broken. Two, they were running out of air. Three, someone, eventually, would rescue them. Four, he wasn't the killer.

Anything else, everything else, was speculation. He needed to stay aware and alert. He needed to remember that perhaps it wasn't over. If it wasn't, any of the remaining three might be the killer. He had to watch them carefully, keeping his gun within reach.

In the bunkroom, the lights were on, dimly, each of them taking on a strange halo from the dust. All three still-living men were there. Durham sat on the edge of his bed. Lewis was at the desk and seemed to be writing. Jansen just stood there, arms loose, pretending to do nothing.

Suspicious, Orvar thought.

"Where've you been?" asked Durham.

"Nowhere," said Orvar. He moved slowly toward his bunk. How could it already be time to wake up? Where had the night gone?

"What's on your sleeve?" asked Jansen.

Blood, thought Orvar. But said, "Nothing."

He unbuttoned the shirt, slowly stripped it off, draped it on the post of the bed. *It had to be Grimur,* he thought. *It had to be.* But each time he thought it, he felt less sure.

He kept his movements succinct, steady, trying to give the others no sense of what he was thinking. He took off his gun belt, laid it flat on the bed. He shucked his boots. *Don't be paranoid,* he told himself. *You're not thinking right. It's the lack of oxygen. The dust.* He pushed the gun belt over and sat down. *A little sleep and you'll see things more clearly.*

But he was not given a chance to sleep.

"You found your gun," said Lewis.

He could tell by the way Lewis said it that that wasn't all he meant. In a brief flash he saw it all: he had no choice. In a few hours there would be three more corpses, followed by days of him wandering the complex alone, slowly going mad, head filling with dust, oxygen slowly draining away. In the end, with a little luck, Grimur's calculations would be correct, and the ship would arrive well before he ran out of air. And then he would explain. *It was Grimur, not me. It was the dust, not me. I'm no killer, I swear. I'm just a man lucky to still be alive.*

He blinked. The other three were watching him, frozen, waiting. Jansen was poised on the balls of his feet, tense. He would probably give Orvar the most trouble and so should be taken care of first. Durham was standing now. He could be easy or hard, too early to say. Lewis, clueless, was still in the chair. He would be the easiest.

It wasn't me, he told himself again. He reached casually over, pulled the gun belt into his lap. "Yes, Lewis," he said. "I found my gun." *It was the dust,* he practiced, and tried to make himself believe it. And then he smiled and drew his weapon.

BearHeart™

The Donners, Michael and Lisa, first heard about BearHeart™ when they were at the obstetrician's office, about four months into the pregnancy. They were waiting at the counter, behind an almost-due Brazilian woman, and while the receptionist tried to locate some staff member named Marlie, who apparently could speak broken Portuguese, Michael started looking at the brochures and flyers spread to one side of the reception window. There was an invitation to be part of a study on weight gain and pregnancy, and a flyer for an exercise class. There were glossy trifold pamphlets for IUDs and other contraceptives, as well as special high-resolution color ultrasound packages that produced the image of your baby in the womb matted with a pink or blue border, or, if you wanted to keep relatives guessing as to the gender, yellow.

And then there was BearHeart™. There was a single flyer for it, battered and a little wrinkled, with phone numbers at the bottom that you could tear off. BearHeart™ offered an ultrasound that would, they claimed, be covered by most insurance. They would not only provide the client the usual ultrasound image, but in addition, for a small fee of fifty dollars, they would make a high-resolution recording of the heart of the baby in question. This would be placed into a device that would be sewn into a silken fabric heart. This in turn would be placed inside a teddy bear, in its chest. Squeezing the chest just right would start the recording of the heart beating, which would run for thirty minutes.

A perfect gift for your newborn! it exclaimed near the bottom of the flyer. *Babies find great comfort sleeping next to a bear that beats with the rhythm of their own heart! Give your child the gift of postwomb womblike comfort! Only fifty American dollars!*

Grinning, Michael showed the flyer to the other half of the Donners, to Lisa, and watched as she read it.

"Weird, right?" he said.

"That can't be good for the baby," said Lisa. "Having its heart both inside and out at the same time. It'd be confusing."

"Sweetheart," said Michael. "The heart's not actually outside of the baby. It's just a recording."

"Still," said Lisa. "Would you want to curl up with a recording of your own heart?"

"I don't know," said Michael. "How do I know? I've never tried it."

They kept talking about it in the waiting room once they were checked in. It was just something weird to talk about. They talked about it too once they were in the examination room and waiting for her doctor to come, and then the doctor came. Among other things, she squirted gel on Lisa's belly and pushed a pocket ultrasound against it. It was connected to a little speaker in her jacket pocket. She turned the sound up and they heard the rapid, rhythmic sound of the baby's heart.

"Some people think it sounds like a stampede of horses," said the doctor.

There were other things, measurements, questions about diet, a little discussion, then the visit was done. The doctor was gone, and Michael was helping Lisa into her clothes again.

"Maybe we should just record a stampede of horses and put that in a bear," said Michael.

"Very funny," said Lisa.

But on the way out, after giving the receptionist his credit card for the co-pay, Michael reached over and tore off one of the tabs from the BearHeart™ flyer. "Just as a joke," he explained to his wife as she rolled her eyes. "Just so we have a story we can tell at parties. Just so we can say we did."

Which was why, when the baby was born premature and stillborn at six and a half months, they still had a bear containing a recording of the baby's heartbeat. They had called the number on the paper tab and made an appointment. They had gone to a body-imaging facility at around eight o'clock one night, where a nervous technician wearing ash-colored scrubs had met them at the front door, unlocking it for them and locking it again after them. He hustled them into a basement ultrasound room and did a quick sonic scan. He put a binder with laminated pictures of teddy bears in front of them and told them to choose one. They were obviously not supposed to be there.

"But that wasn't thirty minutes of heartbeat," said Michael.

"What?" said the technician. "Oh, no, we only need about fifteen seconds. We just take that and loop it."

Michael wondered if he should complain. It felt like a mistake now to have come; what had started as a joke now just seemed odd. But they were far enough into it, far enough along with it, that it seemed like they should finish. Lisa was just barely tolerating it— this was not her thing, but Michael's; she had made that very clear on the drive over. And now, when he tried to get her involved in choosing a bear, she just waved the book away. He looked quickly through the pages, but what did he know about choosing a bear? He hadn't even had one when he was a child. They looked all more or less the same as far as he was concerned. In the end he chose one with small black eyes and dark brown fur that was described as "tight nap." He chose it partly because of the thought that he'd be able to make a joke about it when the baby was napping with the tight-nap bear.

Before they left, the technician took Michael's fifty dollars, then grabbed his insurance card and wrote down the numbers.

"It'll show up tomorrow," he said.

"Why?" asked Michael. "Why not today?"

The technician looked furtive. "That's just the way we do it. Anything freelance shows up as tomorrow."

And then they were standing out in the improperly paved parking lot watching the technician relock the door.

The bear, when it arrived in the mail, wasn't dark brown at all but more a kind of streaked pale brown. The nap too couldn't be properly described as tight since it was basically not a nap at all but just fabric. It was, no question, a cheap bear. It looked worn too, like maybe the technician had just gone and bought the first used bear he'd seen out of a thrift store.

"That's it?" said Lisa, rubbing her stomach. She was maybe six months pregnant at the time. "Hideous."

But she had stayed and listened as Michael had pushed on the bear's chest repeatedly, trying to switch on the heartbeat. It took a while to make it go, but when it finally started, even she had to admit it sounded remarkably clear.

"But even so, why would a baby want to listen to that?" asked Lisa.

Michael shrugged. He had no answer. He toyed with it a while, turning the heart on and off, and then he'd tossed it in one corner of the crib, to wait for the baby.

For all intents and purposes, the Donners forgot about the bear. Instead, they prepared for the baby. They read online about what they needed and what they should expect. They filled the house with baby things, slowly settled into the idea of a baby coming. They did another ultrasound, this one at the obstetrician's office,

and found out they were having a girl. Michael was surprised—
he'd expected a boy, had directed his thinking toward that the
whole way along. But then he began to get his mind around the
idea of having a girl and grew to like it.

Indeed, it was all going smoothly—a *textbook pregnancy* the obstetrician liked to say—and then, suddenly, it was not. Michael Donner
came home from work and called out to Lisa Donner, and there was
no answer. He thought she'd gone out. He went into the kitchen and
poured himself a drink. He took off his tie and placed it over the
back of a chair. He wandered into the bedroom and then he saw her,
collapsed on the floor, unconscious, her thighs stained with blood.

He called 911. Then he checked to see if she was still breathing.
She was. He slapped her and talked to her and chafed her hands until
she started to come around, but even then she was confused and didn't
seem to know where she was. And then she saw the blood and became
hysterical, and it was all he could do to control her until the para-
medics arrived and sedated her and bundled her off to the hospital.

"Sometimes," the pediatrician told them a few hours later, "the
pregnancy just doesn't take." It wasn't their fault, there was nothing
they could have done differently. Sometimes the body just decides
to let the developing fetus go.

"But we heard the heart," protested Lisa. "We saw her on the
monitor. She was alive."

The pediatrician shook her head. Who knew what had gone
wrong with the fetus? Something had, and that had stopped the
baby from going to term. They shouldn't blame themselves; they
should just understand that this was something that happened.

But Lisa had a hard time not blaming herself. It was her body after
all that had been holding the baby and thus, she reasoned, her body
that had killed it. Michael tried to comfort her, to hold her, but
quickly came to realize she did not want to be comforted or held.
She wanted to be alone with her grief.

There followed days when she almost didn't leave the bed, days when Michael had to force her to eat. They were told, after the loss of the baby, that she had been old enough that they could get a birth certificate, and so they filled out a birth certificate and a death certificate at the same time, marking a one-minute difference between when she had been born and when she had died, even though to Michael it seemed as if the baby had been born dead. But this, they were told in the hospital, was the custom. They were asked if they wanted to have a funeral, were told that too was something that could be allowed, but Lisa couldn't face it. Instead they had the body cremated and took the ashes home. He didn't know what to do with them and couldn't get Lisa to say what she wanted done, so he placed the urn temporarily upstairs, on the changing table in the nursery.

When the baby had been born stillborn, Lisa had held it—one of the nurses said this was sometimes done, was one way of saying good-bye—but it hadn't seemed to do Lisa any good. And it had ended up giving Michael nightmares. It was hard not to think about: the child, obviously dead and not fully formed, pressed against his wife's skin as she wept.

They left the baby things just as they were. At first Michael had suggested taking them away, storing them in the basement, but when he began to gather them, his wife had given a strange, keening cry that had frightened him as much as anything ever had, and he put everything back.

So there they were: Lisa barely functional, Michael trying to live on tiptoe so as not to make it worse for her, the baby things for a missing baby all neatly arrayed in the nursery, both of the Donners waiting, hoping for a time when they would feel better.

II.

About three months after losing the baby, Michael woke up to a noise. He could barely hear it, wasn't sure for a while that he wasn't imagining it. He lay in bed, his wife crumpled beside him, either asleep or pretending to be, and listened. For a while he thought he might drift off again, but there was something about the sound he couldn't quite put his finger on that continued to keep him awake.

Yawning, he finally got up and went in pursuit of it. He opened the bedroom door and went into the living room, but he wasn't hearing it nearly as well there. He went into the kitchen and stood, holding his breath. Still nothing. Same in his office.

In the end, he went back into the bedroom and lay down. Immediately he started to hear it again.

He was wide awake now. He tried to find the sound and this time walked from place to place in the room, listening. Until, finally, he realized he was hearing it through the heating register in the ceiling, that it was coming from upstairs, from the nursery.

He went upstairs, opened the nursery door, and waited. There it was, a sound like white noise, but softer, a strange thrumming to it. He walked around the darkened room, slowly homing in on it, only realizing at the last moment that it was coming from the crib.

For a moment he experienced sheer panic. It flashed through his mind that they had had the baby after all, but that both he and his wife were in denial that the baby existed. They had left it up here, alone, to die. And then he reached out and felt around and found the body of the bear.

Its heart was beating, slowly and regularly. Its borrowed heart, rather, since it was the sound of his dead child's heart. He'd completely forgotten about it. There must be something wrong with the mechanism that had caused it to go off at random, he thought.

He held the bear for a few minutes until, as suddenly as it had begun, the beating of the heart stopped. Had it really been thirty minutes? Perhaps there was a glitch somewhere. He placed the bear gently back in the crib and went back to bed.

The next day he didn't think about it. He left as usual to go to work, spent the day at the office. But when he came home for lunch, he found his wife wasn't asleep. She was up and functioning, had showered, had even tidied the house. Something had begun to change. For the better.

He took a deep breath. In the months after the baby's death, watching his wife struggle, struggling himself, he had told himself that they, the Donners, would make it through, but he hadn't exactly believed it. But now he thought it might be possible.

He kissed her, they ate the lunch he'd picked up at the Vietnamese place, then he went back to work, whistling. The rest of the day was a good day, one of the best he'd had in a while. He felt good all the way up to the moment when, at the end of the workday, he walked through the door and found his wife sitting in the living room rocking the bear, listening to the beating of its heart.

"Ssshh," she said. "She's almost asleep." And smiled.

He had stopped dead in the doorway. He just watched her from there, wondering what he should say, what, if anything, he could say.

"Do you want to hold her?" she asked.

"Lisa," he said. "You know that's just a toy, right?"

She looked down at the bear in her lap. "Yes," she said. "You're mostly right."

"Mostly?" he said.

She nodded. "Only it has her heart," she said.

"Just the sound of her heartbeat," he said. "It's a recording."

"Sure," she said, after a long pause. "I know that."

He waited for her to go on, but she didn't say anything more, just kept rocking softly, looking down at the bear.

"Lisa," he said.

"She was calling to me," she finally said.

"Oh, honey," he said. He moved to take the bear, but she was clutching it now, not letting it go.

In the end, after a lot of talking, he got her to relinquish it of her own accord. Yes, she said, she understood. She hadn't meant to scare him. Of course she understood—it wasn't their daughter, it was just a teddy bear. She hadn't meant to suggest anything beyond that, she claimed.

"What did you mean when you said it was calling to you?" asked Michael.

"She, you mean," said Lisa, her eyes not meeting his.

"What?"

"I didn't say *it*," she said. "I said *she*."

He gestured with his hand. "Does it matter?" he said.

For a moment she looked at him with a shocked expression, but then slowly it vanished and she looked away. "No," she said. "Not really."

And then she became listless again, like she had been before. She let him lead her back to bed. *Maybe it would have been better to let her keep the bear,* he couldn't help but think. But another part of him was worried about what would happen if he did.

"What did you mean when you said she was calling to you?" he asked again, tucking her in.

"Just that," she said. "I heard it. I heard something and went up to see what it was. It was the beating of her heart."

"It just started on its own?"

She nodded. "I didn't do anything. It just started on its own."

And having experienced something similar himself, he felt he had no choice but to believe her. There was something wrong with the player inside the bear, some sort of glitch. They would have to fix it. Either that or get rid of the bear. Probably better to do that, he thought, to just get rid of it.

But a few days later, he still hadn't gotten rid of the bear. Once it was back in the nursery, he simply forgot about it. Lisa was spending most of her time back in bed again, but she was getting up a little more, and Michael told himself she was slowly getting better.

He would have completely forgotten about the bear if, three days later, he hadn't awoken in bed again knowing he had heard something. It was louder this time. Half in a daze, head throbbing, he made his way out of the bedroom and up the stairs to the nursery, but when he got there, the bear was nowhere to be seen. The sound too had diminished. He looked for the bear for a few minutes before returning to the bedroom. Only then did he realize the bear was in the bed.

Furious, he woke Lisa up. She looked sleepy and confused. He brandished the bear at her.

"What do you have to say about this?" he said.

"About what?" she said.

Couldn't she just admit she'd gotten the bear and brought it into the bed? What was wrong with her?

"But I—" she said.

"No buts," he said. He continued to excoriate her until, furious herself, she yelled, "But I didn't go get it!"

Then how had it gotten there? he wanted to know. Stuffed animals don't just walk around the house. One of the two of them got it, and God knew it wasn't him. Which left her.

"No," she shouted. "I swear. I didn't get it!"

He took a deep breath. All right, he said, finally calming down a little, maybe she didn't go get it. Or didn't know she had. He was willing to accept that as a possibility. Maybe she had done it in her sleep, without thinking.

"No," she said, calming down a little herself. She had been in the bed the whole time. She was sure of it.

He shook his head. There just wasn't any other explanation, he told her.

"What about you?" she said. "Why couldn't you have been the one to do it in your sleep?"

Without thinking, he said, "I'm not the one who's sick." He immediately regretted it, but it was too late. It was the beginning of an argument that ended with the bear in the outside trash, his wife livid, and him having to sleep upstairs on a pile of blankets in the nursery.

The first thing he saw when he woke up was the bear, in the crib, pressed against the bars, like it was watching him. He realized, with a dull fury, that his wife must have gotten up once he was asleep and gotten the bear out of the trash and put it back in the crib. It had been a bad idea to purchase the bear in the first place, he told himself. At the time it had just seemed like a joke, and it would have been a joke if their child had survived. But considering all that had happened, it had been a very bad idea.

He thought about going down and yelling at her about it, but wasn't that exactly what she wanted? No, he told himself, he would handle it like a grown-up: he would pretend not even to have seen the bear. He would simply put it back in the trash where it belonged, and then, since today was trash pickup, stay home long enough to make sure it was taken away. That would be the end of the bear. They wouldn't have to think about it anymore. They could go on with getting back to the way their lives had been.

And indeed, he managed to do all that. He showered, had some breakfast. He took a bowl of cereal in to his wife, but she was still asleep—or perhaps pretending to be asleep so she wouldn't have to speak to him. He kissed her on the cheek and then went upstairs and got the bear and put it, heart now beating, in the trash can. Then he got into his car and waited there behind the wheel in the driveway until he saw in the rearview mirror the garbage truck arrive, the mechanical arm pick up and dump the can. *There*, he thought, starting up the car, *over and done*.

And that might have been the end of it. In normal circumstances it would have been. When he came home that night, he apologized to his wife and she apologized to him. She cried, and he had the decency, if that was what it was, not to accuse her of bringing the bear back into the house. And she, in turn, had the decency not to acknowledge that he had put the bear back in the trash again. She promised to make more of an effort, and he promised to be more patient. In short, they did all the things that each half of a couple does, out of fear or out of love, after being afraid of having gone too far.

But that was not the end. Three nights later, or four, when Michael had let his guard down, when he was beginning to feel that they were returning to their normal life, he again awoke in the middle of the night knowing he had heard something.

No, he thought, still mostly asleep. *Just imagining it. Dream.*

He tried to go back to sleep, he really did, but the sound wouldn't let him. Not a sound, really. More the ghost of a sound. But it would not leave him alone. Slowly, it began to fill him with dread.

He got out of bed. He listened in the bedroom, but the sound wasn't coming from there. He listened in the living room, even though he knew the sound wasn't there either. He listened everywhere in the house except for where he expected the sound to be coming from and then, in the end, he went to listen there too.

He opened the door to the nursery. Yes, there it was, the sound was here, the faint beating of a heart. There was the bear, in the crib, just as it had been for months now. But how had his wife gotten the bear back? Had it somehow gotten caught in the can and hadn't been thrown away? Had it ended up not making it into the garbage truck, and she'd found it in the street? There must, he hoped, be some logical explanation.

He turned on the light and stared at the bear through the bars. The heart now had stopped, just as suddenly as it had begun. The bear, he saw, was filthy, covered with a layer of gray dust as fine as ash. He would have to destroy it, but before he did, he felt his wife owed him an explanation. He would wipe the bear off and then show it to her, get her to explain, and then, in front of her, he would destroy it.

But when he picked it up to clean it, he realized something had changed. The bear felt different now, heavier, and when he moved it something seemed to sift through its body, as if it was now filled with sand. He moved it closer to his face and sniffed it and realized that no, its covering wasn't an ashy layer of dust, it was simply ash. And when, making a face, he laid the bear on the changing table to wipe it clean, he realized where the ash had come from. The lid was loose on the urn, a scattering of ash spilled around its base, and when he looked in, he realized it was mostly empty.

His limbs felt very heavy. He could see, now that he was looking for it, where the seam in the fabric had been torn open and clumsily unstitched to fill the bear with his daughter's ashes. Things were, he suddenly knew, much worse than he'd realized.

Trying to think, he opened the urn and held it just under the edge of the changing table, slowly sweeping the loose ash into it. Then he put it back on the table and began to unpluck the new seam on the bear.

As soon as he did, the heart began beating again. And then, in a way he didn't understand and found he never properly could describe later to the police when they were questioning him as to the death of his wife, the bear smiled at him.

He pulled his hand back as if bitten. He stared at the bear. *This is the moment,* he thought hopefully, *when I wake up.*

But he did not wake up. He was already awake. And as he reached out again, this time to tear the head off the bear that had stuffed itself with his child's ashes and that contained a sonic replica of her heart, he had no way of knowing that this would be the last moment when he still felt as if he had control of his life, that from here on out, things would only get worse.

Scour

1.

When the rain came it was not rain at all, but a pale scouring dust or sand. They watched it strip the paint off the car and slowly grind the windscreen opaque. For a while he kept driving, though he couldn't really see the road and kept slipping off it and back on. But then dust started seeping through the vents and the car died.

"What do we do?" she asked.

"Do?" he said. "What can we do but wait?"

"We have to get out of here," she said.

"No," he claimed. "We have to wait."

And yet, he was the one—after an hour, after perhaps two, the air of the cab already grown stifling—to open the door and step out.

*

By the morning the storm had died down somewhat, and by the time the sun was high overhead, it had stopped entirely. She had to force the door through the grit to get it open and then saw more grit piled all around the car, in drifts against it. She found the remains of a body 100, maybe 150, meters away, but it was so scoured and stripped of flesh and clothing she could not be sure it was his. Probably it was, she told herself. She left it where it was.

*

She regarded the sky, but there seemed to her no way to tell if the storm would return. And the landscape too was so flattened and beaten down that if it did return, there was no place to hide. *Which way to go?* Perhaps in the direction the car was pointing, unless they had gone off course in the storm. But if not there, where?

She set off, traveling as quickly as she could, the landscape unvarying and flat, never changing, revealing nothing. Still, she kept walking, kept on.

*

When the wind began to rise, she started to panic. There was still no sign of shelter, no place to hide. The dust, or sand, if it was either dust or sand, began to rise in flaccid tourbillions around her, almost immediately collapsing but staying aloft a little longer each time. Her skin began to sting. She started to run. And when it became clear running wasn't enough, when the grit had begun to eat away at her face and arms and eyes, she fell to her knees and burrowed as quickly as she could, digging through the sand, trying to cover her head and chest and yet somehow preserve a space to breathe. And even though she felt the grit strip the shirt from her back and then flay off strip after strip of skin, she stayed balled and folded in on herself, concentrating on breathing in the small space of air between her hands and her knees, until she passed out.

*

That was how they found her. They lifted her unconscious body up and carried it across the waste for several hours, and she did not wake up. They stopped and tried to feed her, but she would not swallow food. They eased the spout of a water skin between her lips and massaged her throat, and finally she did swallow some—her throat convulsed, in any case. And it was for this, and only this, that they did not leave her to die.

II.

When she awoke, it was days or perhaps weeks later. She was in a shelter, a room of some sort, and for a moment she thought she was back again in the car, but the shape of the space around her was wrong. But she told herself, *No, it's the car,* that it was her vision that was wrong. And yet the colors were wrong as well. It was not the car. No, definitely a room.

*

She was lying on a bed, she finally determined. The room was dingy and low-ceilinged, and only barely bigger than the bed. More like a cell than a room. She climbed out of the bed and went to the door to see if it was locked. Or would have done so, anyway, had she not been strapped to the bed.

*

For a while, she shouted. Nobody came. She shouted some more, then tried simply asking for someone to release her. Nobody came. Then she lay in bed and tested the strength of her straps. She tried to wriggle out of them without success. Then she just lay there, not doing anything. Then she fell asleep.

*

When she awoke, a chair had been brought in, crammed into the narrow space between bed and wall. A man was sitting in it, smiling. He looked somewhat like the man she had lost, the man who had been driving and who had then left the car. But it was not him:

he had different eyebrows. And maybe other things different about him as well.

*

"Hello," the man said, the new man, his voice vaguely friendly. He held his hands neatly in his lap.

*

Many things she could possibly respond with rushed into her head. *Who are you?* for instance. *Where am I?* for instance. *What am I doing here?* for instance. *Am I a prisoner?* Or *Release me this instant.* Or.
    She said none of them.

*

"Hello," she said.

*

The man smiled. "I'm sure you have a lot of questions," he said. "For instance, who am I? Where are you? What are you doing here? Are you a prisoner? I must ask you, for the moment, to be patient, to wait."
    She closed her eyes. This man, or any man, for that matter, shouldn't be able to say so directly what was in her head. *Is this a dream?* she wondered. *Am I dreaming?*

*

When she opened her eyes, the man was still there. He had removed his hands from his lap and was now resting them lightly on one of her arms. For a moment she couldn't think if it was her right or left arm. *Am I dead?* she wondered.
    "Doing all right?" he asked, then he smiled again before she could respond. "Of course you are," he said. "Why wouldn't you be?"

*

"Where," she finally managed to say, "where am I?"

He applied a little pressure to her left or right arm. "Hush," he said. And then, after a long moment, said, "You're here."

*

But where? she wondered. *Where's here?*

III.

In time the man, or a man very much like him but still not exactly like the man who had been driving, loosened the straps. She was allowed to chafe her wrists until the numbness left them. And then the straps were tightened again.

*

The first time this happened she resisted and then another man, nearly identical to the first and second, came in and pressed her shoulders hard into the bed while the other tightened the straps. He bared his teeth at her while he did it. After that she let them tighten without resisting.

*

And then that too stopped. One day one of the men loosened the straps and did not tighten them again. And then he left.

*

For a while she lay in the bed chafing her wrists, but then all the feeling she could stand was back in them, and she saw no reason to chafe them further.

*

She got out of the bed. Her legs were weak and looked like sticks rather than legs. She could not walk far, but she could walk as far as the door and put her hand on the doorknob and twist it.

*

Only it wouldn't twist. It was locked.

*

And then one day it was not locked. She twisted the doorknob and the door came open, and she saw that it led into a simple, unadorned hall.

*

The first day she simply looked out into the hallway and then closed the door and returned to sit on the bed, her hands held motionless in her lap like two dead birds.

*

A man came, just as a man came every day, and gave her some food, sitting in the chair crammed beside the bed as she ate. Then, when she was finished, he took her bowl and spoon away and carried them toward the door.

*

As he opened the door and closed it behind him, she waited, listening for the sound of his keys jangling, for the sound of the lock tonguing into its groove. This was a difficult moment for her, and she all but cried out. But she heard no sound, and though she feared this merely meant he had one key and thus it would not jingle, that the lock was freshly oiled and as silent as a fish in deep water, when at last she could bring herself to stand and again twist the doorknob, she found it was still unlocked, and she was flooded with relief.

*

Or at first she was flooded with relief. For she began to think to herself that if they had left the door unlocked, it was because they wanted her to go through it, that it was a trap of some kind.

*

Or maybe, she told herself, they had made a mistake not once but twice, so that tomorrow the door would again be locked, and locked forever from then forward.

*

Or maybe, she told herself, *I am not a prisoner at all.*

*

But nevertheless, trapped between these possibilities, she found herself for several hours hesitating between staying in the room and exiting. In the end she succeeded only in stepping briefly into the hall and looking down it, first in one direction and then in the other.

*

The hall was poorly lit. It looked the same to her in either direction and seemed to go on as far as she could see. After a few minutes, she came back in and shut the door again and then sat on the edge of the bed, waiting.

*

What she was waiting for she didn't know, but whatever it was it didn't come. Or if it did come, she didn't recognize it.

*

They kept coming to her room, just as they had before, bringing her food, bringing her water, sitting in the chair crammed alongside the bed. They all looked the same to her, or nearly the same, and she was unaware of how many had care of her. Maybe just two or three, though perhaps several dozen.

*

They would come and they would go and then she would go to the door and pass through it into the hall and look first in one direction and then the other. Then she would return to the room and lie down on the bed and wonder what exactly was wrong with her, why she couldn't bring herself to leave.

IV.

And then one day, if it was day, the men did not come. She waited for them to bring her food, and they did not bring her food. *Perhaps,* she thought to herself, *something in my head has slipped and I am confused about time.* And so she waited. She waited for them to bring her water, and they did not bring her water. It was only when her throat was parched and her tongue sticking to her teeth that she admitted to herself that no, something in her head had not slipped, that the problem was outside, was with them. The problem was they had abandoned her.

*

How often in my life have I been abandoned? she thought, and could not help but think that *abandonment* was a word jotted not just on one or two moments of her existence, but scrawled heavily across her life as a whole.

*

She thought again of the man in the car and how he had driven with her for miles, and of how, without explanation, after having first prevented her from doing it herself, he had stepped out of the car and abandoned her, and died.

*

Only what if he had been trying not to abandon her, but save her? What if he had left the car so there would be air enough for her? So that she would survive? Did it make a difference? He had still abandoned her, hadn't he, even if only to save her?

*

And who was to say the same hadn't happened to these men as well? If she were to go down the hall, would she find them, bodies scoured or stripped or broken, dead for her sake without her knowing why? She was, she finally realized, afraid of going down the hall. Afraid of what she would see.

*

Such thoughts, she thought. But they had already begun to feel as if they did not belong to her.

V.

And then at a certain point she either died or seemed to die, and she was never in a position after to say which, if either, it was. Perhaps her life drained out and was gone and then, slowly, replaced by something else. Or perhaps she slipped from one level of life to another, then yet another, becoming slowly less and less present but still managing to persist. It did not matter which it was. What mattered was what seemed to become of her.

*

After this she could not move, except for her eyes. What became of her was that she was in a room, or thought she was. Only the room at times had no walls and indeed seemed to breathe and flex from being a room to being, simply, the outside. A steady rain was falling—or what she thought was a steady rain but feared instead would be, if she looked too closely, a pale scouring of dust or sand.

*

But no, when she was outside, it was rain, cool against her face. And when she was in the room, it was nothing at all.

*

And soon there was nothing more than that, a coolness against her face and then nothing at all, back and forth, back and forth, less and less of both each time, slowly vanishing but never quite gone, and she too going with it. *What can I do?* a scrap of herself wondered. *Do?* another scrap answered. *What can you do but wait?*

Torpor

When they slept, she had gotten into the habit of resting both her hands on his arm. Now that his arm was gone, what was she to do?

Before, they had had a good arrangement, or had come to have one once she had sorted through matters. She had begun with splints, using them first for just one hand and then for both. They kept her from waking up in the middle of the night with stabbing pains. But still, even with the splints, her hands would eventually start to throb, and that was enough to awaken her. More than enough. She tried drugs, but they did nothing but make her groggy. *What you need,* a friend told her, *is better drugs.* The doctor she approached for a prescription told her instead that it was simple: she just had to keep her hands elevated. So, she had tried to keep her arms bent at the elbow and the elbow planted on the bed, to sleep with her hands waving in the air on the stalks of her forearms. Either they fell down as soon as she fell asleep, or she awoke with her arms locked and sore. She stacked pillows next to her and splayed her hands onto them, but it didn't elevate them enough. Nothing worked, nothing at all. But then one night, his back had been turned to her and he was sleeping with his arm hemmed to his side, and she had simply reached out and placed her hands on his arm, and he, sleeping, had let her. She slept the sleep of the dead all the way through to morning.

It had gone like that for many nights in a row: she lying awake, restless, until he rolled over and pressed his arm along his side and then she could wriggle her way toward him and lay her hands on his arm. Then sleep. She had grown not only to like it, but to need it, and the few times he had been gone at night and not in the bed, she had not been able to sleep at all. Those nights, the stabbing pains had been worse than ever.

For better or for worse, she had promised. She knew that was what she had promised, but how was she to have known that worse meant there would one day suddenly be less of him? It had been like that: one day he was whole and complete, and the next day his arm was three-quarters gone. When he first came home, the stump wrapped in gauze, she had of course understood that she couldn't touch it, that it would hurt him to do so. She had respected that, kept her distance. But then the wound had annealed, the scar tissue had thickened and then hardened, and the stump became just that: a stump. By that time, it felt as if she hadn't slept for a year. It hadn't of course been that long, but that was what it felt like, and that was what she meant when she'd said it to him. But, touchy, he'd misunderstood. *The tragedy here,* he'd claimed, *is not whether you can sleep. This,* he said, shaking the stump in her face, *is the tragedy. Stump,* he claimed, *trumps stabbing hand pain.*

But did it? Were they really playing at some game that had trumps? A game in which only the person with the missing arm, the three-quarters-missing arm, was allowed to feel pain? She hadn't thought so. And indeed, with a little time, a little patience, as his own pain lessened and he learned not to try to pick up, say, a glass with his missing hand, he went from feeling offended to saying—quite sensibly, he believed—*But I still have a good part of my arm left. Use that.*

But no, it wasn't the same. When he turned now, as he always did, to sleep on his side, and she scooted closer across the sheet and rested her hands on him, she could, true, fit both hands on what remained of the arm. But one hand always slipped off the stump to fall lower, against his ribs. And if she scooted higher in the bed so that that hand wouldn't slip off, it was the other hand that did so, spilling off the shoulder and down against his neck. Either made it too low. Admittedly that meant she was throbbing in just one hand instead of two, but she still couldn't sleep. *Can't he just wear his prosthetic through the night?* she found herself sometimes wondering at two or three or four in the morning. But this, she knew, would be asking too much. If he wore his prosthetic during the night, the doctor had told him, had told *them*, he wouldn't be able to wear it through the whole day without having aches and strain and even, potentially, shooting pains of his own. No, despite their relationship, she just could not ask—and even if she did ask, she felt, he would almost certainly say no.

So, for months she was sleepless. She placed one hand on her husband and then held the other there in the air, over the place where the arm used to be. She held it up as long as she could, or placed it on a pillow balanced on her husband, if he was asleep enough that she could get away with it. But it was not the same. The best she could manage was a kind of grumpy torpor. And it was not, she became more and more convinced, enough.

And so, late at night, listening to her husband breathing beside her, one arm already tingling, sleep refusing to come, she found herself imagining what it would be like to be in bed with a man who had not one arm, but two.

From this, everything else followed, inexorably. It was a simple thing to take a lover. Not because she was sex starved, or to find passion, or for anything of that sort—for indeed, so she told me as she again pulled the sheet high enough to cover her breasts, she loved her husband passionately and desired him and always would.

No, she did it for afterwards. For the moment when, both of them spent, her lover would roll away.

As he perhaps dozed a little, she would stealthily slip on her splints and then, carefully, place both her hands on him. And then, finally, if all was just right, if he stayed there on his side, if he didn't move, if he didn't mind having her there pressing on him, then she, at last, would once again be able to sleep.

Past Reno

I.

Bernt began to suspect the trip would turn strange when, on the outskirts of Reno, he entered a convenience store that had one of its six aisles completely dedicated to jerky. At the top were smoked meat products he recognized, name brands he'd seen commercials for. In the middle was stuff that seemed local, with single-color printing, but still vacuum packed and carefully labeled. Along the bottom row, though, were chunks of dried and smoked meat in dirty plastic bags held shut with twist ties, no labels on them at all. He wasn't even certain what kind of meat they contained. He prodded one of the bags with the toe of his sneaker and then stared at it for a while. When he realized the clerk was staring at him, he shook his head and went out.

I should have known then, he thought hours later. At that point he should have turned around and driven the half mile back into Reno and gone no farther. But, he told himself, it was just one convenience store. And it wasn't, he tried to convince himself, really even that strange. It just meant people in Reno liked jerky. So instead, he shook his head and kept driving.

It was the first time he'd left California in a decade. His father had died, and he'd been informed of it too late to attend the funeral, but he was driving to Utah anyway, planning to be there for the settling of the estate, whatever was left of it. He was on his own. His girlfriend had intended to come along and then, at the last moment, had come down sick. What she had neither of them was quite sure, but she couldn't stand without getting dizzy. To get to the bathroom to vomit she had to crawl. The illness had lasted three or four hours and then, just as suddenly as it had come, it was gone. But she had refused to get in the car after that. What if it came back? If it had been bad while she was stationary, she reasoned, how much worse would it be if she was driving? He had to admit she had a point.

"Do you even need to be there?" she had asked him. "Won't they send you your share wherever you are?"

Technically, yes, that was true, but he didn't trust his extended family. If he didn't go, they'd find a way to keep him from what he deserved.

She shook her head tiredly. "And what exactly do you deserve?" she asked. Which was, he had to admit, a good question. "And didn't your father tell you never to come back?"

He nodded. His father had. "But he doesn't have any say," he said. "He's dead now."

But in any case, she had not come with him. And maybe, he thought now as he drove, his girlfriend's illness—miles before Reno—was the first indication the trip would turn strange. But how could he have known? And now, well past Reno, already having gone so far, how could he bring himself to turn around?

Back at the beginning, just past Reno, he drove, watching Highway 80 flirt with the Truckee River, draw close to it, and then pull away again. Then he hit the scattering of houses called Fernley, and the river vanished too. For miles there was almost nothing there, just a ranch or two and bare dry ground. He watched a sagging barbed wire fence skitter along the roadside, then, when that was gone, counted time by watching the metal markers that popped up every tenth of a mile. After a while those disappeared too, leaving only the faded green mile markers, numbers etched in white on them. He watched them come, his mind drifting in between them, and watched them go.

He thought of his father as he had been when he was young, a man who wouldn't leave the house without ironing creases in his jeans. His boots he made certain were brought to a high polish before he left, even if he was just going to the back acres, even if he knew they'd be dirty or dusty the moment he stepped off the porch. That was how he was. Bernt hated it. Hated him.

He remembered his father lashing a pig's hind legs together and running the rope over the pulley wheel screwed under the hayloft floor and winding the rope onto the handcrank. His father had made him take hold of the crank and said, "You pull the bastard up and hold it, and don't pay no mind to how it struggles. I'll get the throat slit and then that'll be the worst of it done. Your job's nothing. You just keep on hold to it until the fucker bleeds out." Bernt had just nodded. His father said pull and Bernt had started cranking. There went the pig up, squealing and spinning and flailing. His father stood there beside it, motionless, knife out with his thumb just edged over the guard and touching the side of the blade, waiting. And then, with one quick flick of his arm, he opened its throat from ear to ear. The pig still struggled, the blood gouting from the wound and thickening the dust. Bernt couldn't understand how his father didn't get blood on his boots or his pants, but he just didn't.

It was always that way, every time he killed something. Never a drop of blood on him. Uncanny almost, it seemed to Bernt, and he had spent more than one sleepless night as a teenager wondering how that could be, why blood would shy from his father. The only possibilities he could come up with seemed so outlandish that he preferred to believe it was just luck.

That was the kind of man his father had been. Now, dead, what was he?

He shuddered. He watched the mile markers again—or tried to, but they simply weren't there anymore. For a moment he thought he might have left the highway somehow, by accident. But no, he couldn't see how he could have, and whatever road he was on had every appearance of a highway. Then he flicked past a sheared-off metal stub on the roadside and wondered if that wasn't what had once been a marker, if someone had been systematically cutting them down. Bored kids, probably, with nothing to do.

He gauged the sun in the sky. It seemed just as high as it had been an hour before, not yet starting its descent. He checked the gas gauge: between a half and a quarter tank. He kept driving, wondering if he had enough gas to get to the next station. Sure he did. How far could it possibly be?

He opened the glovebox to take out the map and have a look, but the map wasn't there. Maybe he had had it out and it had slipped under the seat, but if it had, it was deep enough under that he couldn't find it, at least not while driving. No, he told himself, there would be a gas station soon. There had to be. He couldn't be that far off of Elko. It was less than three hundred miles from Reno to Elko, and he'd filled up in Reno. And Winnemucca was somewhere in between the two. Had he passed that already without realizing it?

He had enough gas, he knew he had enough. He shouldn't let his mind play tricks on him.

His father had told him that if he was going to leave, he should never come back.

Fine, Bernt had said. *Wasn't planning to come back anyway.*

And then he had left.

Or wait, not that exactly. It had been so many years ago now that it was easier to think that was how it had ended, but it hadn't been quite so simple. He hadn't said, *Fine.* He hadn't said, *Wasn't planning to come back anyway.* What he had said, "Why the hell would I want to come back?"

His father had smiled. "Thought you'd never ask," he said. "Come along," he said, and he made for the door, waving to Bernt to follow him.

Perhaps an hour later—maybe more, maybe less, it was hard for him to judge time driving alone—he called his girlfriend to tell her she had been right, he shouldn't have come after all. He was hoping that maybe she would talk him into turning around, inheritance be damned.

But she didn't answer. Or no, not that exactly: the call didn't go through. It seemed as if it was going through—he dialed the number, he heard it ring a few times, then the call disconnected. His phone had no reception.

Well, what's strange about that? a part of him wondered. He was out in the middle of nowhere—of course service was bound to be bad. He'd have to wait until he was near a town and then he'd try her again.

All that sounded right, rational, correct. And yet another part of him couldn't help but worry that something was wrong.

The radio too faded in and out, the same station one moment seeming quite strong, the next little more than static, then quite strong again. *Not strange*, a part of him again insisted. Must be the mountains, he told himself, the signal bouncing around in them. He told himself this even though it seemed to happen just as regularly when he was in open country as when he was skirting a mountain or when one had just hove into view.

There were moments too when there was nothing but static. When he turned the knob slowly but found nothing. When he could press the search button and his tuner would go through the whole band from beginning to end without finding anything to settle on, and would start over again, and then again, and again, and again. It might go on for five minutes or even ten, then suddenly it would stop on a frequency that, to him, still seemed to be nothing but static, but it stayed there. After a while, he became convinced there must be something beneath the static, a strange whispering that surely would slowly resolve itself into voices. Though it never did, only stayed static.

He checked his gas gauge. It read between a quarter and a half tank. Hadn't it read that before? He tapped on it with his finger, softly at first and then harder and harder, but the reading didn't change.

When he came to Winnemucca, he would stop for gas, just in case the gauge was broken. He probably didn't need gas to make it to Elko, but he would stop anyway. He tapped the gauge again. Had he already passed Winnemucca? He felt like he should have, but surely he would have noticed?

He watched his father check the crease of his trouser leg. He watched him stop on the porch and raise first one boot and then the other to the rail, quickly buffing them with the yellow-orange cloth draped there before he stepped off and went down the path leading out to the road.

Bernt followed.

"This here is all mine," his father was saying, gesturing around him. "This, all of this, belongs to me."

But of course Bernt knew this. His father had been saying shit like this ever since Bernt was a child. It was not news to him. When his father turned to see how Bernt was taking it and saw his son's face, his lips curled into a sneer.

"What in hell do you know about it?" he asked Bernt.

"What?" asked Bernt, surprised. "I know you own the land. I already knew that."

"Land," said his father, and spat. "Shit, that's the least of it," he said. "I own anything that comes here, plant or animal or man, including you. If you leave, it's because I let you. And if I let you, you sure as shit ain't coming back unless I say."

Almost before Bernt knew it, his father's hand flashed out and took his wrist in a tight, crushing grip. Bernt tried to pull away, but his father was all sinew. His father nodded once, his mouth a straight, inexpressive line, then he cut off the path, toward the storm cellar, dragging Bernt along with him.

No, he should have reached a town by now. Something was wrong. The sun was still high. It shouldn't still have been high. It didn't make sense. The gas gauge was either broken or for some reason he wasn't running out of gas. He tried again to call his girlfriend and this time, even though his phone didn't have any bars, the call went through. He heard it ring twice and then she picked up. She said "Hello," her voice oddly low and almost unrecognizable—probably because she was sick, he told himself later. He said, "Darling, it's me," and then the call disconnected. He couldn't get it to reconnect when he called again.

His father took Bernt across the yard, pulling hard enough on his arm that it was difficult for Bernt to keep his balance. Once Bernt stumbled and nearly fell, and his father just kept pulling him forward, and he had to struggle to stay upright. He got the impression from his father that it didn't matter to him if Bernt stayed upright or not.

They went past the barn and around to the back of it, to where the storm cellar was, a single wooden door set flat into the ground and kept closed with a padlock. Bernt had always known it was there, but he had never been inside. His father let go of his arm and thrust a key out at him. "Go on," he said to Bernt. "Go and look."

II.

Just when he started to panic, he came to a town. He didn't catch the town's name—perhaps the sign for it had been vandalized, like the mile markers. He came over a rise and around a bend and suddenly saw the exit sign and the scattering of buildings below, windows shimmering in the sun. He had to brake and slide over a lane quickly, and even then he hit the rattle strip and came just shy of striking the warning cones before the concrete divider. But then he was on the ramp and going down, under the bridge and into town.

He pulled in at the first gas station he saw. He stopped at the pumps, turned off the car, and clambered out, only then realizing the shop was abandoned and empty, the pumps covered with grime, the rubber hoses old and cracked. He got back into the car and started it again, then drove through the streets of the town looking for another station. But there didn't seem to be one.

What had he seen in the storm cellar? He still wasn't quite sure. He unlocked it and went down, his father standing with his arms crossed up top. It smelled of dust inside, and of something else— something that made him taste metal in his mouth when he breathed the air. It made his throat hurt.

He went down the rickety wooden steps until he came to a packed-earth floor. There was just enough room to stand upright. Even with the door open, it took a while for his eyes to adjust, and once they had adjusted, he didn't see much. The floor was stained in places, darker in some places than others—unless that was some natural property of the earth itself. He didn't think it was. There was, in the back, deeper in the hole, a series of racks, and there was something hanging on them. He hesitated and from up above heard his father say, "Go on," his voice cold and hard. He groped his way forward, but because of the way his own body blocked the light, it wasn't until he was a foot or two away that he realized that what he was seeing were strips of drying meat. Hundred of them, sliced thin and sometimes twisted up on themselves, with nothing really to tell him what sort of animal they had come from. Though it was a large animal, he was sure of that.

His mouth grew dry and he found himself staring, his eyes flicking from one strip to the next and back again. He almost called out to his father to ask him where the dried meat had come from, but something stopped him. In his head, he imagined his father answering the question by simply reaching down and swinging the door shut and leaving him in darkness. The feeling was so palpable that for a moment he wondered if he wasn't in darkness after all, if he wasn't simply imagining what he thought he was seeing.

He forced himself to turn around very slowly, as if nothing was wrong, and climb up the stairs. His father watched him come but made no move to reach out and help him as Bernt scrambled out of the shelter.

"You seen it?" asked his father.

He hesitated a moment, wondering what exactly his father had meant for him to see—whether it was the strips of meat or perhaps something else, something behind the racks, even deeper in. But almost immediately he decided it was safer to simply agree.

"I saw it," he said.

His father nodded. "Good," he said. "Then you understand why you have to stay."

Bernt made a noncommittal gesture his father took as a yes. His father clapped him on the shoulder and then began walking.

Why his father felt he understood that, what his father thought he'd seen, what he'd thought the storm cellar had done to him, Bernt couldn't exactly say. Indeed, he would never be sure, and ultimately he felt it might be better not to know. He went after his father back to the house and retreated to his room. From there, it was a simple matter to wait until dark and then pack a few things, climb out the window, and leave for good. He had never been back.

After a while he gave up looking for a gas station. The gas gauge read between a quarter and a half full still; probably he had enough to make it into Elko.

He parked in front of a diner on Main Street and went in. It was crowded inside, all tables full. He sat at the counter. Even then, it took a while for the waitress to get around to him. When she finally did, he asked her about a gas station, felt it was par for the trip when she told him there wasn't one. *Used to be one,* she said, *but gas here cost too much. Nobody used it, not with Elko nearby.* No, the nearest one was up the road at Elko.

"How far away is that?" he asked.

The question seemed to puzzle her somehow. "Not far," she said.

He asked what she suggested, and she recommended the soup of the day, which he ordered without thinking to ask what it was exactly. When it came it was surprisingly good, a rich, orange broth scented with saffron and with strings of meat spread all through it. Pork, probably. It made his mouth water to eat it. It seemed a sign to him that his trip was finally becoming less strange, or at least strange in a way that was good rather than bad. When he finished, he used the edge of his thumb to scour the sides of the bowl clean.

He sat there, far from eager to get back on the road. The waitress brought him a cup of coffee with cream at the end without his asking for it, and before he could tell her he didn't drink coffee she was gone again, off to another customer. He let it sit there for a while and then, for lack of anything better to do, took a sip. It was rich and mellow, different from coffee as he remembered it, and before he knew it he had finished the whole cup.

It's okay, he told himself, and found he more or less believed it. *The strange part of the trip is over. Everything will be all right from here on out.*

He had written twice to his father from California. The first time was maybe a year after he'd arrived. He'd wanted for his father to know that he was all right, that he'd landed on his feet. He'd also wanted to gloat a little. Perhaps too he had still been curious. *What exactly was it that you thought showing me the storm cellar would do? What was it in there that you thought would keep me?*

For a month, maybe two, he had waited for a reply. But his father had never answered the letter. The only way he knew for certain his father had received it was because when his father died, his aunt had written to let him know, saying they'd finally gotten his address off a letter he'd written his father.

The second letter, years later, had been more measured, calmer. It was, as much as he could bring it to be, an attempt at reconciliation. It had come back to him unopened, "Return to Sender" written across it in his father's careful block writing.

Everything will be all right, he was still telling himself when he got up from the stool and made his way to the bathroom. He peed and flushed, then stretched. While he was washing his hands, he noticed the mirror.

Or *mirrors,* rather. There were two of them, one suspended over the other, a larger one with a small one screwed in over it so that the larger one looked almost like a frame around it.

He looked at himself in it, his haggard face, but his eyes kept slipping to where one mirror ended and the other began. Was it meant to be that way? Some sort of design scheme? Was the center of the larger mirror cracked or foxed and the small mirror had been hung to cover that? Was there some kind of hole the second mirror was hiding?

He reached out and grabbed the edges of the top mirror. It was affixed in each of its four corners by a screw that went through the corner of the mirror and then through a thin block of wood and then through the mirror behind it. He could just get the tips of his finger in the space left between the mirrors. He tugged, but it was bolted firmly in place.

When he let go, the tips of his fingers were black with dust. He washed his hands again, more slowly this time. His face, when he looked up this time, looked just as haggard. He turned off the taps, dried his hands, and left the bathroom.

A moment later he was back in. He had the penlight on his keychain out and was shining it at the gap between the top mirror and the bottom one. He pressed his eye close, but no matter where he looked, no matter where he shone the light, the mirror behind it looked whole and complete.

III.

At first, he lied to his girlfriend, claiming he had gone to Utah and to his father's ranch for the reading of the will, but had received nothing. But then, when the box came, he finally came clean. It was an old box, starting to collapse, and smelled dank. It was very heavy. The words "Bernt's Pittance" were written on the side of it in his father's careful hand.

He left the box sitting on the table for a day and a half. The evening of the second day, they were both sitting in bed, both reading, when she asked him when he was going to open it. He put the book down on his chest and began to talk. She let him, interrupted only once, and when he was done she curled up beside him, one hand touching his shoulder softly, and said nothing. That surprised him—he'd thought she might be angry that he had lied to her. But if she was angry, she kept it to herself.

Of course, he told her, *nothing was really going on, it was just my imagination. It was just an ordinary trip. I was just noticing the things that under normal circumstances I wouldn't notice.* But as he told the story, moved bit by bit across the landscape between Reno and the small town whose name he had never quite figured out, it was all he could do not to panic again. He didn't believe it was a normal trip. He believed it was anything but. And he believed that somehow, his father was to blame.

The hardest part was explaining why seeing that, seeing the one mirror placed atop the other mirror, had been the thing that had turned him around and made him drive back to Reno, made him stop and rent a hotel room and drink himself nearly blind until he ran out of liquor and sobered up enough to realize enough time had elapsed to give his girlfriend the impression that he had gone to Utah. There hadn't, he had to admit, been anything really wrong with the mirrors—but that, somehow, had been *exactly* what was wrong with them.

That was the one time she interrupted him. "Was it like what you saw in the storm cellar?" she asked.

But what had he seen in the storm cellar? He still didn't know, and never would. Was that like the mirrors? No, that had been a hole in the ground containing curing strips of dried meat. How could twinned mirrors be like a hole in the ground and strips of meat? No, the only thing they had in common was that he felt as if he couldn't quite understand what either one was telling him. That he felt he was missing something.

He'd left the café, climbed into the car, and driven. His intention at first, despite the way he was feeling, was to keep driving, to continue on to Utah, to see the trip through. But as he took a left out of the parking lot and headed down Main Street, he felt as if he was being stretched between the mirror and wherever he was going now. That a part of him was caught in the mirror, and the link between that and the rest of him was growing thinner and thinner.

And so instead of getting on the highway, he circled back to the café. He took the tire iron out of the kit nestled beside the spare tire and walked into the café and straight into the bathroom. He gave the top mirror a few careful taps with the tire iron and broke out each of the four corners, then lifted it down and set it flat on the floor. The mirror beneath was complete and whole. This mirror he simply broke to bits, just to make sure there wasn't something behind it. There wasn't. Only blank wall. So he broke the first mirror as well. And then he left just as quickly as he had come, the waitress staring at him open mouthed and the burly cook hustling out of the building and after him, cursing, just as he turned the key to his car and drove away.

Even then, he might have kept going, might have kept on to Utah, he told his girlfriend. But the trip—all of it, not just that last moment of finding himself doing something he'd never thought he'd do—seemed to him a warning. It was a mistake, he felt, to go on. So he turned around.

And indeed, almost before he knew it, he was back in Reno, the car all but out of gas. He found a gas station, then found a hotel and settled down for a few drunken days to wait. Both because he was ashamed he hadn't gone all the way to Utah and because, to be frank, now that he was back in a place that seemed fully real to him, he was afraid to get in the car again.

But then at last, head aching from a hangover, he had climbed into the car and driven. A moment later he had crossed over the state line. He wound his way up into the mountains, went past Truckee, skirting Donner Lake, through Emigrant Gap, and then slowly down out of the mountains and into more and more populated areas, ever closer and closer to home. By the time he had pulled onto their street, it almost seemed as if he had made too much of it, that he had just wanted an excuse not to go to Utah after all.

The more he talked, the more he tried both to explain to his girlfriend how he felt and to dismiss it, to relegate it to the past, the more another part of him felt the event gather and harden in his mind, like a bolus or a tumor, both part of him and separate from him at once. He did not know if speaking made it better or made it worse.

When he was done, he lay there silent. Her girlfriend was beside him, and soon her breathing had changed, and he could tell she was asleep. He was, more or less, alone.

There was the box still to deal with, he knew. He knew too that he would not open it. He did not want whatever was inside it. In his head, he planned how to get rid of it. Just throwing it away did not seem like enough.

Careful not to wake her, he got up. He slipped into his jeans and found his car keys. He put on his socks and a shirt, and at the door he slipped on his shoes.

No, he needed to get it as far from him as he could. He would take it back to Utah, back to where it came from.

Or maybe not, he thought a few hours later, well into the drive and recognizing nothing as familiar, completely unsure where he was. Maybe not as far as Utah, but certainly somewhere past Reno. That would have to be far enough.

Any Corpse

When she awoke, a shower of raw flesh had fallen in the field. She watched the furnishers sweep their way slowly toward her, moving awkwardly in their armatures, prodding the rended bits where they lay. What seemed fresh and unmaggoted and was large enough to grasp they gathered. They would smoke and preserve it, then try to sell it as provision. What was rotten they kicked dirt over, lifting their faces to the sky as they scraped the dirt along with their feet.

There was nothing for her here. No, nothing. The furnishers could not understand this. They could, in fact, understand very little, she had come to realize, and were it not for their armatures, they would not be able to make pretense of being human, the air pressing too heavily upon them. One of them, indistinguishable to her from the others, approached, bowing and scraping, and said in its gargly voice, "Query: shall person be furnished?"

"No," she said. "What do you have, meat?" It gave the flinching gesture she had come to understand as assent. "I don't need meat," she said. "I need a body."

"Body made of meat," the furnisher said. "So too meat made of body. Let it be written and beads exchanged."

"No," she told him, "I need a whole body."

"Whole," it said. Unless it was "hole."

"Complete. Someone recently slaughtered, one of the newly deceased," she continued, trying now to ape the spirit of their own locutions, to make them understand. "One whose flexible organs would yet be capable of speech, not with lineaments already hardened in the sun."

"Organs," he said. "Yes. Lineaments, yes." He barked something and the furnishers behind him began rooting through their bags.

"A complete body," she insisted. "Who are you?" she asked. "Which one? Are you the one I spoke to last time? Do you have a name?"

"These are many queries," he said, and hastily retreated.

The rest came at her bowing and presenting their bags to her, but she waved them away. Confused they turned in circles a moment and then bowed and presented again, but she had already turned and walked back into her cave, where she knew they would not follow her.

There were other fields, other caves. Everything told her there must be. Her tablature could be moved—she could probably hire the furnishers to do so. Or the slaughter would change, and bodies would again present whole, or nearly so if she were to wait a little. A few days maybe, or a few weeks. Was she willing to wait? Soon her provisions would dwindle and then she would be forced to go hungry or buy from the furnishers. Or leave.

She watched the furnishers from the darkness of her cave, crouched and aimless near its mouth. Why did they not enter? What were they afraid of?

Soon, she strode out to the mouth, standing still in its shadow where they would not approach. This time she had her stick with her, and as she spoke she struck it against the rock of the mouth. They gave little shivers with each blow, but whether they were of pleasure or pain, she did not know. Once she had a corpse, she would ask it. Perhaps it would know.

"A corpse," she said. "Bring me a corpse."

They mumbled to one another and then one approached. Whether the same as before or different, she couldn't tell.

"Person, excuse," the envoy said. "Person will be furnished in meat."

"Not meat," she said. "I shall not buy meat from you. Never. But I shall buy a corpse."

There was much confusion at this. "Query: person pay well?" the envoy asked.

"Yes," she claimed. "Very well."

"Person will have corpse," it said, giving the flinch of assent.

She had just begun to turn away when the envoy continued. "Query," it said. "What corpse?"

"What corpse?" she said. "It doesn't matter what corpse. Any corpse. As long as it's freshly dead."

"Query: any corpse?"

"Yes," she said.

"Freshly dead," it said.

"Yes," she said.

"Queries: person pay well?" it said. "Any corpse?"

"Correct," she said.

For several hours they conversed, using that strange gargled speech so distant from her own language that she couldn't even make out the parts of it, couldn't really decide if they were speaking in discrete words or in something else entirely, a kind of warble of sound that couldn't be parsed. She observed them from the shadow of the cave. Then again they fell silent, and one made its way to the cave's mouth.

"Query," it said. "Any corpse?"

"Are you the same one?" she asked. "I already answered that query," she said. "Any corpse, as long as it's freshly dead."

It turned and mumbled something at the others. When they responded, it turned back to her.

"Person, please to proceed out of cave," it said.

"Why?" she said. "Do you know where to find a corpse?"

"Yes," it said. "Any corpse."

She wondered at the locution, then shook her head and slung her grapple over her shoulder. She stepped out into the sun. "Well," she said. "Where is it?"

They crowded around her, jostling her, pressing her tightly. They were awkward, ungainly in their armatures, but by the time she realized what they were doing, it was too late, there were too many of them. She struck a few away with her stick and managed a few steps, but several had already taken their place, and there was nowhere to go. They kept clawing at her, dragging at her, trying to pull her down. She fell quickly to her knees. She tried to turn back to the mouth of the cave. She got her hand on her grapple, but her arms were pressed down now, and she couldn't raise it to strike. She opened her mouth and screamed, and something filled her mouth. A few moments later she was dead.

Soon everything was as it had been, the furnishers standing at a distance with their cloth bags, bowing. One of them, a representative or envoy, approached and spoke to the woman's body.

"Any corpse," it said, and extended what in the armature passed for a hand. "Person pay well."

It stayed there, false hand extended, patiently awaiting its reward, its fellows attentive and eager behind it.

II.

When he awoke, a shower of raw flesh had fallen upon the field. It lay there, glistening in the sun. Where were the furnishers today? he wondered. Usually they were here and eager, scavenging the fields and then trying to sell to him. Sometimes, he had to admit, he bought, but only after the flesh was smoked. One smoked meat was like another, he had come to feel, and if you were to eat any flesh, what did it matter what flesh it was? He had even, he had to admit, acquired a taste for it.

In the back of his cave, he blew the embers into flame and heated water, adding the old and sodden leaves to it. They barely changed the water's color now, even when he squeezed them. No, he would have to go back soon. There was little for him here.

Some of the ports of the tablature were starting to rust, and these he rubbed with sand until they shined. He polished the surface, rubbing it with the chamois, then nicked his arm slightly, just below the elbow, and let a few drops of blood fall on the surface. These he rubbed over the surface with the chamois, until they were spread so thin as to be invisible.

He went back to the mouth of the cave. Still the furnishers had not come. Flies had begun to gather on the hunks of flesh.

He slipped into his boots and began to walk the field, careful where he stepped. No, only bits and pieces, hardly anything recognizable, nothing large. A finger there, but stripped mostly of skin and the nail and bits of its meat gone. Even with a full finger he might have been able to get the tablature to do something. He searched and prodded, but no, nothing.

Near the edge of the field, he caught sight of a group of furnishers. They were on the edge of the next field, the ditch lying between them and him, and there were more of them than he had ever seen in one place, several dozen at least. One was beckoning to him, or gesticulating in a way he took to be beckoning. He still wasn't altogether sure how to interpret their gestures.

"Person," the creature started saying when it believed it had gotten his attention. "Person, hear and see!"

He walked to the edge of his field, heard the startled gasp of the furnishers as he crossed the field's border. He stood on his side of the ditch, looking over.

"What is it?" he asked.

"Query: person buy?" the furnisher asked, the horde behind him rumbling some muted variation of his words, like an echo.

"What do you have?" he asked. "Flesh?"

"Flesh," said the furnisher. "Flexible organs still capable of speech. Whole flesh."

"Whole flesh," he said. "What do you mean? A body?"

The furnisher flinched. "Query: person buy?" it said again. "Query: person pay well?"

"There is no occupant of this field?" he asked.

"No occupant of field," the furnisher confirmed.

He slid down the bank of the ditch and up the other side and into the other field.

The body was fresh, as fresh as any he'd ever seen. It was a woman's body. It did not look as if it had fallen; the limbs were intact, the bones seemingly unbroken, the lips blue, cuts and a few deeper wounds running up and down the arms and torso. He could not tell what had caused them.

"Where did you find this?" he asked.

"Field," the furnisher said. "A good find. Query: you pay well? Let it be written and beads exchanged."

He nodded and asked how much. When the envoy told him, he reached into his purse and fished out a handful of beads, which he piled in a heap beside the body.

The furnisher refused to take them. It was, he remembered too late, the haggling that they enjoyed as much as the beads themselves. And so he put most of the beads away and started dickering.

It was hard not to be impatient. Every moment they delayed, the body lost tractability. The skin was already lying differently on the bones. But he bargained back and forth with the envoy until, at last, the furnishers had a neat stack of beads and were satisfied.

He left them gathered together staring at the pile of beads. He passed the hook beneath the jaw of the corpse and up through the bottom of the mouth until he could see the tip of it glinting between the teeth. Fastening his cord to the hook's eye, he flung it over his shoulder. He dragged the body through the scattered flesh and along over the dips and swells and grasses and rocks and stones, then down into the ditch and back up again and back to his own field and to his cave.

There, he slung the dead body onto the tablature and worried it. He suppled its wounds and infused a clear fluid into its veins. He washed the dirt from the body and cleared its skin of clotted gore. The lungs he inflated with a small bellows inserted down the windpipe, watching the chest rise.

He struck the chest twice, muttering. The jets of the tablature began to hiss lightly. He carefully opened the body cavity and reached in, slitting the integument surrounding the organs, and grasped the heart, slowly massaging it. He rearmed the tablature, then withdrew his hand and sprayed foam into the incision.

He waited. At length the congealed blood became liquid and warm. It oozed out of the wounds, slowly becoming paler, finally stopping. The fibers were called to action beneath the gelid breast, and the nerves mimicked the instinct of life. The eyes shuttered open, like the eyes of a doll. They roiled independently in their sockets, only slowly coming to focus on him. The eyeballs were already losing their turgidity, he saw, beginning slowly to deflate.

"Awake," he said. "Ye who lie dead."

The corpse tried to speak, sputtered, coughed out a plug of black bile. Bloody flux welled from the hole beneath her chin. She swallowed, tried again.

"Dead?" her broken voice said with a kind of wonder, as if she didn't believe.

"Where are your treasures?" asked the man. "What are the mysteries of this place? Show me." He tugged on the hook run through the jaw.

"Who are you?" asked the corpse. "And what are you to me?"

"You must tell," said the man. "I control thee."

But the corpse was trying to rise, was grasping at his hands and arms. "Here," the corpse was saying. "I have been waiting for you. I have spent many days hungry and waiting, and now you are here. You have fallen from the sky. Lay yourself upon my tablature, and soon we will both have what we want." But her movements were muddy and sluggish, and it was easy for the man to shake her off.

This corpse has gone mad, he thought. Another part of him thought, *This corpse thinks she is me and knows my thoughts.*

"The mysteries," the man said again. "You shall tell me of them and then I shall be your voice to the living, to tell the living of what you were when you were alive."

The corpse stopped, hesitated. Slowly the mouth split wide, and she began to make a choking noise the man took some time to realize was laughter. "Ah, very good," she said in between gasps. "They had me good and proper. Very good indeed."

He applied pressure to one temple with the chisel, breaking just through the bone, and the corpse stopped laughing.

"Speak!" he commanded again.

For a long time she was silent. Just when he had decided she had become a simple corpse again, she spoke. "I shall tell you a story," she said.

"A story?" he said.

"A story," she said. "About a man and a woman, in which one could be the other and the other could be the one, and each to each, and both puppets of a handful of beads."

"What do you mean?" he asked, raising his eyebrows with surprise. "I do not understand this story. Is your only treasure beads? I warn you, do not try to deceive me."

"I do not deceive you," she said. "You deceive yourself."

"Speak clearly," he said. "No parables, no stories, no riddles, just plain speaking from beginning to end."

She raised her head slightly and moved her lips, and he, thinking she was whispering something, leaned closer. But when he did, she spat full in his face with a force and vehemence he had never known the dead to possess. He stumbled back, wiping the spittle away. She tried to stand again and this time sat up and slid jerkily off the tablature. She took a step toward him and suddenly stopped, then spoke, swaying.

"There, in the distant city, there came . . ." she said, and trailed off.

And then she collapsed in a heap. Despite his best efforts, she could not be revived again.

III.

He made a fire and roasted her, the black smoke pouring out of the mouth of the cave. She would last him many months, he thought. As her skin split from the heat and her flesh bubbled, he jotted notes to himself about what she had said, what he had said and done. He had, he told himself, made progress, even if he had little, if anything, to show for it. Next time would be different.

When he judged her cooked, he rolled her body out of the fire with his boots, left her steaming and smoking on the stone beside, the fat rendered from her flesh darkening the cave floor. Furnishers, he saw, had gathered around the mouth of the cave, eager and attentive but unwilling to disturb him.

"Person: good flesh," one of them called.

"Yes," he said. "Very good flesh."

Later he would cut and joint her. Some could be eaten immediately, the rest he should carefully preserve. No doubt parts would have to be cooked longer, smoked. It was just meat, he told himself, meat like any other. Though that was not, he knew inside, why he chose to partake of it.

"This was a good one," he said again, turning to the mouth of the cave. "Can you bring me another as good?"

"Query: as good?"

"As whole," he said. "As complete."

The furnisher envoy shivered. What did that mean? Was it the same furnisher he had spoken to in the fields, or did they take turns serving as envoy? He couldn't tell one from another.

"Query: any?" it said.

"What?" he asked, confused.

"Query: any corpse?" it asked.

"Any corpse?" he said. "I suppose so, as long as it's a whole corpse. As long as it's a good one."

"Any corpse," it said.

"Yes, any."

It turned to consult with the others. They conversed for a long while in their odd language. They kept gesticulating, arguing among themselves, or so it seemed to him. Finally the envoy turned back.

"Please to proceed out of cave," the envoy said.

"Why?" he said. "You know where to find a corpse?"

"Yes," it said. "Any corpse."

"As good as this?" he said, gesturing to the charred meat beside him.

"Any corpse," it said, and flinched. It raised its armature in a way that revealed a series of barbs on the dark body enclosed within. "Person, please out of cave."

The Moans

At first everyone told him the back porch was haunted and invited him to throw his rucksack in one of the other rooms, share an already shared bed or curl up on the floor. But when he pressed them, they said, well, no, not haunted exactly, not haunted all the time, anyway. You only felt it was haunted when you were flying.

"Flying?" he asked, thinking his English must not be as good as he'd thought.

"Tripping," said the woman whose name was Hannah but who called herself Little God. "Stoned."

Ah, yes, he had learned those slang terms, he understood. Flying was the same? But in that case he would be okay, he would not be haunted, for he was here to observe the community, to be in it for a time but not part of it, and he was a teetotaler.

"A what?" whispered Little God, smoke curling out of the corners of her mouth. Was it the wrong word? "Whatever, man," she said, "it's all good."

It *was* all good, for now he had a room to himself. Or something like a room, since the way they had nailed up the scrap lumber to close off the porch still allowed the wind to whistle in. He bought a lamp from the thrift store down the street and ran in an extension cord; there was half a mattress in the porch room, and if he put his rucksack at the bottom just right, he could sleep comfortably enough. There was a stack of broken chairs that Summer or Fawnstar—could that possibly be her name, anyone's name, a name someone had actually chosen?—claimed to be planning to repair but never looked at. Other than that, there was just him.

During the day he moved through the collective and observed. At first he made notes on what everyone was doing, but then the man called Big Dig told him no, it wasn't cool, observation could mess with their rhythm, that you start writing things down and they change, recording something changes it, so he stopped taking notes. He just watched and then later, on the porch, he would write down what he could remember, whatever he thought might be important.

And Big Dig was right. Before, everybody had been playing to him and his notepad. Now that he wasn't taking notes, after a while everybody just kind of ignored him; they bumped and jostled around him, passed the pipe right past him, reached around him for a glass or a plate. It was as if he wasn't there, as if he was a ghost. Which was funny in a way, considering he was living in the haunted room. *In the community but not part of the community,* he thought. He liked it. It was like being alive and dead at the same time, or being alive but being the only one who knew you were.

He got so used to them not noticing that it was a surprise when, suddenly, one did. It was Little God, sitting cross-legged on the floor. She was stoned, even more so than usual; her dull eyes swept past him and then swept back, made an effort to focus as if seeing him for the first time, as if he was difficult to see. "You're still here?" she said. "I thought you'd left."

Yes, he claimed, he was.

"Still writing about us?" she asked.

Yes, he admitted, though in a way he wasn't anymore, had stopped recording much of anything in his notebook. He was still there, but wasn't sure what exactly he was doing now.

Little God nodded. She turned and stretched backwards, grabbed a sheet of pink paper covered with a series of blurred, blotted red images from behind her. She tore a square of the sheet off and handed it to him, but even looking at one of the images up close he wasn't sure what it was. It was a face, maybe. Maybe human, maybe not.

"Thank you, no," he said and pushed the square back toward her.

But Little God just shook her head. And when he kept his hand held out, she lazily reached out with both her own. With one, she took the square; with the other, she reached out as if in slow motion and touched his lips, parting them with her fingertips. He let her do it and let her, a moment later, place the paper on his tongue. It tasted slightly bitter, but only slightly. She kept her finger there, just inside his mouth. "Just hold it there," she said, "don't swallow it." And when he nodded, she slowly withdrew the finger.

Maybe it was a defective tab, because nothing was happening. "Just wait," Little God said. "It'll come." But it didn't come. How much time went by? It felt like a lot of time, hours perhaps, but the hands on the clock hadn't seemed to move much. What time had it been when she gave him the tab? He couldn't remember. But every time he looked at the clock, the hands seemed to be in the same place.

"Where are you going?" Little God asked.

What? He hadn't been aware he was going anywhere, but yes, it looked as if he was on his feet. He was so concerned about what would happen once the drug started working that he wasn't paying attention, really. He was anxious. He needed to stop being anxious since the drug wasn't working, it was a defective batch, or his tab hadn't gotten painted properly, if that was how they got the acid on it—how was he supposed to know how they got the acid on it? He wasn't an expert, he never claimed to be.

A voice was calling from behind him, and it took him a moment to realize it was Little God. *Where are you going?* she was calling out, or rather had called out—it was hard to know if it was happening or already had happened. And there was his own voice, coming from a place where he knew his body not to be. Who had gotten hold of his voice? *To my room,* the voice said from behind him, and yes, that made sense, because his body already was there, already in the porch room, waiting for the voice to catch up.

Once there, once around his familiar things, everything seemed fine again, normal. Yes, that was all he needed, some time to himself. He'd just imagined everything, nothing was really happening, he was just fine. He picked up a book, began to flip through it.

For a moment the letters had a startling crispness and clarity, then they began to pulse slightly. *When I have killed,* he read, *I make a pile of stones, a cairn, and I set in my memory who it was, what it was died there and how. My mind is shaped like a map of these cairns.*

Excuse me? he thought. What book was this? He tried to turn it over to look at the title, but no matter how he turned the book he couldn't see the cover. And when he turned the page of the book, it was still the same page and the same words, and somehow he knew they were words of a book that hadn't been written yet, that what he was reading wasn't a book, or not yet a book, but that he'd plucked something out of a web of a future time without getting entangled himself, like a ghost might.

And when he thought that word, *ghost,* he remembered that this was the room that was haunted. *My mind,* he thought, *is shaped like a map of these cairns.*

What cairns? The room flickered around him. He found he couldn't move his arms—and then, unexpectedly, he knew now he could, but he had to move them carefully if he was to keep them from breaking off. He moved them so slowly it was as if they weren't moving at all. There were shapes all around him, and he moved his arms through them so slowly that he did not disperse them; they were all his own shape, all the places his body had been in the room, a strange, fleeting rustling in the air, time overlapped and smearing together. There were other shadows too, and perhaps these were the ghosts the others had meant. But he was more frightened by being surrounded by a dozen versions of himself, some paralyzed, some moving so fast they could barely be perceived.

And there was a sound too, a moaning that part of his mind knew he always had heard, a moaning he had thought to be caused by wind through the gaps in the walls, but now he wasn't so sure. When he brought his ear close to the outer walls, the moans weren't any louder and maybe softer. There was wind whistling through the gaps, but this moaning, moans, and not just any moans, his mind told him, but *the* moans. Part of him was terrified to realize this, but another part was more terrified because it wasn't sure what exactly it was that had been realized.

He fell back on the half mattress. Around him the room throbbed, and his own shapes circled him, and the moans grew. He felt it all swirl around him, the room growing darker and darker until it seemed there was no room but only blackness and the moans.

Then for one brief moment there was Little God over him, slapping him, and Big Dig there beside saying, "What else was in it, do you think?" and the improbable Fawnstar—Fawnstar?— rubbing his temples. He turned his head weakly to one side and retched, but nothing came out, then he drily retched again and blacked out.

He awoke in the hospital, his rucksack stuffed into the space beneath the end table. Eventually the nurse came and nodded and smiled and spoke to him like this wasn't the first time they'd had a conversation. He apparently had been speaking to people, speaking for hours, or his voice had; he had—so the doctor told him—been only technically dead rather than actually dead. An important difference, the doctor claimed, especially for him. What was it that he had ingested exactly? How had he gotten to the hospital? Had he walked? Had someone dropped him off?

After a few days he felt all right. Eventually they let him leave, though he had nobody to pick him up. His rucksack had all of his possessions except for his notebook, and when he went back to the house to get it, he found the place abandoned. The porch was as it had been—boarded over to form a room, same stack of broken chairs, same half mattress—but his notebook wasn't there. The rest of the house was an empty shell mostly taken by fire, apparently a long time before, though he didn't understand how this could be.

For years he forgot about it. He wandered through the rest of his life, dabbled a little in this, a little in that; for a time he was a step away from the street. He learned to hide his accent, then learned when it was advantageous to bring it out, even exaggerate it. He published a number of articles, then a book, then another.

Then, suddenly, it became clear that he knew just enough about any number of things for someone to decide he might be useful. He was hired to wear a suit and tie and sit in a room for eight hours a day with five other people, considering ethical and political problems, some practical, some abstract. A question would be posed, and they would think it through aloud until their voices were hoarse. They talked and argued, and a microphone with a green light in the center of the table recorded the discussion, and, presumably, someone transcribed it, and it was shared with the people who had paid to have the question discussed. It was a strange profession, and sometimes he wondered if he wasn't in some very special sort of hell.

And then one day, in the middle of considering the best way to warn people thousands of years from now—when perhaps language no longer even exists—that an area is dangerous, that the ground and air and water are shot through with deadly but invisible poison, he flashed. He remember the trip, the ghosts in the room, and the moans; and all of it, despite the time passed, was so vivid, so real, that for an instant he was sure he was still in the porch room, flying. *My mind is shaped like a map of these cairns,* he thought. The moans were terrible, and he could feel his vision tunneling down to darkness, and knew he would soon black out.

Until a hand touched his shoulder. "All right?" the woman next to him asked, a behavioral psychologist who often acted as if she were in charge, though whether she actually was, nobody seemed to know. The woman was looking at him with what he suspected was supposed to be *relaxed calm*, though it was slightly too studied to come across that way. His vision still throbbed slightly. *She looks like Little God*, a part of him thought, though he knew that part of him was wrong; Little God and this woman were not remotely alike.

Aloud, he didn't express any of this. Aloud, he said, "Fine." Then he began to speak not to the woman beside him or to the rest of the group, but to the microphone with the green light on it. *Recording something changes it*, he thought, and imagined aloud black basalt monuments, leaning columns that would be perceived as threatening to collapse, electrical barriers somehow powered by lightning and by machinery capable of staying functional for thousands or tens of thousands of years, the slow release of noxious gasses and smells, and, above all, stone carved and sculpted just right so that the instant it was touched by the slightest wind, it would begin to moan.

And then he opened his mouth and let the moans, lodged inside him all these years, come out.

The Window

He was all but asleep. Or he was asleep and then the sound woke him. Or he was dreaming and never awoke at all. All three possibilities occurred to him later, when he was telling the story to a friend after realizing he had nothing to show for what he'd experienced, or thought he'd experienced—no proof, nothing but a dull and slowly fading sense of fear. Without proof, he began to doubt himself. For surely what he thought had happened couldn't have actually happened, could it? Wasn't it better to think he was dreaming or crazy than to think that things like that could happen?

He had been in the bedroom, down the hall at the far end of his apartment, when he had heard a noise. The lights were off, but they had been off for just a few moments, so he didn't think he was asleep yet. Even if he was, he was pretty sure he had woken up immediately. If not, how was he to explain the fact that he was later standing there, in the living room, staring.

Sleepwalking? the friend he was trying to explain it to speculated.

But no, he wasn't a sleepwalker, he'd never been one, no history of it in his family either. His friend had been watching too much TV. He hadn't dreamed it. Even if part of him hoped he had.

He had been in the bedroom when he had heard the noise. The air conditioner wasn't on even though it was a hot evening, the sort of evening when he usually would have turned it on—if it had been on, even on low, he wouldn't have heard the noise. He remembered it being hot but couldn't remember feeling any discomfort—which was surprising, he had to admit, but there it was. He had to tell it as he remembered it if he was to have any hope of making sense of it. He had to trust his impulses—if he didn't trust them, what, if anything, was left for him to rely on?

Just tell the story—this from his friend. The friend did not understand that this was all part of it for him, that sorting through the tangled impressions was something he had to do to know how much to trust what he was telling, how much to believe what he'd experienced. But yes, all right, he would try to tell it the way the friend wanted to hear it: clean. He would do his best.

He had been in the bedroom when he heard a noise. At first he thought it was from outside, a bird banging against the living room window—that was the first thing that had come to his mind, a bird striking the window hard, once, twice, a third time. But then it had kept up, and the sound had changed too. For a moment he lay in bed, drowsy, just listening, a little curious but also half asleep, not really taking it in. For a moment his mind went from thinking about a bird on the outside of the window to a bird on the inside of the window. And then his mind focused and he realized that no, it wasn't a bird: there was someone in the house.

Nothing like this had ever happened to him before. He wasn't sure what to do. Even as it was happening he couldn't quite believe it. He got up, left the bed, and made for the bedroom door, but once there he hesitated just shy of the sill, waited. He didn't know how exactly he was supposed to act, what he was supposed to do. Should he call the police? No, his phone was in the living room, where the noise was coming from. Should he stay in the bedroom until they were gone? No, there were too many things that he couldn't afford to have them (whoever *they* were) steal. He had no gun, no weapon of any kind, and the kitchen, where he kept his knives, was in the other direction.

In the end, he simply grabbed a book from the nightstand, the largest and heaviest in the stack, and moved as quickly and silently as he could toward the living room.

At first, with the room mostly in darkness except for the slight light shining through the windows, he didn't see anything. The room was a strange crisscross of lighter and darker shadow, some parts of it visible, others not visible at all. The end window was up, propped halfway open. There was a smell to the room, bitter and pungent, that he wanted to take as the smell of the outside air. But no, it was more than that.

At first the room seemed empty. He stood in the doorway hesitating, wondering if he'd just been imagining the noise. But then he saw something move. One of the shadows in the far corner flowed out, and he saw a dim, vague shape. It was more or less the size of a man, though crouched and almost toppling forward in a posture he felt would be difficult for a man to maintain. But maybe what he was seeing was partly shadow rather than body. It moved slowly, seemingly unaware of him. It traveled slowly along beside the wall. It knocked against the objects near the wall, rattling them—this, he realized, must have been the sound he had heard—but it seemed to be unaware of this too, and did little to alter its course. Instead it simply pushed forward the objects rattling in its path.

He tried to speak, but his throat was dry, and all that came out was a kind of inarticulate barking sound. Somehow the intruder didn't seem to hear this. It continued to move forward, around the edge of the room, at exactly the same pace it had been moving before.

I should be afraid, he thought, then suddenly he realized he *was* afraid—that was the strangest thing. He felt as if the fear was happening to another person, *like I was at a distance from my body, observing it.*

Maybe it was a dream, his friend said.

No, he said. Yes, of course he had considered this, but no, he didn't think it was a dream—though he would prefer it if it had been. But that wasn't all, he said to the friend, that wasn't the worst yet, he said, just be quiet and listen, that's only the beginning.

He spoke aloud, but the figure didn't notice, and he felt a strange sort of distanced fear—as if the fear was all around him, but he was swaddled from it somehow, insulated. He had, of course, already been afraid. The moment he thought someone else might be in the house he had been afraid. But this, this wasn't the same sort of fear. This fear was of another order entirely.

Then the figure passed before a window—not the open window, he explained to his friend, but a closed one—and the fear rushed closer. For when the figure crossed into the light, he realized he could see through it. It was the shape and size of a human but indistinct, its edges blurred somehow, as if it were not existing here precisely at all, but instead existing somewhere else, in a place that happened, somehow, to overlap with this space. Its edges were blurred, and even within its boundaries its features were shifting and unclear, as if he was watching something in the process of becoming real. Or, another part of him thought, ceasing to be real. But even then, with the figure indistinct, he could tell it was the size and shape of a human but not human at all, and he was terrified of what it might be.

The figure seemed to be shining slightly, vaguely glowing, though a moment ago in the shadows it hadn't been. And this luminescence seemed to be emanating from somewhere within its person, right about where the head, such as it was, met the body, such as it was. This puzzled him for a moment until the figure moved farther, and he abruptly realized that what he was seeing was coming not from the shape at all, but from behind it, that he was seeing through it to the streetlight shining outside. That he could see *through* it.

Almost without knowing what he was doing, he hurled the book at it. The book struck but went right through, not even slowing down, and struck the window behind it, making it shiver before then falling to the floor. The figure stopped abruptly as if it had finally heard something, and turned to face the window, its arms twitching, but it paid no attention to the book itself. When it continued, it was moving more quickly, heading toward the other window, the one that was open.

A moment later and it was starting through the opening, squeezing through it before he had thought to move. He rushed toward the window itself and reached it with the figure halfway in and halfway out, eager to close and lock it as soon as the figure was out. But in his rush to shut the window, he managed to close it right on the figure itself.

But just as with the book, the window passed right through the figure. He felt no resistance at all, as if the figure wasn't really there. For a moment the window was open and the figure stretched out across the sash. Then the window was closed and the figure split, bisected by a piece of glass.

Considering the way the book had passed through it, he expected the figure to just keep going, to move slowly out through the glass and away into the night until it became lost among the other shadows. Instead, it hesitated for a moment and then suddenly began to flail its limbs. A moment later it divided into two halves, one on either side of the glass. The one on the outside fell down somewhere into the bushes and was lost. The one on the inside slipped down the sash, spilled onto the floor, and lay still.

When he rushed over and turned on the light, he found the wall and floor where the figure had been were covered with what looked like a swath of blood. That was all that was left of it.

He called the police, reported an intruder. He waited patiently for them to come and while he was waiting stayed staring at the bloody wall and floor. The color of the blood, he noticed, seemed to be fading, the stain diminishing as well. As he waited and watched it faded entirely, leaving only a dampness on the floor. Then that too faded and was gone.

By the time the police arrived, there was nothing to suggest there had ever been anything there at all. Had there been? He had to wonder. Had he perhaps dreamed it all?

If not, what on earth could it have been?

Whether he had dreamed it or not, he admitted to his friend, he hadn't slept that night, nor the next, nor the next, because he kept expecting it to happen again. He was afraid to go to sleep, afraid to turn off the light. He felt that by closing the window on it he had made it aware of him somehow, and now he could feel it somewhere, just out of sight, trying once again to become real, starting to push its way back into the world. He had hurt it, and now it would hurt him. He lay awake, listening to his heart pounding in his chest, waiting for it to come. So far it hadn't. But it would come again, he felt that somehow, feared that, and when it did he knew that this time it would come for him.

Which was the other reason he was telling his friend the story: not only was he trying to figure out what had happened to him, whether it was real or not real—he wanted at least one other person in the world to know what had happened, what he thought had happened, so that at least one person in the world would know later why he had disappeared. Soon it would come for him, though he didn't know how. Soon it would be his blood on the floor and wall. Perhaps it would fade and perhaps it would not, but in either case it wouldn't matter, at least not to him, because by that time he would be dead or gone or both.

Click

I.

He had been given a notebook to write in, and the lawyer had loaned him a brushed-steel mechanical pencil with golden accents that he claimed were real gold. "I am loaning you this," his lawyer told him when he handed it over, "so you will know how important and serious the matter is, and so you will do your best to remember everything you possibly can and write it all down as it actually happened."

The lawyer leaned down close and looked at him without blinking, his eyes steady. *He doesn't blink as much as normal people do,* the man thought. Sometimes he felt as if the lawyer was not even a person at all, as if he was simply pretending to be a person, and not very well.

"Life and death," the lawyer said. "That's how important this is."

All right, he told the lawyer. He would do his best. He would try to remember.

And that is exactly what the man is trying to do. *Anything that you remember,* the lawyer had said. If he felt compelled to write down something but didn't understand why, he shouldn't try to figure out what the thing meant, he should just write it down. They could sort it out later. *I'm your friend,* the lawyer insisted, *I'm on your side.* Other people, the lawyer claimed, might try to insinuate things, to convince him that certain things had happened. It was better to let the real things come back on their own instead of making up things that never happened.

"I don't know why I'm here," the man had admitted.

"All right," the lawyer said. "That's just what this is going to help us figure out," he said, tapping the notebook. "Write. And don't show it to anybody but me."

The doctor has told him that it is common for individuals with head trauma not to remember what happened to cause it, nor even to remember the days surrounding the trauma. But then sometimes something suddenly just clicks and it comes flooding back. Maybe not everything, maybe not even most of it, but some of it, anyway. It would be nice if he could remember at least some of it.

From what he knows about the rest of his life, he doesn't see how he could have done anything wrong. If he did, he's sure it must have been by accident.

He has said this over and over to whoever will listen. They just nod as if they want to believe him, but don't. Sometimes they even seem a little afraid of him. When he said this to the lawyer, the lawyer didn't even bother to nod. He can't tell what the lawyer thinks. "Don't tell me. Just write it all down," the lawyer insisted. "Whatever you can remember."

And what if he really did do something wrong? Does he really want to know?

He thinks so. Even if he did something very wrong indeed, like, say, murder. Even then, he thinks he would rather know than not know. Right now, the man doesn't even know who he is. They tell him who they think he is, they pronounce a name, but it doesn't sound right to him. It is as if they've written a name on his forehead that doesn't belong, and they can see it and he can't. His life was apparently going along like normal, then suddenly there came a black patch. After the black patch everything seemed wrong, as if he was leading someone else's life. As if he was possessed. Or maybe had taken possession of someone else.

The doctor also warned him that sometimes things never click. Sometimes you never know what really happened. He tried to feel something about that, some worry or anxiety, but he was still medicated enough to make it hard to feel things when they were happening. He only starts to feel things later, once it's too late.

II.

When he first woke up, he didn't even know where he was. His eyes had a hard time focusing. His jaw hurt and his throat was sore. He tried to swallow a few times, gagging before he realized there was a tube running down his throat and he couldn't swallow, not really. He remembered—if he is remembering correctly now and not making just a little of it up—that he was staring up into a round, blurred light that slowly went from a bright white to a pale orange red, like a dying filament.

Then he blinked and his vision cleared, more or less. There was a ring of faces all around him, but the bottom halves of these faces were gone—all he could see were their eyes. A whole circle of eyes, intense, intent, all staring at him.

Maybe, someone prompted later, *these were doctors, and their faces were just covered by surgical masks?*

Who suggested that? he wonders now. *And why did they want me to believe it?* In any case, at the time he didn't think of them as doctors. At the time, he thought of them as men who were missing the bottom halves of their faces.

This terrified him.

And then these half-faced men started to make sounds. Which terrified him even more.

He fainted.

. . .

The next time he awoke, it was a little better. There were not so many half-faced men, not so many eyes. No eyes, in fact, none at least that he could see. He was alone.

He was lying on a bed of some kind, but it was not his own bed. There was a curtain on a fixed track around the bed, but it was mostly pulled open. He could see things: white walls and a metal tray and a shiny floor. It was as if there was a whole world around him again. Not just a half world full of half-faced men.

He closed his eyes. Probably he slept. When he opened them again he saw, past the end of the bed, a guard near the door. He seemed to have a whole face. He was sitting in a chair, his arms folded across his chest. Half asleep but still stiff as cardboard.

The man tried to speak, but no words came out, only strange, half-choked sounds. The tube, he only then realized, was still down his throat, his cheeks stiff where they had taped the thing to his face to hold it in place.

The guard was awake now and staring at him and speaking into his shoulder radio.

Everything started to blur.

The last things that happened before the man's eyes rolled back into his head were that the guard's radio crackled, and the bottom half of his face started to fade away, and then, mercifully, the man passed out.

Probably between those times, between when he awoke a first time and when he awoke a second time and then when he awoke a third time, there were dreams.

But if there were dreams, he doesn't remember them now. Not a one. But he's sure that if he could remember them, they would be nightmares.

A little later, someone was touching him softly. Then, very gently, they began shaking him.

"Honey," said a woman's voice. "Honey, wake up."

It was his mother's voice. For a moment he thought he was back in his bed at home, asleep, and she was waking him up for school. That was how she always used to wake him up. A gentle touch at first and then gently shaking him awake. But why wasn't she calling him by his name? And what was his name again?

"Honey," she said again, more insistently, and he opened his eyes.

Only he was not at home. He was in the hospital room, and it was not his mother. It wasn't even a woman. In fact, there was no one there at all.

He lay there, head wrapped in gauze, almost anonymous, afraid.

If he squinted his memory enough, he seemed to remember the chief of police standing beside the bed and reading charges to him. Murder, was it? Several counts? Four, say? He was not sure when that had been exactly, where it fit with everything else that had happened. But he remembered it. He was almost certain he did, anyway. Unless it had been something he had seen on TV.

If you feel compelled to write it, write it. "Murder?" the man had said when the police chief finished. His voice didn't sound like his voice anymore, still hoarse from the tube they had snaked down his throat. "Are you sure you have the right person?"

The chief just nodded grimly, his lips a thin line. The man heard his mother start to cry. His dad awkwardly put his arm around her shoulder, tried to comfort her.

Of course that last part was all in his head, since his parents both had been dead for years now. But he was almost certain the rest of it could have been real.

Murder? he thought. No, it didn't sound right. Even now it still doesn't. But what else does he have to cling to?

Another early memory. A man parted the curtain and came close to the head of the bed, pulling up a chair so close that it was almost as if he was in the bed too.

"Who the hell are you?" the man in the bed asked.

"Language," the other said. "Make a good impression. Every little bit counts. I'm your lawyer," he said. "Your parents hired me."

"My parents are dead," the man said.

The lawyer ignored this. "I will be representing you," he insisted.

"What's this all about?" the man asked. "Is this the way it's usually done?"

"Not usually," the lawyer said. "But you're a special case."

"What's this about murder?"

"A murder? Why don't you tell me?" the lawyer said.

But he couldn't tell the lawyer anything. Which is why he now has the mechanical pencil and the notebook and is trying to write, trying to make things click.

There is a guard. Sometimes he can see the guard and sometimes he can't. He doesn't know if the guard is here to protect him, or to keep him from escaping.

When the guard is here, he sits in a chair just outside the curtain. Sometimes he reads or talks into his shoulder radio or cleans his gun. Mostly he just sits and waits or sleeps. Sometimes, if the curtain is open, the guard glances over at the man.

"What's this about murder?" the man said.

"A murder? Why don't you tell me?" the lawyer said.

But he didn't remember anything about it. Nothing at all. He just looked at his lawyer helplessly.

"All right," said the lawyer after a while, low enough that the guard couldn't hear. "Maybe you don't—"

No, wait a moment, the guard wasn't there when that conversation was going on. That was before the guard was there. He is getting confused again. He and his lawyer were alone. The lawyer must have just said it in a normal voice.

"Maybe you really don't remember," the lawyer said, in a normal voice. "You're accused of killing four people. Who do you think they were?"

He was too stunned to say anything at all.

"How old do you think they were?" the lawyer asked.

"Wait a minute," the man said. "Four people? Me?"

The lawyer didn't answer. "How old do you think they were?" he asked again, as if he were following a script.

"How do I know?" the man said. "Normal age?"

"What's normal age?"

"These are weird questions," the man said. "Why are you asking me them?"

"Do you know how you allegedly killed them?" the lawyer asked. "Gun? Knife? Poison? Bare hands?"

"I don't even know that I *did* kill anyone," the man said.

The lawyer nodded. "That's good. Keep that for when they question you," he said.

"Don't you believe me?"

The lawyer looked at him again with those flat, unblinking eyes, as if he neither disbelieved nor believed. "It doesn't matter," he said.

"Why not?" the man said, confused.

The lawyer gave him a grim smile. "Why do you think?"

And that's exactly the problem, isn't it? He hasn't the faintest idea.

"At least tell me how I did it," he said.

"With a gun," the lawyer said. "You allegedly shot four people and then tried to commit suicide by shooting yourself." He gestured to the side of the man's head, to the bandages there. "You apparently didn't succeed in the latter," he said. "Do you think you were trying hard enough?"

The man took a deep breath. His mouth was dry. *I am finally getting somewhere,* he thought. "Who," he asked, "did I kill?"

"With a knife," the lawyer said. "You allegedly stabbed four people and then tried to slit your own throat." He gestured to the man's neck, which was, the man realized, also wrapped in gauze.

"Wait," he said. "You said it was a gun."

The lawyer smiled. "With your bare hands," he said. "You beat four people to death and then tried to commit suicide by striking your head repeatedly against a cement wall." He gestured again to the side of the man's head.

"Wait," the man said. "I thought you were here to help me. Why are you trying to confuse me?"

"With poison," the lawyer said. "You allegedly poisoned four people, one after another, and then tried to commit suicide by swallowing poison yourself." He gestured to the man's throat again. "It hurts to swallow, doesn't it?"

"Stop it!" the man said, closing his eyes. "Stop!"

When he opened them again, he was alone.

III.

Sometimes the lawyer does help. The lawyer, for instance, warned him that the doctor would be coming to see him. If the man passed an examination, he would be moved. *Where?* the man wondered. "Are you sure you're ready to be moved?" the lawyer asked. But anywhere, the man had to believe, was better than here. "Just remember not to go along with everything they suggest to you," the lawyer said. "Resist. No might haves. No could haves. Stick to what you remember, and if you don't remember just say you don't."

"But I don't remember anything," the man said.

"All the better," the lawyer said. Then he held his hand out for the notebook.

The man almost couldn't give it up. Even when he managed to hold it out to the lawyer, the lawyer had to pry it out of his hands.

The lawyer began to read. Watching him, it seemed to the man that the lawyer could read quicker than anyone the man had ever met—either that or morphine or some other drug the man had been given was accelerating the world around him. Almost as soon as he had begun, the lawyer had reached the end. When he closed the notebook and looked up, the lawyer's face was so distorted and angry that it was hard to think of it as a face.

"No! No!" he cried. "Not 'he'! Call yourself 'I'!"

"Yes," the man said. "I'm sorry."

"What's wrong with you?" the lawyer said.

"I don't know what the rules are," the man said. But something in his head immediately translated it into: *He doesn't know what the rules are.*

The lawyer is going to speak when there comes a noise from the hall. The lawyer shakes his head. He hands the notebook back. He presses his finger to his lips and backs slowly out of the room, leaving the man alone.

I need to think about what really happened. I need to try to remember instead of making up situations in his head. *My* head. I—

No, *I* doesn't sound right. I can't do it: he.

He needs to try to remember instead of making up situations in his head. But it's hard not to, especially when he's alone.

Now is the time, he thinks, when the voices should start, when faces and half faces should start to well up. Now is the time for him to see himself, pale and washed out as if in a dream, and either see what he did or see some false version of the same, offered to him by whatever devil or god has brought him here to suffer.

But nothing's coming. Not a thing.

"Who can say?" he heard the doctor report in the hall. "Head injuries aren't predictable." The man couldn't hear how the person the doctor was saying this to responded.

"I wouldn't recommend it," he heard the doctor say, then "I could stop you, but I won't."

A moment later someone who looked like a policeman came in. He placed a tape recorder on the bedside table and turned it on.

"Shall we begin the examination?" he asked.

"Examination?" the man echoed.

"State your full name," the policeman said.

The man tried to say something, but his mouth wouldn't move.

"Let the record show the subject has no name," the policeman said.

But no, the man insisted, it wasn't that he didn't have a name, only that he was having difficulty locating it.

The officer smiled, ignored him. "Would you like to confess?" he asked.

"Confess what?"

"We have two witnesses who saw you," he said. "A man and a woman."

"Shouldn't my lawyer be present?" the man asked.

"Your lawyer?" the officer asked. "What good would he do?"

"I just thought—"

"You can't seriously believe that both witnesses, credible people in their own right, would have cause to lie, can you?"

"I don't know," he said. "Maybe they just got it wrong."

"We're just talking here," the officer said. "An informal chat. We're all friends here. Aren't we?"

"If you say so," the man said.

"I do say so," the officer said. "They saw it happen. They hid under a table, but you found them anyway. Fortunately for them, you found them after the others."

"I don't remember any of this," he said. "It doesn't sound like me."

The policeman's eyes tightened slightly. "What they say," he said, "was that you made them come out. You looked at your gun and laughed. 'Only one bullet left,' you said. 'How do I choose?' Ring any bells?"

"No," he said. "So it was a gun?"

"Eenie, meenie, miney, mo. Still nothing?"

"No."

"It was the male witness who ended up 'it.' You pointed the gun at him, and he thought he was a goner. Do people of your generation still say that, *goner?*"

"I don't know," said the man.

"How would that feel? To have a gun pointing at you? Can you imagine how that would feel?"

The man didn't say anything.

"As it turns out, you can," the officer said. "Since a moment later, you turned the gun away and pointed it at your own head and pulled the trigger."

The police officer stayed looking at him, watching his expression. The man held his face slack and still, but inside his brain was spinning.

"Officer, I'd like to speak with my lawyer," he said.

"Officer?" the officer said and laughed. "Just who do you think I am?"

"The police," he said.

"The police?" he said, and laughed again. He laughed so hard his lower jaw disappeared, leaving only the upper half of his face. "Ah," he said hollowly, "you're killing me."

Upon which the man fainted.

IV.

The doctor shined a tiny light into his eyes. "How are you feeling?" he asked. "Are you getting plenty of rest?"

"People keep interrupting," the man said. "They keep waking me up."

"Oh?" the doctor said. "People? Who, the orderlies? I'll have a chat with them."

"Everybody," the man said. "The police. My lawyer. Everybody."

"The police? And why would you have a lawyer?"

"Because of what they think I did," he said.

He knew he'd made a mistake when the doctor stopped shining

the light into his eyes and peered at him closely. "And what would you say they think you did?" the doctor asked.

His voice, the man noticed, had changed. Before it had been off-hand, ordinary. Now it was casual, but deliberately casual—as if he was trying not to startle the man away while he crept closer.

For a moment the man didn't say anything. Then he said, "You're a doctor, right?"

The doctor nodded. "Technically, yes," he said.

Technically?

"And I'm in a hospital," he said.

"Yes," the doctor said, frowning a little. "You could call it that."

"And I'm ill."

The doctor smiled. "I don't think there can be any question but that you're ill," he said.

"You still don't remember anything?" his lawyer asked.

"The doctor told me to rest," the man said. "I'm not supposed to talk to anyone. I don't even know how you got in here."

The lawyer waved the statement away. "Tomorrow we take out all the stops," he said. "Deploy everything we can."

"Please leave me alone," said the man. "Please go away."

"Go ahead, keep it up," said the lawyer. "See if it does you any good."

His head was starting to ache. When he reached up to touch the bandages covering it, his fingers came away bloody. He should have paged the doctor, but he wanted to write more down first, even though his fingers were shaking and the blood was dripping onto the paper. He was afraid of dying, but he was more afraid of forgetting.

He had dreams just before the bleeding started. He was dreaming but he was still awake, hunched in the bed. He saw people rushing out of a building, people hurling chairs through windows and throwing themselves out, the sound of an alarm going off. It wasn't right. It was as if he was watching a bad TV set. There were jerky black-and-white images of people running, and he was there among them. In the dream, he was panicked.

Why does his head hurt so badly? Who is doing this to him? Did someone take his place for a few days and then depart again, leaving him to take the blame? Is he mad? Is it the world itself that's starting to come apart at the seams?

He was still sitting there holding his special borrowed pencil, clicking it to make a little more lead appear so he could write, and suddenly it was as if the whole world started to dissolve. There was a humming in his head, and the notebook seemed too far away to be in his lap, miles away now, and had begun to be eaten away by threads of darkness. And then suddenly it all disappeared, just blinked out.

He woke up having fallen partway out of the bed, the notebook lying on the floor. The guard was still in his chair just outside the door, still sleeping. He hadn't woken up. How was it possible he hadn't woken up? The man didn't know how long he had been there on the floor like that. Enough time for the bandages on the left side of his head to become sodden with blood and for blood to form a small puddle on the hospital floor.

He managed to retrieve the notebook. The pencil too, though reaching for them made a lump of darkness clot his vision for a moment. A numbness oozed out into his arm. He managed to slide the notebook under the covers and pulled himself down lower in the bed until he was lying down mostly flat, his head bloodying the pillow. Then he reached out for the call button, but his fingers found the morphine release button first.

So he pressed it. He wasn't thinking all that clearly. His head felt as if it was muffled in cotton. He knew he needed to press the call button, that he was still bleeding, but he could never quite find it. And then he thought, okay, he'd just close his eyes for a minute, he'd just catch his breath.

The last thing he wanted to do was lie in his bed and bleed to death. The last thing he wanted was for blood to slowly puddle around his brain until he died.

He felt as if he was drowning. Or maybe choking. He still had his eyes closed, but he was starting to wake up, groggy but still alive. He opened his eyes and found something covering them. Something was draped over his face. No, pressed hard against it, smothering him. He tried to shout but could only make a muffled noise, hardly even human. He couldn't breathe. Blood pounded slower and slower in his ears. He was barely there, blood in his throat now too. For a while, it was all he could do to breathe. And then he couldn't even do that.

Perhaps hours later, he awoke to see a doctor's face.

"What happened?" the man asked.

"You tried to die," the doctor said.

"Where are the police?" he asked. "Where's the lawyer?"

The doctor looked at him strangely. "The police are where they're supposed to be," he said. "And what lawyer do you mean?"

But this can't be true. He has a lawyer, his lawyer's been coming to visit him.

"No," the doctor explained, "nobody has come to see you since you were admitted."

But, but, but, he said, maybe they came and nobody saw them. Yes, that must have been what happened, yes.

The doctor shook his head. "No," he said. "We have a very serious protocol here. Nobody could get in or out without our knowing."

Once again, he knew then he should have been quiet, that he'd said too much.

"Language," scolded his lawyer, who was suddenly there beside—

Wait, maybe that was from the same conversation or maybe from a different one. Everything mixes with everything else, and he's so groggy he has a hard time keeping things straight. How is he to know where one thing starts and another ends?

The doctor paid the lawyer no attention. Which means he probably wasn't really there. But since I am telling the story, I am going to keep him there. He, I mean. Since he is telling the story, he is going to keep him there. If he's the man's lawyer, well, he should have been there.

The doctor paid the lawyer no attention. Instead, he stared at the man.

"Where are my parents?" the man asked.

The doctor looked at him quizzically, started to thumb through his file. "I thought your parents were dead," he said.

"That's exactly what I've been telling him," the man said, nodding toward the lawyer.

"Don't listen to him," said his lawyer, but the man wasn't sure if the lawyer was speaking to him or to the doctor.

The doctor, in any case, didn't seem to hear him. "Telling who?" he asked.

"Your parents are exhausted," the lawyer said. "I told them I'd stay with you as long as the hospital let me. They'll come when they're feeling better."

"How can they feel better if they're dead?"

But wait, how had he gotten confused? It had not been his lawyer after all, but a nurse, and she wasn't talking about his parents but making him follow her moving finger with his eyes.

"Good," she said. "Good. Good."

The doctor had withdrawn to one side, scribbling on a pad—the doctor at least was still there. The man looked closely at the nurse to make sure she wasn't his lawyer in disguise, but if it was a disguise, it was good enough that he couldn't see through it.

A liquid touched his lips, and it felt as if his tongue was on fire. Then he was half asleep and half awake and watching a long procession of people who looked as if their bodies had been bled dry. He knew he was observing a battalion of the dead, a long line of ghosts. They nodded to him with their missing jaws. They beckoned and opened their arms wide.

The doctor was there beside him, in his shiny white coat. A nurse was with him too, either the same nurse or a different one.

"How are we feeling?" the doctor asked. "Let's take a look at that head."

Which head? the man couldn't help but wonder, and he kept expecting the doctor to pull one out, but then the doctor reached out and touched him. A wave of pain ran through him, and he realized the head in question must be his own.

Finally the doctor stopped prodding it. "Could be worse," he said.

He began to unwind the dressings from around it. They were sopping with blood. The nurse collected them as they came off, in an enameled bedpan. They made a wet sound as she slopped them in.

The doctor stared at the exposed wound for a while, his brow furrowed.

Then they wrapped the head back up again, and the doctor began to write on a clipboard.

"What happened?" the man finally managed to ask.

"Hmmm?" he said. "Problems with blood pooling. And your brain was swelling. We had to cut a hole and put a shunt in, to take the pressure off. You should be all right in a few days." He smiled. "Then we'll install a plate."

"A plate?"

He nodded. "Sure," he said. "Nothing to worry about. We'll graft skin over it. Nobody will even know it's there." He turned to the nurse. "Let's let him rest for a while," he said. Then he gave the man an injection of something.

But I'll know it's there, he thought as he drifted off. *And the doctor will know, and the nurse too. And anybody who reads this notebook. How can that constitute nobody?*

V.

Morning again, a pale light streaming in through the window, motes of dust whirling in the air. A nurse moving about the room, smiling. She changed the bedpan and then, with the help of an orderly, moved him from his bed to a new, clean one. It hurt a little, was a little jarring, but it didn't kill him. He only began to relax as they set the brakes of the new bed and wheeled the old one out.

It was starting to get dark when the sound of voices in the hall woke him. Soft at first, then growing louder. Soon, his lawyer opened the curtain and came in.

The guard was back. Now that the curtain was open, the man could see he had retreated to the doorway and stood in the hall. He leaned awkwardly against the wall, stiff as a board.

"Hello," the lawyer said. "Feeling better?"

"Not really."

"We won't have long," the lawyer said. "Did you look at the file?"

"File?"

"Yes," he said. He lost just a little of his composure. "I told you I was leaving it. I asked if you understood. You said you did."

"I don't remember any of that," he said. "I never saw any file."

The lawyer regarded him silently. "Well," he finally said. "We don't have anything to talk about, then. Not yet. It's tucked under the mattress," he said.

The man made a move to pull it out, but the lawyer shook his head no. Not until after he was gone.

When the guard still hadn't moved, the man snaked his arm out from under the sheet and slipped it over the side. He pushed his fingers under the mattress, poking around for the so-called file.

But nothing was there.

All right, he thought at first. The lawyer had pushed the file in too far. No problem. He scooted over to the very edge of the bed and made sure his arm was sunk in to the elbow and wiggled his fingers around. But he still didn't feel anything.

All right, he thought. Just because the lawyer was seated on that side in his last visit didn't mean he wasn't on the other side the visit before. So the man labored his way to the other edge of the bed and slipped the other hand in.

Still nothing.

He lay there for a while staring at the ceiling in the slanting light of evening.

Someone took it, he thought.

But who?

The police? A guard? His doctor? The orderly? The nurse?

Or maybe his lawyer didn't leave it after all. Maybe he'd forgotten to. Maybe he just wanted the man to think he had.

All those thoughts spun about in his skull, slowly starting to consume him. Until he remembered that they had changed his bed. They had moved him from one bed to the other and wheeled the first bed out. The file must have been under the mattress of the other bed.

He pressed the call button. He would call the nurse and have her find the bed and get the file for him. He needed the file. He needed to see what he had done.

He pressed the button and waited, but nobody came. He pressed it again. Still nobody.

Was the guard there this time? Sure, why not? Let's put him there. Let's say that the man could see the edge of his shoulder just past the edge of the curtain.

"Hello?" the man called to the guard. "Can you help me?"

The guard didn't move. He stayed exactly where he was.

"Hello?" the man called again.

When the guard still didn't answer, the man very carefully moved his feet to the edge of the bed and then let them slip off. He pushed himself up with his arms until he was sitting. It was almost too much—his brain was sloshing like wet sand. He could feel the blood pounding in his skull and imagined the dressings wrapped around it beginning to saturate. He managed to get his legs onto the floor, and a wave of nausea went through him, only slowly ebbing back.

And then suddenly he was standing, walking, feeling as if his feet were impossibly far below him. It was all he could do to stay upright.

He made his way around the curtain and there, just on the other side, he found not a guard at all. What he had thought was a guard was only a crude figure made out of cardboard. The word *Guard* had been written in the middle of the blob that was its head, the letters like the features of a deformed face.

Panicked, he stumbled out of the room and found only a dimly lit hall, dusty and impossibly silent. Only a few of the ceiling lights still functioned well. Others glowed a dull red and still others had gone completely out. Stacked against one wall were more cardboard figures. Some seemed well used, others almost untouched. *Nurse* said one. *Chief of Police* said another. *Lawyer* said a third. *Orderly. First Reporter,* and on its reverse side, *Second Reporter.* Almost everyone he had met and a few he hadn't, not yet.

Near the back of the stack, one said *Mother* and another *Father.* But both of these figures had had their heads torn mostly free.

Behind these were four more figures, each of them with a quarter-sized hole burned in their cardboard heads.

He looked for a door out, but there was nothing but hall, seemingly going on forever. He started down it and before he knew it was back at the stack of cardboard figures without any sense of how he had gotten there. *Lawyer* was on the top now, though he hadn't moved it. This, he thought, must mean something. And where was *Doctor?* he wondered.

Overwhelmed, he tried to return to his room but found only a piece of cardboard pasted to the hall wall where his room had been.

He pushed at it, but it was just a piece of cardboard with a word on it, the word *Door*. Other than that, it was nothing at all.

"Hello?" he heard a voice say, and when he turned he saw the doctor—flesh and blood it seemed, not cardboard. How had the doctor gotten here, and why hadn't he seen him before? The man felt the doctor touch him on the arm, but the touch felt wrong somehow.

"What are you doing out of your room?" the doctor asked. "How did you get out?"

He tried to respond, but when he did nothing came out. He tried to gesture with his hands to show the doctor that something was wrong, but they were flat and stiff and wouldn't move.

"Come on, then," said the doctor. "Come with me."

When he hesitated, the doctor reached out and effortlessly gathered him under one arm. He carried him toward the word *Door* and somehow—the man couldn't see how—opened it up and brought him back into his hospital room.

The doctor set him upright. For a moment the man saw his reflection in a brown square labeled *Mirror* and realized that he too was a crude figure in cardboard, a name scrawled on his insubstantial chest, the word scratched out and half effaced, illegible.

"There now," the doctor said. "Isn't that better?"

But he couldn't say if it was or wasn't, because he didn't understand what was happening. He couldn't move.

He listened to the doctor chatter on a bit, and then the doctor checked his watch and said, "Let's let you get some rest."

He allowed himself to be placed flat on the piece of cardboard labeled *Bed* because he could think of no way to prevent it. The doctor went out, and when he did the world around the man became even more impoverished.

He lay there, hoping the world still had some tricks left up its sleeve, and that some, at least, would fall his way.

After a time, an hour, a day, a month, perhaps longer, he could move again. He was holding a notebook in his hands. Someone was holding out a pen to him, telling him to write.

This is the extent of his report. He has done as you asked and kept a record of everything he can remember. He has kept it to himself and shown it to nobody but you.

Now, we need you to tell us what we should make of it.

The Blood Drip

1.

They had stumbled upon a town and tried to approach it, but had been driven off with stones. Or Karsten had. Nils had stayed there, at the base of the wall, pleading, and had been struck, and then struck again. When Karsten had shouted to him to come away, Nils had turned and been struck yet again, in the head this time, and had fallen.

There was blood leaking out of his head when he fell, and in the brief flash he caught of Nils on the way down, Karsten thought he had seen bone. But as he hurried away he began to doubt. Were blood and bone really what he'd seen? Or had he convinced himself that he had seen them because he wanted to believe Nils was dead and thus no longer his responsibility? Shaking his head in frustration, Karsten turned around and went back.

He stopped shy of throwing range. Nils lay near the wall, in a heap. Perhaps he was dead, perhaps he was merely unconscious.

He cupped his hands around his mouth and shouted his friend's name. When they heard him, the men on the walls threw a few stones. None came close to hitting him. At the base of the wall, Nils didn't move.

"Nils!" he called out again.

Maybe Nils was unconscious, or maybe he was simply dead. Or maybe he was injured in a way that kept him from moving—a broken neck, say, an injured spine.

But in any case, Karsten could not retrieve him.

"Nils!" he cried. "Can you hear me?"

There was no answer. What was Karsten to do? He would have to leave Nils. There was no choice but to leave.

He started away, but he could not bring himself to go very far. Nils had stood by him, a part of him argued within his skull, and he should stand by Nils.

There were other parts of him that argued differently. But, after a while, that first part won.

He pretended to leave. If Nils was injured but conscious, Karsten hoped he would not see this and think he was actually leaving. But if Nils did think this, there was nothing to be done about it.

He entered the woods and threaded his way through the trees, coming out farther along, near one corner of the wall.

They do not suspect me, he told himself. *They think I have seen my friend struck dead by a stone and so I have fled. But they do not reckon with this: how do I know what I have seen?*

Probably, yes, Nils was dead, but this was not certain. Perhaps he was dead. But *perhaps dead* is not the same thing as *dead,* he thought. Perhaps he was not dead and could be dragged to safety.

Safety? wondered Karsten. *What did that even mean?* They had gone looking for a town because in the forest they were famished and not safe, likely to soon be dead. If a town would not take them, what then?

He stayed crouched in the undergrowth on the edge of the forest. He waited, watching the sun slip along the sky.

I will wait until the right moment, he told himself, *and then I will drag Nils to safety.*

Safety? he wondered again.

How will I know the right moment? he wondered.

The right moment came and he missed it. Or it didn't come at all. How was one to know the right moment? The sun touched the lip of the wall and made everything swollen and red as blood, then it slipped behind the wall and was gone. Then the light was dwindling and the air was still, and he wondered: *Now?* But shouldn't he wait for dark?

He shifted in the bushes and blinked, and abruptly, or perhaps not so abruptly, it was dark, the night bereft of moon. It was almost too dark to see.

He groped his way out of the bushes and forward, stumbling on the uneven ground. He had matches, but too few of them to waste, and the guards were perhaps still on the wall and would see the flame. No, he couldn't use them.

Nils was already dead, he reasoned. *I should simply abandon him. There is no point to this.*

He moved forward.

When he reached the place where he thought Nils was, Nils was not there. He felt around, sweeping his hands just above the ground. He felt the tickle of grass against his palms but couldn't find a body. He paced forward and back and after a while was unsure where the forest was, where the wall was. There was ground and grass, and, sometimes, stones, but that was all.

He kept searching, crouched, his hands held outstretched before him, feeling about.

After a while he stood and walked forward, looking for a new spot to search. Almost immediately, he stumbled over something and fell. He grunted, clattered heavily down.

He heard a voice cry out, saw above him a light. Beneath his touch something other than dirt or grass: the feel of a coarse-woven cloth, maybe. He pushed his hands down, trying to right himself. More shouts. A light fell upon him. And then he was up and running.

Something struck him in the back, hard. He kept running, his back throbbing, was hit again and again. And then something struck the base of his skull, and his vision bloomed into a strangely vivid darkness.

2.

When he awoke, it was light outside. The bones in his hands ached from cold. The rest of his body too was chilled through.

He turned his head slightly, found he was closer to the wall than he'd imagined. Nobody was atop it, as far as he could see. He turned his head the other way, heard a scratching within his skull as the base of it dragged along the ground.

He sat up, looked around. Only bare ground, the grass and dirt crusted with frost and rime. Nils was nowhere to be seen, but the ground was soaked with blood where he must have been lying. Karsten touched the back of his head and winced, brought away a hand filthy with blood and mud.

A moment later he was up and weaving, staggering away toward the forest. He kept expecting there to be a shout, a halloo, and then for stones to start whirring over the wall again, but the only sound he heard was that of his feet through the grass and his own ragged breathing.

Another town, he told himself as he pushed his way through the brush and into the trees. *There are other towns. Other places besides this one. Surely one of them will have me.*

At first he knew where he was going, or thought he did. But as the trees closed around him, he lost his sense of direction. The sun was out: he could follow it, try to derive a compass from its course. But most of the time he could hardly see it through the canopy of red and yellow leaves overhead. Leaves were thick on the ground too. It was hard for him to understand how they could be so thick on the ground and yet still thick on the branches too. It was as if another set of trees had dropped their leaves and then melted away to make way for these trees with their new set of leaves.

He shook his head to clear it. It did not clear. He reached back and touched the back of his skull, and again his hand came away dirty, mostly with blood this time, very little mud.

What's wrong with me? he wondered.

What had they done with Nils's body? he wondered. Had they dragged it inside the walls? He hadn't seen any signs of dragging, but maybe it had been carried or conveyed by some other means, a means that left no mark, or perhaps he simply hadn't looked hard enough. And if they'd taken Nils, why had they left Karsten where he was?

Perhaps Nils had managed to get up and stumble off to die somewhere in the forest. But hadn't there been too much blood on the ground for that?

He was still cold, but the bones in his hands no longer throbbed. He did his best, by what little glimpses he had of the sun, to move east, until the ground began to slope upward and he veered off course. North maybe—it seemed plausible it could be north.

He heard the sound of a stream, or thought he did, and his tongue suddenly felt thick and dry in his throat. But when he tried to look for the stream he could not locate it, and the sound never seemed much closer.

He kept walking. He gathered some pinecones from the ground and crushed them between his boot and a flat stone, hoping to get something out of them, but there wasn't anything inside that struck him as edible. Perhaps he didn't know what to look for, or perhaps they were the wrong sort of pinecone, or perhaps he was simply too confused and tired to make any real sense of the world at all.

By the time it began to grow dark, he was very hungry, thirsty too, but above all cold. He stopped in a small clearing, kicking the dried pine needles and dead leaves into a pile. He gathered sticks, tenting them atop the pile, then a number of larger branches, which he stacked to one side.

He fumbled in a pocket, felt out three slim matchsticks with his numb fingers. Carefully, he extracted one and struck it alight, brought it cupped in his hand over to the leaves and needles.

He watched the flame spread from the match along a leaf, reducing it to a delicate, spidery armature that quickly collapsed. The needles tensed in the flame and flindered away to nothing. He blew softly and steadily and watched sparks careen, the fire grow and crackle, and saw now a scattering of red mites pursuing a line up one of the branches, away from the heat. Before he could decide if they were actual insects or just sparks, the branch caught fire and they were gone.

He fed the fire until it was roaring, then settled down beside it, watching the flames dance. Eventually, exhausted, he fell asleep.

He awoke screaming. The fire had spread somehow from the pile he had made and into his hair. He batted it out with his hands, his head ringing, then was up and stomping out the runnels of flame trying to work their way out of the clearing and into the trees.

When he was done, his hands were blistered, his hair all or mostly gone, and the soles of his boots melted enough to grow sticky, but the fire was again safely contained. He cleared the ground around it again with his boot. For a while he remained upright, breathing heavily, unsure what else he should do, but slowly he settled again, crouching at first, then sitting, then finally lying down on the still-warm ground.

For a long time he just stared into the flames. It was like watching water, he thought, except it was not water. He felt as if he was being hypnotized. How had the flames spread? Had he not been careful enough when he arranged the fire last time?

I should get up and check, he thought. *Walk around the fire and make sure I didn't miss anything.* He did not move. *I'll get up*, he thought again. A moment later he was asleep.

...

In his dream, he was in another time and was another person, though somehow at the same time it was still him, and still here. He and a man whose face he could never quite see were traveling by horse along a ridge trail through a bitter wind. The other man had been shot in the thigh. In the dream, Karsten wondered idly if he'd been the one to shoot him. He asked the man, who was always traveling just a little ahead of him, if this were the case, but the man didn't answer. He just kept following the trail, hunched over the saddle horn, with Karsten behind, watching the man's back, babbling, not sure if he was talking to the man or to himself. The man's trouser leg had become soaked through with blood, and Karsten could see the blood now welling up through the fabric and leaking down the horse's side, as if it were the horse rather than the man who had been injured.

"Hey," said Karsten. His own voice was unfamiliar to him. "Hey. You got to bandage that. You don't and you're gonna die."

But to this too the man said nothing. He just kept riding, an impossible amount of blood seeping from his leg and down the side of the horse, the blood painting a shape on the horse's ribs, a vaguely human figure, like a man in a robe or an angel. Though no, Karsten was seeing things—it was just blood, he told himself, just the slow, regular brushing of a blood-sopped leg against a horse's side. It didn't mean anything.

And yet he kept staring at it, at the man on the horse, at the blood smeared thick on the horse's side, the blood now reaching the bottom of the horse's belly and beginning to drip off. Karsten hardly saw the path anymore. All he was watching now was that slow drip, drip, drip of blood off the horse and the drizzle of it into the dirt of the trail, the blood drip that his own horse now followed as if it were the real path.

Even when the dream was over, the dripping didn't stop. When he opened his eyes, there was a little dark puddle before him, something still drip, drip, dripping into it from somewhere up above.

He turned his head away from the puddle and slowly looked up. Above him, just visible, he saw the branches of a tree. Something was in it, some animal, its teeth or eyes just catching the light of the fire.

For a moment he was confused, didn't know the dream was over. He reached for his gun, but no, he didn't have a gun, that was in the dream. So he held still, then wondered if he wasn't imagining it. Maybe nothing was there.

But no, the puddle was still there in front of him, and something still dripping down into it. He reached out and touched the puddle and brought his finger close to his eyes. The liquid was dark, thicker than water, sticky. He touched his finger to his mouth, tasted metal.

Slowly he sat up. With the tip of his boot, he stirred the fire, then loaded a few more branches onto it. Once the flames were high again, he took a brand out and quickly turned around, holding it up.

There was something in the tree above him. But it wasn't an animal. It was a man.

3.

"Nils?" he said.

Nils didn't answer. He seemed at once dazed and watchful, holding perfectly still and staring down at him from where he was spread along the branch. His jaw moved strangely, as if it had been broken, and blood was dripping from the side of his head down onto the ground. Yet he didn't seem to be in any pain.

"What's wrong with you?" asked Karsten, his limbs feeling suddenly heavy. "It's me, Karsten. What are you doing up that tree?"

"Hello, Karsten," said Nils. He turned Karsten's name around curiously in his mouth as if not quite used to saying it. "I'm glad I found you."

"You're bleeding," said Karsten.

"Bleeding?" said Nils, and no, Karsten saw, whatever bleeding there had been seemed now to have stopped.

"What's wrong with your jaw?" asked Karsten.

"My jaw?" asked Nils. He reached up and prodded it, and Karsten thought he saw a jag of bone push up beneath the skin. Then, with a swift movement, he crunched the jawbone back in place. "What do you mean?"

"Why are you up there?" asked Karsten.

"Do you want me to come down?" said Nils. "Are you inviting me to join you by the fire?" And then, when Karsten didn't say anything, "Karsten, invite me to join you by the fire."

Something's wrong, thought Karsten, *but the worst part of it is that I don't know for certain what or how much. Maybe everything*, he thought. He lifted the brand higher, expecting Nils to turn his head away or shield his eyes, but he didn't move, didn't even blink. Karsten took a step back and nearly stumbled into the fire.

"What are you doing in that tree?" he asked again.

"What tree?" asked Nils.

Very carefully, Karsten made his way around the fire and to the far side of it, putting the flames directly between him and Nils. From there, he could barely see Nils.

He looked at what remained of the pile of wood. There wasn't much, but he wasn't anxious to leave the fire to look for more. Maybe it would be enough to last until morning. He sat down, pulling his knees up close to his chest, and stayed there, staring up at Nils. He laid his brand back in the fire, then let his hand run idly over the ground until it found and closed upon a stone.

"Shall I join you by the fire?" asked Nils after a time.

"Are you asking me to invite you to join me?" asked Karsten.

For a moment Nils remained motionless and then he nodded.

Karsten thought, chose his words carefully. "Who am I to tell you what you can or can't do?" he said.

Nils made a little hissing sound that made Karsten sick to his stomach. Only after a moment did he realize it was laughter.

"Ah, very good, Karsten," said Nils. "Who indeed?"

For a time they were both silent.

"Are you coming down?" Karsten finally asked.

"What do you have in your hand, Karsten?" asked Nils.

"My hand?" asked Karsten. "Nothing," he lied.

Again that little hissing sound, abruptly cut short. Then just silence except for the crackling of the flames. *How long*, wondered Karsten, *until morning comes?*

He didn't fall sleep, he was sure of that, more or less sure. Maybe he closed his eyes a moment, or maybe he just blinked. When his eyes were open again, Nils was down from the tree and sitting on the other side of the fire. In the firelight, Karsten saw he was very pale, the front of his shirt stiff with dried blood. His jaw had slipped out again, and one side of his head looked as though it had been dented in. Maybe it had always looked that way, Karsten hoped.

Nils smiled, but reservedly, in a way that kept his teeth hidden. "You can go to sleep," he said. "I'll tend the fire. I'll make sure it doesn't go out."

"Is that what you were doing in the tree?" asked Karsten. "Watching the fire as it caught in my hair?"

"It didn't go out," said Nils. "It was a healthy fire."

"I don't mind staying awake," said Karsten, a vague panic beginning to build within him.

"What's the matter?" asked Nils. "Don't you trust me?"

Karsten didn't bother to answer. He pretended to watch the fire, all the while watching Nils. He suddenly realized he was gripping the stone tightly enough to make his fingers ache.

"Shall I come around the fire and keep you warm?" asked Nils.

"I'm fine," said Karsten as calmly as he could manage. "Don't trouble yourself."

"No trouble," said Nils, and he began to stand. Karsten stood too. Nils smiled, sat back down again. Slowly Karsten sat too.

"Then I'll tell you a story," said Nils. "Something to keep us entertained."

"There's no need," said Karsten. "Please don't."

"What are you afraid of?" asked Nils. "It's just a story. A story can't hurt."

Can it? wondered Karsten. But before he could decide, Nils had begun.

A man was shot, *he said,* or perhaps struck by a rock, and killed. No, shot, let's tell it that way, like a dream rather than real life. He and his friend had come to a town to retrieve something, or rather to steal it, but they did not call it stealing because they had a high opinion of what they deserved. The townsfolk saw what they were doing and prevented the doing of it and then shot one of the pair as they tried to escape.

The man who was shot and killed did not realize he was dead.

What did you say? *Karsten interrupted.*

You heard me, *said Nils.*

Why would you tell me this? *Karsten asked.*

It's just a story, *said Nils.* We're just having fun, aren't we? Why wouldn't I tell you?

The man who was shot dead did not realize he was dead. Like the other man, he ran to his horse and leaped onto it and galloped out of town and into the mountains. The townsfolk gave chase, but both men, the dead man and the living one, rode hell for leather. Soon the townsfolk turned back. The two men, not knowing if they were pursued, rode on.

They rode a narrow trail, dead man in front and living man behind. Slowly, as more time went by without sign of pursuit, the man riding behind began to relax. Only then did he notice that the other man had been shot in the leg—

—in the what? *asked Karsten.*

The leg, *said Nils.*

Who told you this story? *asked Karsten desperately.* How do you know it?

Perhaps you are thinking, "A man isn't killed by being shot in the leg." Perhaps the dead man was thinking this also, and this was the explanation for why he didn't know he was dead. But he had turned toward the gun as it fired, and the bullet, in entering him, severed the artery, and with each step he took, each step the horse took, more blood left him. Soon his trouser leg was sodden. Soon too the side of his horse had grown bloody, blood awash all down its ribs. It took a very particular shape, and to the man riding behind him, when he finally noticed it, it reminded him of something.

Stop, *said Karsten.* Please.

No, *said Nils.* Don't interrupt. It reminded him of something, *he said,* but for a long time he didn't know what. In trying to think of what it was, he kept himself from thinking about how much blood there was, about how any man who had lost as much blood as this was not just as good as dead, but, in fact, dead.

He rode behind the other man, wondering about the shape on the side of the other horse. And then all at once it came to him. It was like the shapes he had made as a child when he lay down on the ground after a snowstorm, moving his arms and legs back and forth to clear the snow away. A snow angel, he thought. And then thought, no: a blood angel.

And only once he had thought this could he admit to himself the other man must be dead. But since the dead man himself did not know, that was where the trouble started. He watched the way the blood had run around the belly of the horse and begun to drip down, *Nils said, and smiled in a way that showed his teeth.* It slowly drizzled a path in the dirt—

But at this point, Karsten bolted into the night and kept running until he ran face-first into a tree.

When he awoke, he was back before the fire, the flames very low. Nils was there with him now, on the same side, kneeling over him but not touching him. Karsten wanted to push him away, but was afraid to. Besides, he wasn't sure he could move.

"There you are," said Nils.

Karsten tried to open his mouth to speak, but nothing came out. He tried to turn his head, but it didn't turn. Nils was peering at him, smiling slightly. And then Nils leaned in close to him, almost touching his lips, and drew in a deep breath.

When he straightened up and Karsten could see his face again, he looked different, not quite like himself.

He leaned in again, and this time did touch Karsten's lips, and drew the breath out of him. When he raised his head again, he was different still. It was as if Karsten was looking into a mirror.

No, said Karsten, but no sound came out.

"Shall I finish my story?" the face looming over him asked in a new voice, in the voice it had stolen. "In a way, it's the least I could do."

He stayed there hunched over Karsten, waiting for an answer. When no answer came, he smiled and nodded. Then, making that same soft hissing sound, he leaned in.

LITERATURE
is not the same thing as
PUBLISHING

Funder Acknowledgments

Coffee House Press is an internationally renowned independent book publisher and arts nonprofit based in Minneapolis, MN; through its literary publications and *Books in Action* program, Coffee House acts as a catalyst and connector—between authors and readers, ideas and resources, creativity and community, inspiration and action.

Coffee House Press books are made possible through the generous support of grants and donations from corporate giving programs, state and federal support, family foundations, and the many individuals who believe in the transformational power of literature. This activity is made possible by the voters of Minnesota through a Minnesota State Arts Board Operating Support grant, thanks to the legislative appropriation from the arts and cultural heritage fund and a grant from the Wells Fargo Foundation Minnesota. Coffee House also receives major operating support from the Amazon Literary Partnership, the Bush Foundation, the Jerome Foundation, the McKnight Foundation, Target, and the National Endowment for the Arts (NEA). To find out more about how NEA grants impact individuals and communities, visit www.arts.gov.

Coffee House Press receives additional support from many anonymous donors; the Alexander Family Foundation; the Archer Bondarenko Munificence Fund; the Elmer L. & Eleanor J. Andersen Foundation; the David & Mary Anderson Family Foundation; the Buuck Family Foundation; the Carolyn Foundation; the Dorsey & Whitney Foundation; Dorsey & Whitney LLP; the Rehael Fund of the Minneapolis Foundation; the Schwab Charitable Fund; Schwegman, Lundberg & Woessner, P.A.; the Scott Family Foundation; US Bank Foundation; VSA Minnesota for the Metropolitan Regional Arts Council; the Archie D. & Bertha H. Walker Foundation; and the Woessner Freeman Family Foundation.

The Publisher's Circle of Coffee House Press

Publisher's Circle members make significant contributions to Coffee House Press's annual giving campaign. Understanding that a strong financial base is necessary for the press to meet the challenges and opportunities that arise each year, this group plays a crucial part in the success of Coffee House's mission.

Recent Publisher's Circle members include many anonymous donors, Mr. & Mrs. Rand L. Alexander, Suzanne Allen, Patricia A. Beithon, Bill Berkson & Connie Lewallen, the E. Thomas Binger & Rebecca Rand Fund of the Minneapolis Foundation, Robert & Gail Buuck, Claire Casey, Louise Copeland, Jane Dalrymple-Hollo, Mary Ebert & Paul Stembler, Chris Fischbach & Katie Dublinski, Katharine Freeman, Sally French, Jocelyn Hale & Glenn Miller, Roger Hale & Nor Hall, Randy Hartten & Ron Lotz, Jeffrey Hom, Carl & Heidi Horsch, Kenneth Kahn & Susan Dicker, Stephen & Isabel Keating, Kenneth Koch Literary Estate, Jennifer Komar & Enrique Olivarez, Allan & Cinda Kornblum, Leslie Larson Maheras, Jim & Susan Lenfestey, Sarah Lutman & Rob Rudolph, Carol & Aaron Mack, George & Olga Mack, Joshua Mack, Gillian McCain, Mary & Malcolm McDermid, Sjur Midness & Briar Andresen, Peter Nelson & Jennifer Swenson, Marc Porter & James Hennessy, Jeffrey Scherer, Jeffrey Sugerman & Sarah Schultz, Nan G. & Stephen C. Swid, Patricia Tilton, Joanne Von Blon, Stu Wilson & Melissa Barker, Warren D. Woessner & Iris C. Freeman, and Margaret & Angus Wurtele.

For more information about the Publisher's Circle and other ways to support Coffee House Press books, authors, and activities, please visit www.coffeehousepress.org/support or contact us at info@coffeehousepress.org.

Coffee House Press began as a small letterpress operation in 1972 and has grown into an internationally renowned nonprofit publisher of literary fiction, essay, poetry, and other work that doesn't fit neatly into genre categories.

Coffee House is both a publisher and an arts organization. Through our *Books in Action* program and publications, we've become interdisciplinary collaborators and incubators for new work and audience experiences. Our vision for the future is one where a publisher is a catalyst and connector.

Praised by Peter Straub for going "furthest out on the sheerest, least sheltered narrative precipice," Brian Evenson is the recipient of three O. Henry Prizes and has been a finalist for the Edgar Award, the Shirley Jackson Award, and the World Fantasy Award. He is also the winner of the International Horror Guild Award and the American Library Association's award for Best Horror Novel, and his work has been named in *Time Out New York*'s top books.

A Collapse of Horses was designed by
Bookmobile Design & Digital Publisher Services.
The text has been set in Adobe Caslon Pro,
a typeface drawn by Carol Twombly in 1989
and based on the work of William Caslon (c. 1692–1766),
an English engraver, punchcutter, and typefounder.